Praise for *Sweet La...*

A *Kirkus Reviews* Be...

"Millet deserves to be celebrated. . . . [R]emarkable."
—Lisa Zeidner, *Washington Post*

"Gripping, smart, beautifully written."   —*Wall Street Journal*

"Few novels surprise me. . . . But Lydia Millet's *Sweet Lamb of Heaven*
confounded me, delightfully so."   —Laura Lippman,
New York Times Book Review

"Millet's sense of pacing is acute and her prose is glittering and exact."
—*The New Yorker*

"A rare pleasure to read. . . . Millet's fine prose . . . is as rich with fresh
imagery as it is open-minded to life's hidden possibilities."
—Matthew Gilbert, *Boston Globe*

"An extraordinary metaphysical thriller."   —Laura Miller, *Slate*

"If Millet's title and premise . . . primes you to expect genre conformity,
prepare to be surprised by more than plot twists."
—Boris Kachka, *Vulture*

"Striking. . . . [W]e have a real thriller on our hands."
—Laird Hunt, *Los Angeles Times*

"Unpredictable in the best sense, Millet's eye-opening stories and
conceptions are irresistibly interesting. This may be her most beguiling
and accessible creation yet."   —David Wright, *Seattle Times*

SWEET
LAMB
OF
HEAVEN

A NOVEL

LYDIA
MILLET

W. W. NORTON & COMPANY

INDEPENDENT PUBLISHERS SINCE 1923

NEW YORK | LONDON

Deepest thanks to Maria Massie and Tom Mayer, beloved agent and beloved editor, and to all at Norton who worked on this book, including Elizabeth Riley, Ryan Harrington, Nancy Palmquist, Don Rifkin, Ingsu Liu, David High, Bill Rusin, Deirdre Dolan, Dan Christiaens, Golda Rademacher, Karen Rice, Meredith McGinnis, Steve Colca, and Julia Druskin.

For information about permission to reproduce selections from this book,
write to Permissions, W. W. Norton & Company, Inc.,
500 Fifth Avenue, New York, NY 10110

For information about special discounts for bulk purchases, please contact
W. W. Norton Special Sales at specialsales@wwnorton.com or 800-233-4830

Manufacturing by Quad Graphics Fairfield
Book design by Chris Welch Design
Production manager: Julia Druskin

Library of Congress Cataloging-in-Publication Data

Names: Millet, Lydia, 1968– author.
Title: Sweet lamb of heaven : a novel / Lydia Millet.
Description: First edition. | New York : W. W. Norton & Company, [2016]
Identifiers: LCCN 2016000554 | ISBN 9780393285543 (hardcover)
Subjects: LCSH: Marital conflict—Fiction. | Psychological fiction. |
Domestic fiction. | GSAFD: Suspense fiction.
Classification: LCC PS3563.I42175 S94 2016 | DDC 813/.54—dc23
LC record available at http://lccn.loc.gov/2016000554

ISBN 978-0-393-35418-8 pbk.

W. W. Norton & Company, Inc.
500 Fifth Avenue, New York, N.Y. 10110
www.wwnorton.com

W. W. Norton & Company Ltd.
15 Carlisle Street, London W1D 3BS

1 2 3 4 5 6 7 8 9 0

CONTENTS

SWEET
LAMB
OF
HEAVEN

1

HALLUCINATIONS, EVEN IN THE SANE

WHEN I INSISTED ON KEEPING THE BABY, NED THREW HIS HANDS into the air palms-forward. He looked like a mime climbing a wall—one of the few times I've ever seen him look clumsy.

Then he dropped his hands and turned away, shaking his head. It was a terminal shake. Afterward his schedule got fuller, his long work hours longer, his attention more completely diverted.

And I have to admit it wasn't just him who turned away. After we differed on that point, the point concerning the baby, I began to give up on Ned too.

So I was alone preparing. It had been an accident, technically more his fault than mine, but who's haggling? And once it happened I felt I needed to accept it—I wanted to. I drove by myself to buy the various infant containers. I chose the doll-sized pieces of newborn clothing, set up a nursery and glued stars on the ceiling; I crept in at night sometimes to see how they glowed. I went alone to doctor's appointments to listen for the heartbeat and see the first pictures, and when the time came I went through labor with mostly just medical staff keeping me company.

Ned did stop by the hospital, apparently, and spent some time talking on his cell phone in the lounge, but he stepped out again for a work lunch, later for work cocktails, and finally for a late work dinner. After dinner he drove home and went to sleep.

None of this was too far beyond the pale, I guess, when it comes to unfortunate marriages. After about twenty hours I lay against the pillows holding her slippery body. Her eyes, against my expectation, were wide open and there was a perplexing chaos of sound in my ears, too many voices in the room for the number of people—soundtracks that overlapped. A kindly nurse was telling me about the other babies he'd seen born with their eyes open when a stream of words intruded, covering his. I heard it most distinctly when the nurse paused.

Later I would hear volumes and forget almost all of it, but the first phrase I picked out stayed with me despite my exhaustion. It started out as a string of foreign words, only one of which resolved, to my ear, into anything recognizable—something like "power," *powa* or *poa*. And then it was English: *The living spring from the dead.*

Delirium, was what I thought, and I dispensed with it by falling fast asleep. It was only when I woke up later, and the baby was brought back to me, also awake, that the stream of chatter started up again and was impossible to ignore.

AT FIRST I was mostly irritated, and went to get my ears looked at. Once, when I was a kid, I'd had an infected ear and heard a wavy music when I pressed my head against the pillow. Maybe this had a physical explanation, maybe some ear-brain interface was being disrupted. But my ears checked out fine. The baby didn't enjoy the doctor's visit, and the voice talked on—only for me, of course—throughout her noisy crying.

Next I made an appointment with a neurologist and insisted on an expensive scan: nothing.

For weeks I combed through psychology case studies, ready to discover the evidence against my sanity. I read up on post-partum depression, though I didn't feel depressed. Of course I might be in denial, I knew; I had a newborn baby, after all, and a husband who had no time for either of us.

But I didn't feel sad. I suffered from no flatness of affect. I was tired and confused—I felt besieged by the noise—but it was frustration, not despair.

I also gave schizoid conditions due consideration. No mother wants a woman with psychotic features bringing up her child, even if that woman is her. So reading accounts of patients who heard voices became my avocation for a while, since, as it turns out, mental illness isn't required to hallucinate. Hallucinations, even in the sane, are quite common. They accompany certain drugs and medicines and an impressive list of diseases; they can be caused by blindness or sensory deprivation or even seem to come out of nowhere.

A stream of advice is often heard by people in extremis, fighting injury or the elements. Voices are heard by the sane in wartime or under other forms of duress, prison or isolation or grief. Sometimes the voices have no obvious cause, their origins buried in the electric labyrinth of the brain.

I was prepared to accept the hallucination hypothesis—the baby's presence, her rapt attention caused me to hallucinate voices speaking to me—but I was curious beyond that and needed to cover my bases. I also went to worst-case scenarios, to the bizarre and outlandish. I studied the occult, including demonology, for instance—spent hours on the Internet reading myths and legends of demonic possession. I made trips to the library, the baby snug in her carrier, and moved from articles about people with auditory hallucinations to those who identified their visitors very specifically, brooking no disagreement.

Demons, they said.

They saw demons with claws, horns and pointed teeth, of course, but often demons appeared in the shape of seductive women and yet others were amorphous shapes that shifted beneath the faces of loved ones. Briefly those faces would distort, then swiftly resume their devious guise, pull over themselves the skin of normalcy.

Or people heard demons that had no physical form but only spoke, mostly in biblical tongues like Aramaic or Hebrew. Experts were consulted and that was often their verdict: what the demon-visited persons were hearing was Aramaic or Hebrew or Greek. The demons tended to speak in dead scripts, as though frozen in the time of early Christianity—the demons clung to the old, reluctant to embrace the new.

I was glad Lena's mouth didn't move when the words issued, as in some possession stories. Because it was only sound and words, invisible, the experience also conjured TV shows involving ESP. I looked into spoon-bending hoaxes and watched shows that featured ghost-finding teams that crept through haunted houses trying to capture stray ectoplasm.

I was worn down by the elements of my routine—the stream of words and my bewilderment during the days, the nights half-sleepless, a mesh of hours spent fitfully dozing or nursing my daughter when she woke up. Ned had moved out of our bedroom while I was pregnant and never moved back, claiming his restless sleep would bother me. Often he didn't come home at all, in those first months when Lena's crying disturbed the nightly peace, but stayed over at the office. It wasn't long before I began to understand that *at the office* was a euphemism.

And when the baby was sleeping but I couldn't sleep, I wallowed in pulp fiction. I read thick paperbacks set in old houses, where the devil took the form of flies and buzzed on windowpanes, or in upscale prewar apartment buildings in Manhattan, where babies were fed evil baby food and raised by Satan cults. Plus there were the movies about antichrists and child possessors, the one with the black-haired boy named Damien, the one with the blank-faced girl who floated over her bed, rasping obscenities. When I was too tired to read, with the baby mostly sleeping and the speaker fallen silent, I'd curl up in front of the screen with cheese popcorn.

But in the end the B-movie fiends were too showy for me to take seriously, almost self-parodies. Besides, the stream of words wasn't malicious and my daughter committed no alarming actions. She ate and slept, lay bundled in my arms. Time passed and she rolled over, sat up, crawled; also gurgled and drooled.

She never fixed upon me a bold, sinister eye.

So by and by I let the demons go, telepathy I dismissed out of hand, schizoaffective disorders I further renounced.

I went with the hallucination theory.

Hallucination has the qualities of real perception: vivid, substantial, and located in external space. It is distinct from a delusional perception, in which correctly sensed stimuli are given additional, often bizarre, significance. —*Wikipedia 5.10.2009*

PEOPLE WITH MIGRAINES see colors and shapes fading and forming anew on the wall. Others, with visual hallucinations, believe strangers are sitting beside them dressed in old-fashioned garb. Next to these people's apparitions my own affliction didn't seem so grave.

It was true that the disturbance was constant, and I didn't find an identical case in the articles I read, but this struck me as more or less a technical detail. At first I called it the voice, as others like me did.

Because I wasn't alone: there were whole support groups given over to non-psychotics who heard things, including a so-called Hearing Voices Movement (its mission: to empower chronic voice-hearers). There were affirming Listservs.

I avoided them studiously. I began to write in this Word file instead, a diary whose sporadic, rambling texts I'd tinker with for years. Over time I redacted, adding and subtracting until the entries formed a narrative that clarified my own story—at least to me.

I spoke to no one about what I believed I heard. I sought out no company in my infirmity.

WHERE WE LIVE now is a seaside motel in the off-season. We're on the edge of rocky bluffs, so I can see a car coming when it's a speck on the long gravel road.

There are few guests this time of year; in summertime they get the kind of tourists who, says Don the motel manager, bicker sharply over the bright-orange sandwich crackers in the vending machine re: advisability of purchasing.

But in the wintertime it's quiet here and there are weekly rates. The carpets aren't much to write home about, having an ashy cast. The tables in the rooms are brown Formica with black cigarette burns; our shower curtains are mildewed. I like their pale-blue imprint of daisies. I also like the cliffs, the rocks, the trees and the gray water stretching to the east. I like the sharp nearness of pine needles against a blurry sheen of sea.

And my little girl loves it. She loves the people and the place; small events make her giddy with pleasure. She spins, cartwheels, races and laughs easily. She doesn't have much, but she doesn't need much. She has her books and toys and art supplies. Some of the toys are old and bedraggled, since she doesn't want to throw out anything—the second I suggest a disused toy might be taken to the charity bin in town she feels a rush of protectiveness and clings pathetically, lavishing praise upon the object that had been utterly forgotten until then.

Watching her protect a ratty mouse, a dog-eared, broken-spined, finger-smeared picture book, it's almost possible to believe that everything in the world is precious, that each humble item that exists has a delicate and singular value.

It's possible to believe that all matter should be treated tenderly.

LENA WAS BORN in a hospital in Alaska. Up to that time I taught as an adjunct at the university and her father was in business: and he's still in business today, though he's expanded his purview.

I was fond of Anchorage. It's a sprawling city of mostly ugly buildings, but no other city I know has bears roaming downtown. I'd be picnicking with the baby near the central business district, watching the sunset from the Cook Inlet shore, and black bears would come rustling through the undergrowth a few feet away. Feeling a tug of panic, I grabbed Lena and retreated to the car, but still I treasured having them so close. The moose roamed Anchorage too, and you could encounter them on a casual run through city parks—more dangerous than the bears, if you believed the statistics.

Of all the actions I've taken, leaving Alaska was the hardest. Not because I enjoyed living there, though I did, but because it's a bold move to take a child so far away from the man who's her father. Even when he doesn't accept the position.

I did have his approval at first for our departure. The part of the split he resented was financial: he didn't like that I took half the value of our savings account and our CDs with me. (I left the stock, I left the mutual funds, but still.) Aside from money quibbles he was glad we'd left, at first; for more than a year he didn't mind at all. He'd been indifferent to me for a long time, as he's indifferent to most people who aren't of use to him.

As for Lena, he hadn't wanted her in the first place and he never warmed to her. Our leave-taking gave him the same liberty it gave us— namely the open-ended chance to be who we were, instead of trapped.

I'd send him the occasional email telling him what she'd learned, what she was doing, an anecdote here or there to keep her real. I clung to the belief that any father would want that, and more than that I felt I owed it to her, to try to keep him existent as a father, however marginal. He rarely responded to these, and his occasional replies were brief and rife with hasty misspellings.

But over the past few months he's decided to make himself a candidate, and candidates want family since family looks reassuring on them. So now we're useful again and he's searching for us. I think he wants a moving snapshot for the campaign trail, two female faces behind him as he stands on the podium.

When I first met Ned he claimed not to have any politics. I should have known enough to be wary of that, but instead I made excuses to myself. Politics were for crooks, he said. But later politics grew in him like metastasis, branching into a network threaded throughout his veins and nerves and bones. It's not that he's left the business world behind, it's just that he now believes politics are a sector of his enterprise.

His platform includes a prolife agenda, for instance, which "values the sanctity of every human soul," and also "believes in the greatness of the American family." The word *family*, on his glossy-but-down-home webpage in its hues of red, white and blue, is a code for *you*, where *you* also means *right, deserving, genuine* and *better than those others, you know, the ones who* aren't *you*. Ned believes in "the American family" the same way processed food companies do, companies that make products for cleaning floors or unclogging toilets—the kind of easy code that makes public speech moronic.

But even if he'd been a genuine family man, I wouldn't have wanted to be a part of his platform.

Once he nearly caught up with us, before I understood that emails can be traced. It was stupid of me and caused a close call and as a result I'm wiser now—or craftier, in that I don't send emails anymore. We move, we don't use credit cards, I don't write my own name when I sign things. I bought a fake driver's license from a computer-savvy teen in Poughkeepsie. If a cop pulled me over I'd have to use the real one, which matches my registration, but I drive cautiously and keep the car in good repair and so far that hasn't happened.

I'm not in any system, that I know of, I'm not a fugitive. Ned wouldn't report me. It would make him look bad, defeat his whole purpose in reclaiming us.

The only authority I'm running from is him.

EVEN THOUGH it's cold out, we spend a lot of time on the beach, the rocks and pebbles and sand. At dawn we take the first walk, following a narrow path down the face of the cliff. I carry a thermos of coffee and she carries a basket divided into one section for treasures, another for litter. Not every form of litter is welcome: she can't pick up medical waste, newly broken glass, rotting food, or old, yellow-white balloons.

I'd like for us to settle down and live a steady life, so she can go to school and have friends. Lena begs not to go to school and claims she wants our life to stay the same forever.

She's six years old. She doesn't know better.

It seems to me that if we can escape his grasp till after the election, we may have a fair shot at an undisturbed existence. If he wins he won't need us.

On the other hand, if he loses and decides to take another shot in another cycle, he may search harder. He may get more determined.

When we discuss her father, who's only a vestigial memory for her, I rely on platitudes like "Our lives took different paths," or "Sometimes people decide to stop living in the same place." The matter of the separation, unlike the matter of the voice I used to hear—on which I hope always to keep my own counsel—will one day require unpleasant conversation, but so far she's satisfied with generalities. She's not overly interested, since she never saw much of him. Much as she never caught his interest, he never seemed to capture hers either. When we did share an address he seldom came home: he traveled, he worked late, he cultivated his casual friends and many acquaintances. He never read bedtime stories or sat down with us for meals.

He was a sasquatch in a photograph, a fuzzy obscure figure moving in far-off silhouette.

DON, WHO'S BEEN so good to us, is a pear-shaped man. This feature endears him to Lena, whose favorite stuffed animal is a plush, duck-like bird with a small head and giant baggy ass. Don has a shuffling gait, seems erudite by hospitality-industry standards, and like us appears to be hiding here—not hiding from one person but from crowds of people, possibly, or from a faster pace. He has a job that involves people, true, but seldom too many at one time, and when people do show up they're in his territory, his cavernous and dimly lit domain.

I imagine he keeps the motel ramshackle so as not to attract too much traffic—so as to keep the trickle of company thin. His family owns the business and seems to accept the small returns.

When a stray overnight guest comes through, Don's civil but hardly overjoyed. Lena, by contrast, is always excited. She acts as though she, not he, is the owner: she's the mistress of all she surveys, with the hosting duties this brings. To her the motel is first-rate; she sees no mildew or cigarette burns. Because I can't leave her with strangers, this means I meet many guests too, tagging along in the background as she gives them the tour.

Most are highly tolerant of her—eager children receive a plenary indulgence, especially dimple-cheeked girls—and her exuberance is contagious. She explains the rules about clean towels with gusto, as though the rules, if not the towels, are sacrosanct; she showcases the antique ice machine with pride of ownership.

"This ice is only for people's drinks," she says sternly. "So don't pick it up and put it back, OK? And *don't* stand with your hands stuck in the ice, even if you like the shiver."

WHEN NED CAUGHT up with us we were staying at a cabin in New Hampshire near the summit of a low mountain. It was a large, wooden cabin with a dozen bunk beds for hikers and three caretaker-cooks. Only a few dozen feet from the porch was a waterfall with a flat-topped boulder at its edge, where Lena liked to sit trailing her hand in the water and basking in the sun. The water wasn't deep.

We only got away that time because Ned made a mistake; he did a flyover. Maybe he wanted to preside from the air while his employees cornered us; maybe not. I still don't know if he was personally there.

But helicopters were rare along that part of the Appalachian Trail, coming in only with major equipment or for medical emergencies. I was on the porch with one of the cooks when that one chop-chop-chopped overhead and she looked up and said, "Huh, a private helicopter. It's not the local guy."

That was all I needed to pull Lena off her sunny rock and leave our sleeping bags behind. I did it only because my stomach twisted when the cook said what she said: I followed my instincts and we bushwhacked down the mountainside—I said it was a game, going off-trail, and the one who made it to the bottom with no scratches on her legs or arms would win a double-scoop cone. When we reached the road I had some light scratches on my forearms while Lena had none; new mosquito bites itched and swelled around my ankles, and our shoes were soaked from slogging through a stagnant creek.

Still, Lena was gleeful at the prospect of her ice cream reward.

The car wasn't parked in the trailhead lot most of the hikers used but in a shaded pullout I'd found. After a short walk on the shoulder of the road we got in and drove off.

And I knew we'd been right to run when the cook, who had become a friend, called me. She said four men had come, two from each direction since the trail stretched out on either side of the cabin. They converged on it fifteen minutes after we'd left. They weren't dressed for hiking: their shoes were shiny leather ruined by mud. So she told them only that we'd left the day before, and after some unhappy muttering and some prowling around the grounds and questioning of other guests, the four men went away.

NED MARRIED ME for my family's money, because he had none of his own and wanted some; I married him because I thought it was love. I was wrong too, it wasn't love—I don't mean to pin it all on him. I had a crush, if I'm being honest, and I didn't know the difference.

Ned's a very attractive man, a man many people use the word *handsome* or *magnetic* to describe. Even straight men have said this of him, the same way they'll concede it, often grudgingly, of famous actors or athletes. Both before and after we were married, men and women alike would confide in me about their attraction to Ned. He makes people covet him, inspires a desperate greed. And he knows this all too well—it's key to his strategy for gathering investors. Ned is his own asset, his own front man, a property that sells itself. Both men and women want to own him or sleep with him, but failing that they're just grateful to be part of his enterprise.

It goes far beyond standard-issue good looks.

He always had a talent for captivating an audience. From the first moment he meets you he establishes eye contact, and he doesn't relinquish it easily. But he's not only a mesmerist. He can embody *audience* convincingly as well, when listening is called for. When he receives a personal disclosure he seems to listen intently, even adoringly.

In fact he isn't listening but intently, tactically *appearing* to listen— no mean feat in itself.

He's humorless, though, which for me proved slowly deadening. Ned always laughs when others laugh, taking the social cues, but laughter doesn't come naturally to him. And while he could occasionally say a funny thing, back in our early days together, it wasn't intentional.

There were other, more minor details of Ned that should have been red flags for me too—his allegiance, for example, to a certain brand of cologne. Before Ned I'd never been with any man who wore cologne. The smell of it didn't bother me: this particular cologne was inoffensive, even subtle. But once, when a bottle of it was knocked off a bathroom counter and broke on the tile floor, I saw a strange edge of rage in him.

In general I had no eyes for red at all in the infatuated months before we got married. Any flags of bright color were lost in the hills and dales of a hazy, indulgent country.

And my feelings were irrelevant, in the end, since he had close to none for me. I was surprisingly late to this realization. We tend to believe what we wish to, and I was no exception. I hoped that Ned loved me, and hope shaded into assumption without me recognizing it.

Before I got pregnant he found me attractive enough too, I guess, but this disappeared with the pregnancy, which he found repulsive. He pursued other women with unqualified success. He had no lasting feelings for any of them either, as far as I could tell, but each was new in her turn, and Ned prizes novelty. Novelty and momentum are his two passions.

In saying he married me for money, I don't mean to imply I was an heiress—my family had the complacent, middling inherited wealth that passes without much notice unless you happen to be Ned, brought up in poverty, entrepreneurial, and with an incentive to research. He could have held out for someone with far more money and far, far better connections, for I had none.

Now, looking back, I'm surprised he didn't. I was a small fish, very small. I had barely enough. But he was impatient to get his enterprises off the ground. And his disinterest in the marriage probably reflected his own awareness of that hasty choice—the fact that he'd settled for much less than he was capable of getting.

WITH A HANDFUL of exceptions I found that when I tried to write down what the voice said, I couldn't. A fog would descend. Phrases that seemed sharply etched to me when I heard them, sense and structure cut like a skyscraper against a crisp sky, would crumble and fade as soon as I tried to record them.

I heard the words in the stream as English or French or Spanish, or sometimes it would be modern English in an accent or dialect, say Australian English or an English with Welsh accents. Other times it was English that sounded like Shakespeare or Middle English, like Chaucer maybe, which I'd read in college. But whenever the format changed I half-forgot what had come before, as though the switch between lexicons and grammars occurred imperceptibly. Since I couldn't identify the languages that weren't English or Spanish or French I figured my imagination was making up a stream of nonsense, sounds that resembled other tongues but were only a sham.

That was a game I'd liked to play when I was a kid. I even played it a few times with Lena, speaking in rapid-fire gibberish, pretending it was an unknown exotic language, say Urdu or Tahitian.

And the voice never went silent, except when Lena was sleeping. It changed from low tones to high, speech to singing, singing to humming to clicking sounds that had a rhythmic quality, on occasion devolving into grumbling or even yelling. I drew the line at yelling—at those times I'd call a babysitter and go out.

I'd shut the door behind me and step into the street, and right away I didn't hear a thing.

WHEN I LEFT Ned, I took enough money to live on for a while. It was only a fraction of the legacy from my family that he'd funneled into his businesses, but I didn't want to fight over money. Ned wanted it more than I ever had and taking too much would bring out the edge in him.

So I took only what I felt I needed. I made a budget carefully, knowing I wasn't going to work again until Lena started school. I'd worked steadily all my adult life and I thought I could use a break; I was well pleased to be only her mother and teacher for those years. I didn't plan to have a second child.

The money keeps us afloat, Lena and me, and in that respect we're fortunate.

I PUZZLED OVER the link between the baby's presence and my hallucination. There wasn't generally supposed to be such a clear connection, in the hallucinations of the sane, between what was heard or seen and the fixations of the hallucinating person—not in the descriptions that I read, anyway. This made my case seem more psychological than purely neurological, and I worried about it periodically. Because the presence of my infant carried with it a voice that had the appearance of fluency in all tongues and gave an impression of encyclopedic knowledge—some kind of frightened projection of my overpowering responsibility as a mother, possibly, was one of my interpretations.

Sometimes the stream of sound wasn't a voice but music, welcome relief: old standards, dramatic epics by well-known composers, folk tunes, pop riffs. It liked Woody Guthrie, whose music I didn't remember encountering before except for the song "This Land Is Your Land," which I knew from summer camp. Research on the snatches of lyrics I could recall yielded his name, and I thought I must have been exposed as a child, and quashed the recollection.

But most often the content was words—what sounded like recitations of texts of all kinds, poems, fictions both literary and mass-market, movie scripts and stage plays, histories, dictionaries, textbooks, biographies, news stories. The subjects were as diverse as the genres: single-celled organisms, hockey scores, feathers on dinosaurs, celebrity suicides, the pattern of Pleistocene extinctions, the fate of the tribe known as the Nez Perce; relativity, particle accelerators, Greek myths, the troubled term *Anthropocene*, the chemistry of a callus on the hand of Heidelberg man.

I was impressed by the knowledge base from which my mind appeared to be drawing. I marveled at it, even. Buried in my unconscious must be some capacity for photographic memory, I thought.

That surprised me.

Nothing salacious ever came from the voice—that is, there were curses, there was profanity, there were even vague references to sex and reproduction, but there was never a suggestion of lechery directed toward me personally. Still, I felt perversion was implicit in the combination of a baby nursing while a stream of elevated diction flowed up from somewhere beyond the O of her mouth. I had to distance myself from the voice when I was nursing her: it might be my hallucination, but, much in the way I might detest *my* head lice or *my* chicken pox, should those happen to manifest, I was forced, at those times, to treat it as a pest.

On occasion I'd try hard to write down what I heard despite my confusion, with doggedness but a lack of clarity, determined to record the substance of the hallucinated event. I still carry with me some scraps of paper—deep in the trunk, where I stuck the file after the last time I picked through it. I'd had to write the words down fast to get any of them, seldom had time to get to the keyboard, so the notes are scribbled on the backs of envelopes, grocery and housewares receipts, once along the edge of a worn dollar bill. Many seemed nonsensical: *Windlessness = illusion planet is static in space ∴ windlessness entropic.* Or *"social animals + writing: ERRATUM."*

Neighbors and friends came over fairly often in the first year of Lena's life and (of course) they never heard the voice, not even the faintest hint of it—I made sure. I'd ask, in a roundabout, casual way, if anyone was hearing anything unusual as we sat there, but my questions always met with offhand dismissals.

Joan of Arc had heard a voice advising her to help raise the siege of Orleans, but as far as I could tell the voice had no specific instructions for the likes of me.

I PASSED THROUGH stages with my hallucination. Sometimes I wished I could hide from it, other times I was determined to study it steadfastly until I could pick out the details and know it more perfectly. After almost a year I fit myself into a certain orbit, adjusting my routine to its disruptions. I shrank and disappeared in the brightness of its perpetual day but at night, when it was silent and so was Lena, I tracked across the dark relief in solitary flight.

I relied heavily on the fact that babies sleep for longer than adults and I also depended on her midday nap, an hour and a half like clockwork. The babysitters gave me some time off, and for the rest I'd found ways to fit myself into the spaces between words, to distract myself sometimes, at other times to tolerate nearness and even, when well-rested, to listen.

In general I felt besieged, my defenses walled up around me, but every now and then something in the fall of words would strike. I'd feel my throat clench in grief or recognition, be on the brink of tears and then not be.

At those times—it's hard to describe and I feel like a fool even trying—I didn't understand why emotion was overwhelming me but I also didn't waste time belaboring the question. I had distinct sensations and I stilled everything to feel them: sometimes I thought I was being cut bloodlessly, cut so that a clear, frigid air entered me and the rest of the outside followed; or possibly I spilled out, it may have been the other way around. I'd feel as though I had the long view, past the end of my life, past the horizon, dispersing into ether.

I loved that feeling the way a drug might be loved, I think, quick as it was, freeing—but also with an icy burn, a searing touch I imagined as the cold of space and couldn't stand for long. There was the euphoria of ascent, the vertigo of height.

Then the feeling would vanish abruptly. I'd just be there, in my house or on the street or in a store, wherever, with Lena. And I'd be desperate to see her clear eyes gazing at me with no interference—to be alone with her instead of in the company of slime molds, cyanobacteria genomics, cuneiform or the dancing of bees.

And finally it wasn't the substance or character of the voice I resented but its proximity—the fact that it was so close, and that it never ceased. I urgently wanted to be rid of the torrent of sound and image, the stream of convoluted murmurings that often evoked either oppressive problems or, at the very least, the broad dramatic canvas of a universe that went on forever beyond our cozy walls. What I wished for was my child by herself, the child I'd counted on only with me—the two of us in peace and privacy.

I wanted the normal pleasures of babies, the smell of her soft cheek against my face, to hold her in my lap at bedtime and be able to read picture books to her without hearing, as I read, the constant burble of a parallel story.

But I adjusted, for the most part. I felt I knew the voice for the invention that it was, unconscious, a product of haywire neurology; with some resistance, with some anxiety, I'd learned to live around it.

And then that changed.

· · · · ·

WE WERE HAVING a rare family moment. One of Ned's affairs had just ended in a mildly humiliating way (I figured out later) and at the same time he'd had a major setback at work—failed at a takeover of a small company that made some minor machine part for shrimp trawlers. He'd flown in that afternoon from Dutch Harbor and was home for dinner, albeit with the crabby attitude of someone who's racking his brain but just can't think of somewhere else to be. I stood at the stove cooking as the baby sat in her high chair eating spinach puree and cheese; as always, in those days, the voice was droning on in the background.

"Turn off that racket, for Chrissake," said Ned irritably, before he'd finished his first drink.

At first I didn't know what he was talking about. I was accustomed to talking over the noise in the background when I had company.

"Turn what off?" I asked, and looked around me as if to see the source.

"That AM radio, that shock-jock shit you're listening to," he said.

I cocked my head and caught a few obscenities. The voice didn't shy away from coarse invective: this piece must have been some standup routine, a foulmouthed rant. It liked to take a run through those, from time to time. I was pretty sure the FCC wouldn't have let those words onto the airwaves and got distracted for a second thinking Ned should've realized that too.

Then I realized the implications of what he had said—the sheer impossibility—and after a double take I walked away from the stove and sat down, stunned.

He was hearing it.

"Well, shit, OK. I'll turn it off myself," he said, and went to the radio on the stereo, where he overlooked the darkness of the control panel and spun the volume knob to zero.

The voice didn't miss a beat and Ned said fuck, it must be coming from the neighbors' and he wasn't in the mood to walk over there and yell at them. There followed a tirade about said neighbors, who were hippies, a category Ned reviled. He ranted about their refusal to wear deodorant and their seaweed-harvesting business; he shoveled his dinner down, took an aspirin and went to bed with earplugs in.

Earplugs had never worked for me.

I'd lifted Lena from her high chair and she was sitting on a mat with arches over it, soft toys that dangled from the arches. When Ned disappeared down the hallway I heard the voice, rising again and switching into a milder patter. For once I was able to record what it said—a couple of quotations. On my laptop I found attributions to famous writers, and I wrote the quotes down. "It requires wisdom to understand wisdom: the music is nothing if the audience is deaf." "None so deaf as those who will not hear."

While Ned and Lena slept I went into a panic. I stayed up all night; I tried to fall asleep again and again, but I couldn't, and so by 3 a.m. I gave up and put sneakers on and went walking—at times even running—in the dark, in the cold, through the silent neighborhood.

The houses all seemed like statues, the cars, the trees all seemed deliberately placed to me. Of course, most of them *had* been deliberately placed, deliberately built or planted there, and yet their placement suddenly possessed a different character. It was as though they watched me, as though their positions had been decided by some unified and motive force . . . I was getting paranoid, I thought: first a delusion of hallucination, and now paranoia had come for me.

Ned had heard it. Ned, indifferent, superficial, and seemingly sane as the next guy, had heard the voice. Someone else had heard it, therefore it couldn't be purely hallucination. I had been wrong.

Starting at that moment when Ned cursed, and on and on forevermore, in my mind, *it could not be and was not a hallucination.*

It was something else.

. . . . .

MY PARENTS' RELIGION had always seemed like a curious habit to me. While I was growing up I drove to services with them on Sundays, I said grace before evening meals, I went through the motions agreeably. But as soon as I was old enough to have my own opinion their church-going fell into a category like the next-door neighbor's golf hobby, the macramé wall hangings accomplished by a wall-eyed teacher I had for fifth grade. I saw the neighbor bundle his clubs into the back of the car on days with pleasant weather; I watched the teacher sorting wooden beads to string into an orange owl. I wondered what shaped the particular details of their interests, where their strange avidity came from.

I thought about mortality, sure, and I felt the pull of soulful music, but I never met with elevated feeling sitting beside my parents and listening to their minister. For me it couldn't be found in the cramped and unlovely building of their church, the boring sermons, the congregants next to us (mostly aged, with skin tags and wadded sleeve-tissues). It would have been as out of place there as it was, for me, in the plaid of the neighbor's golf bag, the yarn of the owl.

What seemed as though it might partake of the awesome or sublime was away from these close-up elements, away from the grainy texture of everyday. It was in cloud passage, in the galactic sweep; it was the stars beyond count, footage of herds of beasts thundering over grasslands or flocks darkening the sky in migration. I saw it in the play of light over rivers, the rush of multitudes, large beauty: a utopian sunset, the black cloudbank of a looming storm.

Meaning can be attached to it or not, I thought when I was younger, but either way the sacred has to live apart.

Later I saw that the sacred *was* the apart, the untouchable and the untouched. Divinity is only visible from afar.

THE NEXT MORNING I watched Ned like a hawk as soon as he woke up. I stared at him when he came into the kitchen and poured his coffee (with the voice nattering on to me the whole time as usual). But he said nothing. He didn't seem flustered or confused in the least, only impatient as he always was to get away—impatient to begin the real life of his day, out of our house, with people who mattered.

He never seemed to hear the voice again, or if he did, he never mentioned it.

Had I believed I was psychotic, no doubt I would have been relieved by what had happened—would have construed his hearing the voice as evidence of my sanity.

But I hadn't gone with the psychosis explanation in the first place, so I hadn't been seriously worried for my sanity. I'd comfortably believed in the power of a faulty and deeply complex neurology, and now that had been taken from me.

2

FIND THEM AMONG THE DEAD

I WAS GRATEFUL THAT I NEVER RECEIVED THE VOICE'S ASSESSMENT of Lena or me, that I was neither mentioned nor addressed directly. There were comments on what we encountered, though, the content of the patter overlapping with an image that flashed across a TV screen, a person driving the car beside us, a squirrel on a branch, a fresh berm at a building site. I'd see Lena's eyes alight on something and seconds later the voice would rush out a series of connected phrases, usually too swift and polysyllabic to be memorable to me, even when they were in English.

I got used to watching Lena's attention fasten onto a scene as only a baby's attention will, without seeming to focus—that round-eyed, often unblinking gaze of passive-seeming intake. But unlike with other babies this would be followed by commentary as the voice bounced over the object or landscape like a sound wave, a light wave, a stream of particles. I didn't get the feeling it was moving her, only that it was following her eyes, her fingers, her tongue. The model was accompaniment, not possession.

And what words came did appear, sometimes, to pass a kind of judgment. Their position seemed to be guided by aesthetics rather than morals—or no, that wasn't it either. More like, the morals *were* the aesthetics. What was ugly was wrong, but what was ugly was not the same as, for instance, what was brutal: ugliness was less the jarring or crude than the false or dishonest. Based on some standard I could never measure, the voice would be dismissive of systems or events, individuals or ideas, *products of human ingenuity.* It would rebuke the odd politician or captain of industry, engineer, or physicist; it would take even artists or musicians to task for *crimes against humanity.* And yet somehow the impressions I took from it were both less and more than opinions. They glittered like sun on water and glanced off again before I could fix my eyes on them.

Only a small number of the voice's observations were given over to the conditions of my life and Lena's, the rooms and scenes we moved through, but periodically there were upticks in interest. For damaged persons we encountered on the street, when we crossed paths with someone sick or in pain or disabled, often the voice would let loose a benediction, recite a snatch of poetry or hum a piece of music. To a shakily walking grandmother: *"Bright star, would I were steadfast as thou art."* To a kid with Down syndrome, *"The Carriage held—but just Ourselves—and Immortality."* Of all the lines of poetry, those were the only two I wrote down right away and looked up.

For an emaciated man we passed in the halls of a cancer ward, where we were visiting someone else, the voice had the famous lines from Chief Joseph after the battle that finally defeated him, which I searched via key words.

> I want to have time to look for my children; maybe I shall find them among the dead. Hear me, my chiefs! From where the sun now stands, I will fight no more forever.

Upon Ned's entry into our space there was always the same phrase, a faintly aggressive chant. In fact the chant was a tipoff that Ned was arriving. Typically it started up on cue a few seconds early, before I even recognized his presence.

> You can keep your Army khaki, you can keep your Navy blue, I have the world's best fighting man to introduce to you.

Google revealed this to be a Marine Corps cadence, one of the verses cadets call out when they're marching.

But Ned was never in the military.

A NEW GUEST came to us today. She's maybe a decade younger than I am, probably in her mid-twenties, and according to Don may stay a while.

She has an air of recovery, or so I thought as my daughter took her through the tour. She was nice to Lena in the cautious way of people who aren't used to the company of children but react graciously when it's imposed on them: patience, no talking down, a genuine interest.

Lena says the woman is a princess—probably because she's slim, tall and pretty, with long hair—and has spun a tale about her already. The princess fell from her throne through the deeds of an evil troll.

She awaits an act of magic, here beside the sea. Lena says a team of seahorses will arrive pulling a giant white shell, and in the shell the princess will be borne away to her own kingdom.

At this point the story gets convoluted, because the princess can't be taken away; that would mean her leaving us. Instead she will sleep in a shimmering palace on the waves, a palace hidden from us now that hovers invisibly beyond the whitecaps. A bridge of waves will stretch from the beach outside the motel to the princess's ancestral home, a white castle of pearl, and we will walk over this bridge to banquets held in our honor, for we may live there too. Inside the castle keep, a special room will belong to us, connected to the princess's royal chamber by a spiral staircase. The chamber is full of sparkling fountains and cushions of cloud. It features a four-poster canopy bed and live-in midget ponies.

The ponies are velvety to the touch and curl up on the bed like dogs, their legs tucked beneath them.

But Lena reassures me that we won't have to sacrifice our lodgings at the motel for this resplendence. No, we'll still treasure our motel home. We'll still frequent these faithful lodgings with their yellowing shower curtain and moldy grout between the tiles. We'll have *two* houses, she says, that's all—"one for regular and one for special occasions."

I'd go with her. I'd take the miniature dog-ponies and the pillows of cloud.

PEOPLE WHO SAY they feel the presence of the Almighty hovering close to them, their personal savior, or tell how faith dwells in their hearts—the advantage they have is that if God overwhelms them, they're free to retreat. Or if the knowledge is so overwhelming it can't be contained, sometimes they let it out with shaking and strange articulations, crying and falling, ecstasy. I admire the idea of this, though I've never shaken in ecstasy myself.

I like to imagine I could, under the right conditions.

My point is, abandon to the spirit has an appointed time and place: the spirit can't be on you all the time. I never thought of the voice as God, while it was with Lena and me; such a thought would have been an outrage. When I write about God right now, that three-letter word—so loaded, so presumptuous—it's a word that I use in hindsight, as close a description as I can get of that stray cascade of ambient knowledge that distinguished itself from the static of everything else and filtered down to me.

So the voice wasn't God to me then, but in the months after Ned heard it, when I couldn't think of it as hallucination anymore, I was confused and stowed my questions in a locked compartment. Some things were unexplained; well, some things had always been. But I listened to it differently once I couldn't believe it was my own confabulation anymore. I gave it more credibility.

My brain's a little above average, according to standard aptitude tests, but not far above: I was always bad at calculus, I had no patience for high school chemistry. Whatever intelligence I have isn't rated for the ornate subtlety of the divine. Most of the time the voice was still wallpaper or elevator music as it streamed past and over me, citing, listing, cajoling, eulogizing, heckling. If I stopped what I was doing and concentrated on it, it quickly dazzled the faculties.

But there was no aspect of feeling chosen, no conviction of being purposefully anointed. We might have been sitting in a lounge chair on the green grass of my lawn, reading, when suddenly a bank of cumulus moved in and rain began pattering onto the pages of my book and the skin of my arms and we had to go in. I never believed the nimbus had chosen her or me or us on the basis of special qualities. I have other failings but I'm not subject to visions of personal grandiosity.

When I looked at holiday crèches or paintings of the infant Jesus I recognized the parallels—that Jesus as an infant had been believed to contain divinity, at least in retrospect—but there the similarity ended for me. I didn't think Lena was a prophet or a messiah.

More or less, in the time after Ned heard, I put off the question of causation, deferring inquiry.

The question of origin was too much for me.

LENA'S SECRET PRINCESS is named Kay and hails from the fair land of Boston. She's a med student there, or possibly a resident or a nurse. She has a hospital job holding babies, according to Lena, so maybe she's assigned to a maternity ward. She seems reluctant to discuss her work so I haven't pressed her.

I let Lena eat lunch on the bluffs with her and they went out wrapped in scarves and wearing puffer coats, though it was mild, for Maine in fall, and the big jackets were overkill. They spread a blanket on the dry grass. I could see them from the back window in our room—the room's best feature, a picture window that offers a view of the cliff edge and the sea. Lena chattered constantly—I watched her small head bobbing and her hands moving—and Kay smiled indulgently as she followed Lena's gestures. And yet somehow Lena seemed to be looking after Kay, not the reverse; the young woman's face was shuttered, and only when Lena spoke did she become animated.

It's one of the bargains I've made with myself, to let Lena have the company of relative strangers as long as I'm nearby and can keep an eye on them. I try to compensate for the lack of other children in her life and the rarity with which she sees her extended family. Of course, it *doesn't* compensate for that; she's an extroverted little girl, always has been, and likes to caper and perform. People are Lena's game.

For her a trip to the post office in town is a trip to see Mrs. Farber, the gum-popping straight talker who presides over the counter; a trip to buy groceries to stock our kitchenette is a visit to Roberto, the skinny cashier with the soul patch and exuberance about cartoons. She knows all the cashiers' favorite colors, pet names, and birthdays. A trip to the big-box store a couple of towns inland is a carnival of anecdotes during which Lena recounts our previous trips at great and exhausting length. She has perfect recall of people she's met even once. "Julio, he's a Pisces that means fish, cars are his hobby, like racing cars that go fast. He has a niece named Avery, the tooth fairy brought her a charm bracelet with clovers on it. Faneesha likes those yucky cookies with figs in them, she learned to tap-dance in Michigan but once she ran over a worm that came out flat."

I COULD OCCASIONALLY discern what I thought were shadings of emotion in the voice, shadings of will. Maybe those shadings were my interpretation, but thinking about it now I'm not surprised, because after all the voice was words, sometimes converted to music or other sound, and I don't see how words can follow each other without implying emotion. Even the effort to control emotion is an act of words, while every effort to control words is an act of emotion.

I didn't catch much at a time but there were recurrent themes in the patter that I learned to recognize. The voice made light of what it held to be false ideas—for example, the yearning for an all-powerful father who grants wishes and absolves. On that subject it seemed to evince something like condescension, rattling off mocking wordplay when we passed a church marquee or once, another time, while I stood at the front door trying to get rid of a Witness. *Omnimpotence,* the voice said more than once. *Omnimpotent being, omnimpotent force. A great and ancient omnimpotence.*

Sometimes it sang an eerie lullaby. *Oh little man, tie your own shoes,* it would sing, on the heels of a passage about the all-powerful father. There was a fire-and-brimstone sermon it liked to recite by an old-time preacher; it interspersed this text with laugh tracks and sang the cradlesong afterward. *Oh little man, dry your own tears. Oh little man, there is no knee. There is no knee to dandle on. Bury your dead, oh little man. Let darkness fall over the land.*

Property was an object of mockery too—the ownership of land, of pets, and even of inanimate objects seemed held to be an elaborate charade, maybe a shared psychotic disorder. The voice inflected words like *owner* or *rich* with irony—as though these should be bracketed, in perpetuity, in quotation marks. Once it said *Fool, you are owned by the sun.*

I couldn't find an attribution anywhere. *No results.*

But in general such great swaths of what it said were borrowed or adapted that they were already familiar—part of the background of culture somehow, part of the landscape of the commonplace. I sometimes wondered if all of it was borrowed, if it was all pure appropriation, a colorful textile made only of copies.

I'd started reading in philosophy, every so often, and that was when I came upon its first word to me, the sound I'd heard in the hospital before it spoke English. That word was *Phowa*, or *poa*, meaning "mindstream" in Sanskrit—the transference of consciousness at the moment of death, was one meaning.

Phowa (Wylie: *'pho ba*; also spelled *Powa* or *Poa* phonetically; Sanskrit: saṃkrānti) is a Vajrayāna Buddhist meditation practice describable as a "transference of consciousness" or "mindstream." —*Wikipedia 6.20.2009*

Sometimes there were brief flickers of foreboding, brief intimations of the voice's departure, but I tried not to invest too much in those. I didn't want to be disappointed so I didn't hope too hard. When I caught a glimpse of a future leave-taking, a tiny slip of possibility, I didn't trot out the streamers or confetti or whistles, the bejeweled gowns and conical party hats, the jeroboams of champagne.

I waited quietly, holding my cards close to the vest.

. . . . .

CURIOUSLY TWO MORE guests have arrived at the motel right on the heels of Kay. By the standards of this place, it's a madding crowd.

They're two middle-aged men, a couple, and I can't help but feel that they, like Kay, are in some state of dismay. Maybe it's conjugal, a conjugal problem, but I feel like it's something else. One of them seems to be consoling the other half the time, he has a steadying hand on the other guy's shoulder practically whenever I see them.

They checked in at the cocktail hour—I have a glass of wine before dinner most days, while Lena and I play "Go Fish" or "War"—and shortly after that we heard a knock on our room door. When I opened it there was Don, the two men standing behind him, politely waiting, and Don peered past me and asked Lena if she wanted to conduct a tour. Typically she has to pester him for that; she'll run along the row of room doors to the lobby as soon as she sees a car pull in and beg to be the tour guide, and Don will check with the new guests to see if they're sufficiently captive to her charms. But this time Don sought her out, and it thrilled her, of course.

So we set out, the four of us—Don peeled off toward the lobby again—and I talked to the balder of the two men while Lena kept up her monologue with the other, a gaunt, handsome blond called Burke who seems to need consolation. The balding one, Gabe, said they wanted to take advantage of the off-season rates, they don't go in for tanning anyway, the cancerous harm of the sun's rays; winter beaches are just fine. Nor do they like to swim, he said, except in pools that are very clean. They also do not fish, surf, parasail, or favor any other ocean-related activities.

It became clear to me—as we stood near the ice machine and I listened to Gabe rattle on about bikini- and Speedo-clad crowds lying on beaches, the rude spectacle of this—that the two men *knew* Don, that Don was a personal friend of theirs, and that was why he'd felt all right bringing them back to our room.

At that moment I saw Don coming out of the lobby again, this time with Kay; they walked with their heads inclined toward each other, talking low. And it struck me with certainty that Don knew *Kay*, too. In fact it could well be that *everyone* else staying here already knew Don; that Lena and I were now the only guests who had not known Don before we came to stay at his motel.

I felt a little jarred.

And now I couldn't remember how I'd found the place, when we first came to stay. Had I driven past a billboard? Had I sorted through online reviews of budget motels? But I couldn't remember a billboard or a review. All I recalled was driving up the long gravel road in an exhausted reverie, hardly thinking, and turning into the small parking lot, shaded with pine trees. I'd liked the peeling wooden sign.

Welcome to THE WIND AND PINES.

I had a feeling of unease, flashing back to the movies I'd watched when the voice was first with me, a vision of black-clad people leaning over a baby carriage. I thought of a sedate old apartment building that was in truth a hive of sinister insects, where behind the ornately carved doors, in sleepy luxury, the neighbors quietly worshiped some dark beast.

I wondered, if I asked Don how he knew them all, whether he would tell me a simple story about how he'd gotten to meet them or would avoid answering my question. I felt a temptation to try this, to confront Don shockingly, demanding information.

But my misgivings are absurd, I realize that. The motel is Don's home, and motel managers can have friends to stay like anyone else.

WHEN THE VOICE fell silent relief washed through me like bliss. I know everyone has reliefs as the days run their course: the feeling of relief is as familiar as a hiccup or jolt of fear. But this relief was the swiftest joy of my life.

Lena said her first word early in a day, so indistinctly that at first I took it for a murmur. She crawled across the rug and began idly banging on my shoe with a red sippy cup. I was skimming the news on my computer, a mug of coffee at my elbow, when she repeated the word, *Ma-ma, Ma-ma,* until I pulled out of my reverie and looked down.

Then she stopped saying it, her mouth falling open as she gazed at me. And in the wake of her utterance a new silence fell around us like a sheath.

I sat in startlement for a few seconds—it seemed to me that the silence had its own soft, rising hum.

This was it, this was how it happened: this was its departure. Her first word had supplanted the voice. And suddenly I knew, in a rush, what had been suggested to me, what had been hinted at opaquely in the preceding weeks—the voice had a life cycle. It passed through those who were newly born, in the time before they spoke, and when they spoke it moved on, displaced by the beginning of speech. It lived in the innocence before that speech, the time that was free of words.

The end, the end, I thought: *the beginning.*

I picked her up and laughed, bouncing us both around.

For a while, after she said that first word and the voice fell silent, I was worried it would return. This reflexive, ritual worry recurred whenever I found myself in an anxious frame of mind.

But the voice didn't return, and by and by I persuaded myself to stop fearing.

And during the new silence I spent weeks, even months in an altered state—the euphoric state of a lottery winner, as I imagine it, or maybe a newly minted Nobel laureate, a state of incredulous rapture. I've never won a lottery, I've never been given a prize, but I had this. I floated wherever I went, my baby in the stroller ahead of me or on my back—my tiny girl toddling contentedly beside me, holding my hand. I smiled a lot, people said, shone like a bride.

Ignorance *is* bliss, few sayings are so demonstrable, and I was blissful without the voice, I drifted on thermals. I loved the freshness of the new quiet and sometimes sat deliberately in a hushed room, picking out faint noises from the street. And the opposite too—I played favorite songs loudly, held Lena and danced with her. Excitedly I prompted her to speak, I asked for repetitions of the word *Mama*, for other words, whatever. I would lean down over her little face with such joy in the movement!—lean close to her, lean eagerly—no one between us, nothing but sparkling air.

Since the voice fell silent I've often been able to put the whole episode behind me. There've been many days, many nights, whole weeks when I've been able to forget the untenable aspects of that time, the first year of my daughter's life.

I've frequently been successful in my denial strategy, and it's probably this success that has allowed me to live a life that, aside from my domestic problems and our flight, could almost be called normal.

SINCE GABE AND BURKE arrived, the routine has changed. Actual maids come now, since the linen laundry is more than Don can handle by himself. They're a couple of teenagers from town who do their work with earbuds in and haven't introduced themselves to us.

Plus Don has opened up a spare room off the lobby and begun to cook. The food he offers is simple and good—special dishes for Lena, a children's menu with pancakes or cinnamon rolls in the morning, macaroni and once bite-sized hamburgers at night. These didn't tempt Lena since she doesn't eat meat and never has; she feels too sorry for killed animals.

The motel guests have been gathering in the café for breakfast and dinner, and since Don keeps limited hours—as befits a chef with a base clientele of five—we're usually all there at the same time. And it's not just the guests anymore; stragglers from town have also been appearing here. First there were two or three old people wanting a break from microwave dinners, then a portly state trooper; Faneesha, the UPS driver, came at the end of her rounds and was instantly commandeered by Lena. Every night there are a couple more customers.

The first evening it felt strange to dine in the room off the lobby. I hadn't realized how much of a restaurant's mood comes from an illusion of permanence. The place seemed like an oversize supply closet, despite the flowers and candles and checkered tablecloths. But already by the second dinnertime it didn't seem preposterous to call it a café— even the lighting seemed altered, though the lamps and candles were in the same places. It had gotten more welcoming overnight.

Lena was intent on the patrons, and on the fourth night she hit the jackpot: a kid came in who was only a year older. He was with his father, whose attention was captured by a cell phone, and the boy too had an electronic toy, a glossy plastic robot that emitted tinny music and recorded the children's voices to play back. The two of them traded it to and fro, giggling at the senseless insults they made the robot pronounce. Lena got so enraptured she forgot to eat.

I was absorbed in the question of Thanksgiving, whether Lena and I should visit my parents. They're not too far from here, but on the other hand Ned knows the house. I was weighing the risks while the guests talked and laughed and Don carried food back and forth with the help of a teenage girl from down the beach. A song was playing in the background, a sad folk song about a love-struck, gunshot bandito dying alone in the hills, and I looked out over the ocean, reached to rest my fingertips on the cold window. I thought of other Thanksgivings, suffused in an amber glow.

When I turned back to the room again, my fingers still tingling, the guests all seemed familiar. It was one of those soft sinkholes of time when separate elements coalesce—we were a blur of sympathy, the air between us pockets of space in one great body, one saltwater being, unplumbed depths where the ancestors came from, primeval well of genes . . . the feeling stretched like a generosity, the gift of oneness. Who cared about those differences we had, those minor distinctions that kept us apart?

But then that lofty idea turned trivial, from second to second its shine faded. It's your *commonality* that's frivolous, I scolded myself, you want to think we're so many eggs under the down of a nesting bird—you want to be held there forever, sheltered in the warmth of a body that watches over you. You want it as almost everyone wants it, to *pretend* that we're one. To let the burden of our separation be lifted at long last.

That was all it was, I told myself: desire. Was it the case that every hopeful sentiment, each stir of communion and vision of eternity, is nothing but a projection of desire?

It's what we want that we see, not what *is*, I thought. Scraped bare, we're nothing but machines for wanting.

I felt a maudlin pity for us. Together now for the blink of an eye, I thought drunkenly, before we tread off into separate futures and one fine day, though motes of our bodies still persist, the last traces of our inner selves vanish. The private selves evanesce, the secret worlds that only *we* knew. The nameless company of ourself, that warm sleeve of being—goodbye, old friend.

With the voice, very rarely, I'd also felt these moments of loss, as though I was looking back at myself from somewhere past my death. At times I'd felt a cold freedom then, when my irritation faded and tears caught in my throat. The long view, the far distance of the stratosphere, clean and thin as high air. The axis where distance and closeness met, the axis on which the world spun.

But back then, at those rare times of elevation, the common ground had felt like truth. Now it was only a wish.

Drunkenness, I thought, could pass for a connection to God.

At my elbow Lena was making the plastic robot dance and laughing at it. There were plenty of people around. I should have felt content but I was distant, like an elder sitting apart, watching others that spun and shrieked, so busy in the midst of life.

IT WAS AT the tail end of that golden summer when the voice went quiet, coming down off the high, that I realized we had to leave Ned. I had no more patience for his complete detachment, his reluctance to come home and rudeness when he did—a rudeness that positioned us as his unpleasant burden. In my own home I had to feel like someone else's dead weight, and I couldn't keep carrying it. We had to leave Ned and the string of young women in whose name he missed our weekly family dinners, who left their sunglasses in his spotless BMW, and after the BMW was gone, in his more electable Ford truck.

Neither the car nor truck ever contained a baby seat. Later I racked my brain trying to recall a single instance when Ned had driven the baby anywhere, but I came up with nothing.

I do remember, though, that one of his girlfriends wore lacy pink boyshort underwear, which found its way into the pocket of a jacket I took to be dry-cleaned—I hadn't checked the pockets beforehand and the panties were handed across sheepishly afterward by a drycleaner. They hung in their own plastic bag, a doll-sized scrap of fabric dwarfed by the hanger.

The drycleaner had cleaned them for free, he said to me shyly.

By then I'd known for a while that I didn't love Ned. But now, rather than existing in an amiable neutrality toward him which I'd tried, even before Lena was born, to cultivate and fit into the space where love should be, I'd come to actively dislike him. I turned the corner one day with nothing else to preoccupy me and caught sight of my own dislike, plain as day.

It couldn't be talked away, couldn't be handled in therapy (which

Ned, in any case, would never have gone in for). It was as solid as a dining room table. His coldness toward me I might have tolerated for Lena's sake, had he been any vague semblance of a father, but his dismissal of her got more and more unbearable. I had the devotional urgency of new mothers and couldn't help feeling that a baby was a standing debt, a debt to a forming soul.

His lack of paternal feeling was unsurprising, in the end, since he'd never promised anything else. And it was true I'd forced him into parenthood by having Lena instead of getting a D&C as he wanted me to. I'd told myself that when the baby was born he'd come around a bit. I never expected him to be a candidate for Father of the Year, but maybe, I hoped, part of a circle would be described, a slow curve into warmth. Surely a real, living child would thaw his chill. It was what happened, I believed.

Now I'm not sure where I got that belief—maybe from a TV movie. I committed a cardinal error of women, by which I mean an error to which women in particular seem prone: the error of expecting some-one else to change *toward* them, to grow into alignment. I expected love, change, and alignment from Ned, and all these expectations were baseless. The category of children was as alien to him as if he himself had sprung fully formed from the forehead of Zeus. His own dim trailer park childhood had ceased to exist after he emerged from it—in his mind, despite the odds, nearly a perfect man.

It didn't help that around that time he was nurturing his budding interest in politics. He wasn't a candidate yet, he wouldn't be for a while, but he was angling, forging careful alliances. Though he'd never professed religious faith, he started attending church "for the connections." He gathered new opinions around him like sacks he was hefting—sacks that bulged ominously, misshapen sacks full of hidden, gross things. Tired catchphrases would spring from his conversation in passing: "No handouts for welfare mothers," say, but also, a fetus was sacred.

It was hard not to take his remarks personally when they concerned, as they often did, categories such as motherhood or women. But at the same time the remarks felt like objects to me—prefabricated items he had purchased quickly in a store, items he was busily stuffing into his shopping cart without close scrutiny.

"BURKE'S BUYING DRINKS for everyone," said Kay, twisting in her chair to talk to me from the next table. "It's his birthday. We only have beer or wine, but Don's serving a pretty good Shiraz."

I accepted the pour of wine into my glass and raised it; we toasted Burke, Gabe saying something I didn't catch about rare hothouse flowers (Burke is a horticulturist). There was a rowdy crowd from town that night, some large-bodied, friendly-looking women out celebrating a remission; one of them had a tumor that had responded well to treatment. Everyone drank on Burke's dime and I embraced once again the sentimental illusions offered by wine—what was wrong with them, after all? I'd clearly been hasty.

"You know what they say about horticulture, right?" Gabe was saying, still on his long-winded toast. "Dorothy put it best: 'Well, you can lead a horticulture, but you can't make her think.' "

I watched Burke laugh and raise his glass; I recalled a half-joke the voice had told. *Have you heard the one about the Buddhist fly?* It was a lovely iridescent fly, ran the riff, that flew through a room buzzing *I am one with the universe, I am one with the universe.* The fly felt the descending peace of its enlightenment, the liberating lift of air beneath its gossamer body. How beautiful it was! How beautiful the very air! How blessed was its flight!

The swatter fell.

You were not one with the universe, my friend, said the voice. *But* now *you are.*

But Don *was* serving a good Shiraz. In its flow I decided Lena and

I *should* go see my family, we *should* sit at the table with them and be thankful for what we had. I recalled our dusty old centerpiece of orange-and-red silk leaves and decrepit Indian corn, which my mother always trots out with an enthusiasm that borders on the poignant.

I HAVEN'T FILED for divorce and custody yet, though I could and probably should—partly because I know it would hurt Ned's career and therefore anger him, partly because it also presents complications for me, since I removed our child from him without a written agreement.

It took me years to leave, years of deciding and planning—far longer than it had taken me to get married in the first place—and by the time I was ready it was past Lena's fourth birthday. I should have divorced him before we left, when he had no legal leverage over me. I don't know why I didn't—ineptitude. I must still have been spellbound, and I didn't know how serious his politics would get, I didn't anticipate a fight. I expected a quiet, long-distance divorce about which he would be indifferent, as he was about me, as long as he got to keep a lot of money.

Or maybe I was afraid, just afraid to take a direct and final action. Maybe it was common cowardice.

When I told him we were leaving he never once objected: there was no tension around our departure. And I only decided to evade him later, when he started stalking us instead of asking for a visit. It was only in the White Mountains that I knew his motives were strong and impersonal, as, with Ned, any motives must be. It was then that unease crept into me.

But there's no proof I didn't spirit her away against his will, only a few emails after the fact that wouldn't bind anyone legally.

WHEN I DECIDED to make the trip I hadn't told Don the details of our domestic situation. He only knew I wanted to keep a low profile at the motel—that much was obvious. So I finally took him into my confidence about Ned, I told him the story. I included Ned not wanting a child, his proven disinterest, until his Alaskan PR campaign, in a family reunion; I left out, needless to say, our visitation by the possibly divine.

To my relief Don didn't see me as a kidnapper. Rather he was alarmed for us, he tried to convince me to skip the dangers of a Thanksgiving in my parents' house and spend the day with him and the other guests. He promised to cook a prize turkey, with something vegetarian for Lena; he would bake pies, pumpkin, fake mincemeat, and pecan.

But I felt bad for keeping her from her grandparents so long, and from my brother Solomon, Solly for short, and others in her family she'd spent too little time with—only a rare Christmas, a few weeks' summer vacation she'd been too young to remember well. Alaska is far from Rhode Island. On Ned's side she'd never known relatives; even if he hadn't been estranged from his parents, he wouldn't have taken her to meet them since he never took her anywhere.

We had to go, I said. I was betting Ned wouldn't dare approach me in my family's presence—my family with whom he'd always played the part of a thoughtful, upright man, my family without whose financial gifts to us he never could have started his first business, from which all else had sprung.

I was more afraid, I told Don, that he would corner us afterward, because it was when we were away from my family that he could coerce me effectively. An in-person encounter between Ned and me is my main anxiety. The prospect fills me with the fatalistic certainty that I wouldn't be able to pull away from him right off, not with Lena's eyes on us. Somehow I'm certain of this despite its weakness, its irrationality, despite the fact that I know it would be wrong, dead wrong for me and for her too.

If Ned gets to us physically I fear he'll outmaneuver me. From the day I left him and felt the welcome release of distance the prospect of his presence has terrified me. Always since then, whenever I think of seeing him again, I'm a deer in the headlights.

If he was watching my parents' house for the holidays, some men in suits and leather shoes might follow us when we left.

"If you have to go, have someone in your family drive back with you," suggested Don.

"But he could still follow us, and then he'd know we were here," I said. "From then on. And we'd just have to move out. I don't want to go yet, and Lena doesn't either."

Don nodded.

"If you want, I can meet you somewhere in my car. We can do a switch—you go into a store, you go through the back, we leave in my car. Whoever was driving your car could bring it back here once he'd given up and stopped following them."

I was startled that he'd go to such lengths to help us.

"There are different ways to do it," he said. "But the key is, you have to be careful. Don't think of complex dodges as ridiculous. It's worth it."

He said he'd known a woman who was abused and had helped sneak her in and out of shelters. But always, sooner or later, she would lose patience and decide to make a generous gesture, she would throw caution to the winds and be caught and beaten again.

SOMETIMES I CONSIDER wishfully whether, when she's grown up, it might be possible to tell Lena about the voice and stop being alone with it. I keep this record for that reason also: not to feel so alone.

Before I had Lena, when something upset me I talked to my friends about it in the standard way. But after she was born, when that ragged, uninvited disruption entered my life, I found I couldn't talk about it to my friends. Maybe we weren't close enough or maybe I was averse to risk. It can't be taken lightly, the rumor of mental confusion.

So this hybrid document is what I have instead, my journal entries mixed with thoughts that came to me later. I don't mean for Lena to read it—it's password-protected—because I understand that even if I fantasize about telling her, it would be the kind of unburdening adulterers sometimes do, a kind of selfishness dressed up as truth. The rules of sound parenting weigh against it. No, I write for myself or for no one. I have no stake in convincing an audience of my trustworthiness; my welfare isn't of general interest. I'm someone who was rained on for a period of months, rained on by word instead of water.

When it comes to my daughter, trustworthiness is the first thing I offer. I value it above all else.

BEING WITHOUT a car made me nervous, but on the other hand I'm nostalgic for trains, and Lena, it turns out, loves them. For her a train is a social bonanza: a long container of possible friends with the added bonus of scenery out the windows. It's far superior to our sedan, where she's limited to my company.

Skipping down the aisle of the café car—where a drooping, whey-faced man looked at us glumly as he wiped down the counter in front of a near-empty display of potato chips—Lena said she wanted to live in the train forever. That's how she expresses approval, sometimes adding a touch of the morbid: "I want to eat ice cream forever and ever, till I'm even older than *you* are," she's said to me before. "I want to stay in the motel that long, I want to walk on the beach." At her age even a day has an eternal quality, so that *forever and ever* is less a linear stretch of time than a form of reassurance. "I want to live on this *exact train* forever and ever till I die. Until I *die*, Mommy! Until I *die*!"

I told her about sleeping cars and she decided we needed *that* kind of train instead, where we would have curtains to draw across our bunks for privacy, supplies of chocolate bars and chips, warm sweaters for fall

and tank tops for summer; we would ride in our train over green hill
and dale, mountain and plain, bedazzled by the sights, enraptured by
our fellow travelers.

We finally stepped out onto the platform of the old station near
my parents' town. The sun was low in the dull-gray sky and a wind
whipped our hair around. Lena was perfectly happy to forget about
trains in favor of the reward of seeing her grandparents again. She
clutched my hand and scanned the station wide-eyed, though she can
only have half-remembered what my parents look like.

But she knew them right off, probably by their tremulous smiles.
I was looking along a row of lockers, past restroom doors and soda
vending machines, trying to cultivate the vigilance Don had urged.
But all I saw was a couple of teenagers slumped on a bench beside their
old-school boombox, belligerent sounds issuing.

"Nana! Grumbo!" cried Lena, and ran forward.

Her pet name for her grandfather, invented I'm not sure how,
has always been redolent of a booze-soaked clown—ill-suited to the
personage of my father, whose bearing afforded him, in the past, a
quiet dignity. These days he doesn't know his name, he draws a blank
equally on his history and the identities of his family, but still the
mantle of that dignity hasn't entirely dropped from him. He holds fast
to my mother when he walks, a dreamy look on his face suggesting a
dim and lovely scene back in the recesses of his mind, a hidden spring
from which he alone may drink.

Lena hugged them excitedly, ambassador of affection. Young
children are the standard-bearers of visible love, I thought, watching.
After we grow up and get sparing with our physical affection, children
are sorely needed to bridge the gap. I love my parents but the urge
to touch them seems to have mostly faded. Without Lena we'd be
stranded in the lonely triangle of adulthood, the lovable child I ceased
to be hovering sadly between us.

"Do you still have the kittens?" squealed Lena, who remembered kittens from a visit when she was three.

One day she'll separate herself with an adult coldness she'll be unable to control, uninterested in controlling; one day she'll probably touch me as rarely as I touch my parents now. She'll come and go, returning only for visits.

The thought is so acute, the outcome so near-certain I cringe, thinking: *This* is why parents want grandchildren. Really they want their own children back again, they long to feel that vanished and complete love.

I watched my parents' beaming faces as they bent to encircle her with their arms—my father doing so in a spirit of general camaraderie, not specific attachment. He doesn't recognize Lena across time but since his memory went he has learned to obey my mother; he simply believes her when she tells him that he knows or loves someone. He has agreed to go along with it. In a way this trust is the crowning glory of their lives, a final achievement. He knows my mother and through her he accepts the rest.

I'm often teary when I first see them again—my mother a little bit grayer but still solid and known, my father a meek shade diminished almost to nothing.

IN MY PARENTS' house, where I grew up, it's hard to convince myself to stay alert for watchers in the shadows. Their neighborhood's staid, the houses upright and boxy and spacious, the trees sheltering. It's well-mapped terrain for me and its textures make for a sense that nothing surprising can happen here.

So I'd relaxed my guard by the time Ned called.

Lena was playing with my brother in the backyard, where a rusty swing set and jungle gym remain from our childhood. Solly's good with children, though he has none of his own—he's younger than I am and prefers the bachelor life, long work hours punctuated by trips to Atlantic City to play poker and weekends drinking and watching sports with college friends—and Lena's smitten with him.

I sat on a stool beside the kitchen island, cutting pie dough, and watched out the window as he lifted her up to the monkey bars. My mother was unhurried in her preparations and the house was quiet, though the next day people I barely knew would come teeming in—old colleagues of my father's, a group from the homeless shelter my mother invites every year, a couple of church friends. When the outdated rotary phone on the kitchen wall rang, she answered it with a voice that faltered at first, though it was perfectly pleasant.

She mouthed *Ned* to me across the room and I slid off the stool, helpless.

"It's so good of you to remember us," she said politely. "Are you having a nice Thanksgiving?"

I went out of the kitchen and lifted the receiver of the hallway phone.

". . . missing my two girls, of course," I heard Ned say.

I recognized his angle instantly: loving husband, abandoned callously.

"You know, Lindsay . . . it's pretty tough to be alone. It's tough, over the holidays."

Ned's automaton nature is well hidden from guileless observers. My mother has never fathomed my leaving him, which was alien to her and which I can't hope to explain fully—especially as I've chosen not to mention, for example, his many affairs or the fact that he pressured me to end the pregnancy. That would upset her too much. I've said only vaguely that there were infractions and that Ned and I don't love each other. But that's an obstacle whose scale, she seems to feel, falls short of the requirements for divorce.

My mother's loyal and chooses to respect my wishes—most recently not to let Ned learn that Lena and I were coming. But she dislikes subterfuge of any kind, which goes against both her instincts and her ethical code; she can't shake off her early positive impressions of Ned, probably shaped by his good looks and the refined manners he affects in certain company (initially acquired from books on etiquette so he could pass among the rich as one of their own; then honed by practical experience). I believe she's always thought of Ned as *that nice, handsome boy.*

And of course my father is now effectively neutral.

My brother, on the other hand, has never trusted Ned; when I first introduced them he said to me privately, "Well, he's sure as shit white! That is some Crest toothpaste, bright-white shit you got yourself there!" He said it in a joking fashion, grinning at me affectionately and cuffing my arm to take the sting off. I knew what he meant: Ned's whiteness, unlike Solly's or mine, has a fifties Boy Scout aspect. It seems to extend deeper than his skin, which is as unblemished as his straight and beautifully formed teeth. And as the months and years passed Solly never warmed to Ned—for which I was eventually glad.

"I can imagine," said my mother weakly.

"I miss them. I really do. I fully understand, Lindsay, you don't like to get into a difficult position, an intermediary position, and I respect that and I would never ask it of you. I just—I miss them"—here a quaver came into his voice—"and I thought I'd feel a little better if I touched base with you. It's a family time. That's all."

"It is, yes," said my mother carefully, after a pause. "Well, Ned. I'm so sorry to hear you're feeling lonely."

"I've got to admit," said Ned, sighing, "part of me just can't believe she doesn't mean to come back. Part of me still holds out hope. I've recommitted myself to the church, Lindsay, and to my faith. And marriage—as a sacrament . . ."

"Yes," said my mother hastily. "Of course. I'm glad for your faith, Ned."

"Faith is what pulls you through," said Ned, "when nothing else will, just . . . nothing. I've had to face that, Lindsay. So in that way, this has been *strengthening* for me. For my *relationship* with *God*. At first I didn't want to see how much I needed this to bring me back to Him . . ."

I felt a wave of nausea at Ned's string of clichés and my mother's vulnerability to them so I put down the receiver. I stood there in the hallway, the faint squawk of the conversation still audible, arrested by an image. Ned's God was a life coach—the kind for whom you had to be at least a mid-six-figure earner. Ned's God was a superstar, a braggart and a motivational speaker, presiding from an office whose walls were lined with awards, diplomas and framed pictures taken with celebrities. Ned's God would have to take an interest in the workings of his personal ego.

Even Ned's Lagerfeld cologne, I thought, would be a matter of no small interest to the God he conceived of.

I smiled at that and the movement of smiling let me lift the receiver again.

Thankfully the talk of religiosity had passed and Ned had moved on to a discussion of his electoral goals, his new mandate to serve the people, and his humble wish for Lena and me to be with him in what was, it turned out, chiefly a humanitarian crusade for public office. He deployed some pieces of text from his website, evoking the twin needs to *restore values* and *build communities* (wisely passing over those pieces of his rhetoric that would not jibe with my parents' political leanings, moderate Democrat). He said the word *humbled* several times: he was humbled by the growing "grass-roots" support for his candidacy and also humbled by the "tireless dedication" of the campaign's volunteers.

Finally, it seemed to me, he was quite humbled by his own humility.

Later I'd try to explain his cynicism to my mother, the connection between his recent discovery of the joys of piety and his career. It was painstaking because she doesn't want to impute evil motives to anyone, much less a son-in-law and in spiritual matters—a generous but inconvenient aspect of her personality. I'd step lightly, not arguing my end too hard, but still she wouldn't be entirely persuaded.

"I'd just ask, if you do talk to her over this holiday weekend," said Ned mournfully, getting ready to wrap up, "I'd just ask that you give her my love. She doesn't take my calls anymore, and so I can't . . . say it to her myself. But I *want* to, Lindsay. You know? I may not have given her the . . . well, the full and complete attention that she obviously needed. I know that now. If I had it to do again, I would. There were pressures, of course . . . but I shouldn't have let my passion for my work come between us. I'd try as hard as I could to give her the attention that she really needs."

There were subtle stresses on certain words. And I knew. I knew *he* knew not only that I was in the house, but also that I was listening.

"WELL, DEAR," said my mother, coming in after she hung up. "Ned tells me he misses you. I *must* say he didn't say much about his little girl. I think that's very strange."

Probably the harshest thing she's ever said about Ned.

I mulled it over in my bed that night, what advantage he hoped to gain by calling. If he *was* letting me know he was watching, why? The element of stealth had been sacrificed, which must mean he wouldn't be showing up in person. So there was that.

I thought of his false regretful tone, saying *the full and complete attention that she obviously needed*. The implication, not too deeply buried, that I was secretly demanding, that I was a woman with hidden and deep reserves of *need*, was intended less for my mother than for me—for me to get a taste of poison, to see how sly he could be.

Maybe coming here physically was too much of a risk, though it was hard to believe his contest for the Alaska state senate was going to expose him to the media in far-off Rhode Island. He's egotistical, but not unrealistic.

But he knows Solly sees through him, and likely he didn't want to have to deal with my family—whose money was still in play for him—on their own ground.

I lay restless on the bed I shared with Lena, who was snoring lightly. I listened to the radiator knock. In the end I decided that, along with laying the groundwork with my mother for our eventual "reconciliation," Ned must want me to feel a threat. To know that he can still touch me.

3

HIGHLY EDUCATED, MODERN PROFESSIONALS

AFTER TEN DAYS AT MY PARENTS' HOUSE WE'VE COME BACK TO THE motel. Snow has fallen and lies in the evergreen branches in perfect white tufts. Meanwhile another three rooms have been filled.

Since it's a small place, rooms numbering one to ten, this means we're close to capacity.

"Business is booming!" I said to Don with forced cheer.

I felt put-upon, since the motel is supposed to be my personal refuge.

He nodded and smiled warmly.

"We're glad to have you back," he said.

Don's elderly father is among the new tenants, so not every new guest is a paying one, I guess. He totters around in faded plaid shirts, leaning on a cane, and smiles apologetically. When his arthritis is bad he lives here so Don can take care of him. There's also a pair of mannish, gangly sisters from Vermont, whom I haven't seen up close but who give an impression of short hair and protruding teeth.

The fourth new resident is a guy not too many years out of college who seems an unlikely person to land alone at an obscure motel on the coast of Maine in early December. He's handsome, with a five o'clock shadow, and unlike Kay—not far from him in age—has an arrogant manner. Maybe he's a drug dealer seeking shelter or a day laborer whose work has disappeared with the cold; maybe he has a trust fund but is aimless and deranged.

But I haven't met the new guests yet, save for sightings of Don Sr., because as soon as we got back from Thanksgiving Lena came down with the flu. Since we went to see the doctor in town she's been confined to her bed. She sleeps for most of the day; I stay with her, I read to her and I write this account. Occasionally, feeling stir-crazy, I emerge for a few minutes, locking the door behind me, and stroll to the lobby or amble to the edge of the bluffs and stare out over the ocean. I leave the picture-window drapes open so I can check on her.

WHEN WE FIRST got here, months ago now, I went over the clutch of notes I'd made during Lena's first year—some from the time of belief in hallucination and some from afterward, the uncertain time.

After the fact it was easy to find a thread that ran throughout them, a thread that reinforced my idea that the voice *had* said "Phowa," that it might have referred, on Lena's first day, to the transmigration of souls. I patched together pieces of text and saw a story there, I thought—did I imagine it, or was it real? I read the pieces as a story of consciousness, believing the voice had always known it would fade when its host began to speak on her own.

I uncovered references to the human brain, to "Broca's area" and "Wernicke's area," which at the time I'd assumed were geographic but which an online search told me had to do with the capacity for speech. There were terms like *remote insult* and *neural plasticity*. Yet there was also a lexicon of religious terms, of Hindu words like *jiva*, mentions of the Sikh brotherhood, the passing along of the soul from one body to another until its liberation.

There were allusions to Jainism and to African faiths—*Àtúnwá*, I was even able to decipher: a Yoruba belief in the rebirth of the ancestors.

KAY OFFERED to babysit Lena tonight while I went to the café to grab some dinner, to give me time out of the room. Lena was already sleeping when I got back after the meal and Kay and I talked in hushed tones, standing near the doorway.

She told me she was a med student and volunteered in a neonatal intensive care unit. There, she said, one of her tasks was "cuddling"— their name for holding babies, just as Lena had said. These were sick babies, some born without a chance of lasting, and they liked the touch of skin. Incubators and other machines weren't enough.

"My shift was late-night," she said. "You know, when the mothers were sleeping. Or some of the NICU babies didn't have mothers who could hold them, they'd be addicts or occasionally they'd have died in childbirth."

She'd hold one of these fragile infants and her next shift, if the infant had gone, she never followed up—it was the policy and she tried to observe it. But this part of her work had proved too much for her. Eventually it had driven her to antidepressants that didn't work and she'd spun out and taken a leave of absence.

She was unfit to be a doctor, she said, shaking her head, but she'd wanted to be a doctor all her life.

"I don't have much longer to decide, the program will give my place to someone else," she said, and looked down at the floor to hide the fact that her eyes were filling.

She's just a girl, I thought with a pang, grown up thin and sad. I wondered where her parents were, if they knew how miserable she was. Since I had Lena I see my own child in any young woman; before that they were only adults, but now they're former children.

How did a young girl come to be alone in a cold motel, I thought, a row of rooms, because she was deemed mature enough? Not long ago she'd lived safely, I imagined, in her parents' home, and now here she was, wretched. Alone.

Not everyone, really hardly anyone, is suited to the job of constant dying babies, I said to her as gently as I could. *Most* doctors wouldn't be equal to that particular task . . . she nodded but I could tell she'd heard this before and it was useless to her, though she was too polite to say so.

I felt low after she went away and curled up next to my daughter in her bed.

DURING LENA'S BOUT with the flu I was more solitary with my thoughts than I am usually, and I don't think it was healthy. I started to wonder if Ned *did* know where we were, if he'd known for ages, if I'd been wrong to think we were on our own the whole time. I felt more and more paranoid and I made up theories—he was watching us using satellites and GPS, he'd turned my laptop camera into a spy device.

In the movies it was easy.

The paranoia's still with me, exaggerated and ridiculous as paranoia has to be. I live alongside it the way I would an unpredictable roommate. A suspicion rises that we're not as far away from him as

I assumed we were, that Ned hovers unseen. Then I reassure myself, which works mildly: the nervousness subsides, until it rises again.

He's always known my parents' telephone number—it's the same number they've had since I was a child, I say to myself. So what if he called while Lena and I were there? It was Thanksgiving and I knew he might call, or worse. Our material circumstances haven't changed, I tell myself, I have no real evidence of his proximity here at the motel.

It's only that his voice—a warm South Carolina drawl that's alluring until you detect the insincere overtone—and his manipulative conversation with my mother have infected me, exactly as he intended. It's me realizing, hearing that voice for the first time in two years, that I've gone from what I thought was love to neutrality to dislike to open hostility. I'm contaminated by the discord between loathing Ned now and once having adored him: I remember my adoration acutely and wince. I don't know how much is shame and how much is confusion. My former, deluded self was a loose construction of poorly angled mirrors and blind spots, I can see that now.

But Lena's better. She woke up smiling and full of energy yesterday morning with no fever, and we've started lessons again. I'm relieved but out of sorts anyway, because besides my paranoia about Ned I'm also grappling to understand the staying of the guests.

In Lena's and my case I know why we're lying low. We have two scarce commodities: disposable income and my willingness to spend it on a dingy motel in Maine in December. I hold my willingness to pay for this cold privilege to be an idiosyncratic feature. But here are the other guests, also apparently willing and able to pay and stay.

They can't all be in hiding from estranged husbands; they can't all be, say, drug dealers on the lam. And even if they *are* all friends or relations of Don's, that fails to fully explain their presence, short of a simultaneous eviction from their homes. It's disorienting and is preoccupying me. Technically it's none of my business, though, and I'm reluctant to broach the subject with Don.

And the college drug dealer with the five o'clock shadow has been making overtures to Kay. He approached her in the café this morning and offered small talk about genres of orange juice.

"Who likes the kind with orange pulp?" he asked. "Where are these orange pulp drinkers? I don't want to drink the pulp. Do *you* want to drink the pulp?"

There was a certain expectant force to his approach that I recognized with curiosity. Pick-up lines have changed since the advent of *Seinfeld*; now they often take the form of one person asking another about a mundane detail, a baffling social or consumer habit. Maybe the idea is to forge an alliance in the face of seemingly senseless choices made by others. Anyway Kay shrugged at the orange-juice pulp opener, but she smiled at him.

Later she told me he isn't a college drug dealer but a guy who makes and spends fortunes selling Hollywood movies to foreign markets. His youth combined with his skill in this realm makes him a prodigy at profit, a producer or studio executive or other dealmaker, I can't recall the title she gave me. So he *is* rich, but not aimless or deranged, and his wealth, combined with the youth and good looks, makes it even more unlikely that The Wind and Pines would find itself by chance at the top of his list of winter vacation spots.

"What's he doing here?" I asked her. "I mean, why *here*?"

I wanted to ask, *Why are any of us here? Why* here? But it was too pointed.

"Not sure," she said, as though it was all the same where he was.

"Well, how about you?" I asked. "I don't mean why aren't you in Boston, I understand that. I mean how did you end up at this motel?"

Again she looked indifferent to the question but passingly curious about why it had been asked, the way a person might look if you asked them, with intense and focused interest, where they bought their toothpaste.

"I was here last summer," she said, flipping through a magazine about trout. "I came back for the rest. It's restful. You know. And Don's such a nice guy. Isn't he?"

"Don's great. But last summer," I persisted—because it was gnawing at me, the casual presence of everyone, their unlikely presence, their stubborn persistence—"how'd you find it in the first place?"

"Just the website," she said, and put down the trout magazine in favor of a yellowing copy of *Cat Fancy*.

As she reached for it one of her long sleeves rode up, and I saw a red scar along the wrist.

BURKE CAME TO HELP with Lena's lessons; he's her tutor in botany. They planted seeds in a doll-sized greenhouse we put together from a kit, Burke bent over beside her, avuncular and kindly. The greenhouse has rows of light-green pots maybe two inches in diameter, a line of small lightbulbs and transparent plastic walls. It sits on our windowsill.

Lena had said she wanted to grow a beanstalk, so Burke brought her several kinds of beans to plant. He cautioned her the stalk might not be large enough to climb on; it might not reach the sky. She nodded and told him that was just as well, because she didn't want to meet a giant or a giantess, she didn't want to hear a cannibal giant say "Fee, fi, fo, fum. I smell the blood of an Englishman."

She isn't an Englishman, she said to Burke, but she still thought the giant might want her, even if she's a girl and an American. She didn't want to hear that giant talk about smelling blood.

Burke patted her head.

"I promise, sweetie," he said, "there won't be any giants speaking to you from this beanstalk."

As soon as he said it his face went pale. He stood there for a few seconds and sat down heavily on my bed, leaned over and stuck his head between his knees.

I was taken aback—Burke had seemed more solid and self-assured lately, seemed to require less comforting.

"Are you OK?" I asked, leaning over him, laying my hand against his back and taking it off self-consciously.

He looked up and nodded.

"Sorry," he said. "Panic-attack type . . . sorry. I'm fine. Heading back to my room."

Lena cocked her head, confused; I watched the door close behind him.

"Here," I said, picking up a library picture book on plants, "let's read this part about how seeds germinate. *Most seeds contain an embryo and food package . . .*"

IT OCCURRED TO ME, reading about the transmigration of souls, that my early assumption of some kind of nonhuman power or supernatural omniscience had been impressively unfounded. It might have been just a *person's* thoughts that had got loose, the memories or knowledge base of, say, some overeducated, possibly unhinged individual whose stream of consciousness flowed along carrying the debris of a lifetime. Could be that Lena caught the ruminations of a scientist or scholar.

Maybe this is a ghost story after all.

Or maybe the information that's now carried by so many frequencies just caught in her as it passed, lodged in her body—the live feed of a humble taxpayer somewhere, erudite but alive. Maybe some unseen field around my infant simply filtered particles from the immense cloud of content carried by those millions of waves that pass through us all the time.

THE SISTERS FROM Vermont, it turns out, aren't sisters from Vermont: I'm bad at pegging guests' identities. Their teeth aren't even protruding, just large and blocky, and they're cousins from somewhere on the mid-Atlantic coast near Baltimore. Both of them are named Linda, a name that's common in their extended family; they're in their early fifties, friendly, good-natured and hearty. One is an administrator at a university while the other is retired from her career at a famous aquarium in Florida where marine animals do tricks for crowds.

When the Lindas went to town for groceries today we hitched a ride with them. They dropped us off at the library so Lena could exchange her picture books—one of which is too young for her, about a bear who's a splendid friend, the other of which turned out to feature cows rising in armed revolt. (They hold roughly drawn Uzis in their hooves; this puzzled Lena's literal mind due to the cows' lack of opposable thumbs.) To answer the question of the guests who don't leave I have to be more outgoing than I have been until now, so I'm trying.

The Lindas, being friendly, are helpful in this chore. Big Linda, as Lena calls her, told us about someone she knew who was bitten by a bull sea lion. "Right on the keester, kiddo. And let me tell you it made a mighty *broad* target," she chortled. She told Lena that performing seals at zoos and aquariums are not seals at all but sea lions; that some sea lions work for the U.S. Navy, finding things in the ocean; and that male sea lions can be four times the size of the females—weighing, put in the other Linda, *up to one thousand pounds. That's half a ton.*

Lena calls the other one Main Linda because she met her first. Main Linda goes swimming in very cold water, Lena said to me, once every year to help raise money for the Special Olympics. Lena's resolved to join her in one of these polar bear plunges, as she calls them. I have to restrain her from practicing.

The Lindas have embraced their nicknames.

When the two of us finished at the library we walked over to the local diner to have lunch. A beefy middle-aged man sat down beside us at the counter—beside Lena, I should say, with me on her other side. He ordered a Reuben, introduced himself as John and proceeded to engage her in a conversation about her gold and silver metallic markers. He was inoffensive, on the face of it, a neighborly fellow patron, yet I thought I detected something off-color in his expression as he glanced over the top of her head at me, a hint of a leer, some glint of beady self-interest.

So I hurried Lena at her lunch a bit. We shared a piece of sickly-sweet cherry pie for dessert, leaving bright jelly smears on the plate. Then we left, with the beefy man smiling after us as the door swung to.

Big Linda was waiting for us in her bulky car; Main Linda, who was buying birdseed in the hardware store down the block, remained to be picked up.

"Big Linda?" said Lena hesitantly, as we pulled away from the curb. "Do sea lions have really *sharp* teeth?"

While we waited in the car again, this time outside the hardware store, the two of them discussed sea lion dentition, a subject that was, to me, of limited interest. I sank into the warm seat in a half-dream, full of the sickly-sweet pie, grown even more sickly in retrospect, and mused on my attraction to the town's librarian, who seems out of place here. He's good-looking; his skin is a coffee shade but the geometry of his face seems less African than Eastern, maybe Malaysian or Indian, I don't know. It's noteworthy mostly because there aren't too many colorful immigrants in this part of Maine—in some parts there are Somalis and Asians but around here most everyone I've seen is plain old white.

When Mainers rise up against immigration it's often been Canadians they accuse of stealing jobs; once Maine loggers blockaded the Canadian border.

I stared out the window, which was fogged up and yielded no defined shapes, only hazy panels of white and gray. I realized I was thinking of sex, of the *idea* of sex or rather, to be precise, the idea of no sex—no sex at all. I mulled over my asexual existence as a mother, gazing at the foggy window, mulled over the asexual existence of many mothers, whose bodies, formerly toasted politely as sex objects when not worshiped outright, had been diverted from the sexual to the post-sexual. In the natural plumpness of motherhood they were summarily dropped by male society like so much fast-food detritus in a mall food court.

I wondered if it was impossible that I would ever be a sex object again, if I should embrace that impossibility or try to reclaim my status as a sex object—by, say, enrolling in pole-dancing classes as one of my old college friends had done after her divorce, enacting a middle-aged crypto-feminist stripper fantasy that seemed to keep her entertained.

I decided I wouldn't enroll in pole-dancing classes.

After a minute along those lines I gave up thinking. As I swiped at the condensation on the car window I caught sight of the beefy man, John, walking toward us down the sidewalk from the diner. A light snow had just begun to fall and his slab of pink face was a blur, so I couldn't tell if the small blue eyes were pointed in our direction; before the blur resolved he turned and disappeared through a door.

The falling snow made me want to shore us up snugly for the winter and brought a pang of homesickness for our house in Alaska, which had always been more mine and Lena's than Ned's, for all the time he never spent there. *Ned* should have gone, I thought, *Ned* should have left.

But I myself had chosen otherwise, no one had chosen my course of action for me, and so Ned had not left the house—rather I was the one who fled. I forsook my existence, my local friends, the belongings I'd slowly and carefully amassed over the years of my life up till then, most of which would mean nothing to him . . . I left it all, except for some file cabinets of photos and documents, a few boxes of books and a handful of childhood keepsakes I'd stowed in a small storage unit. I'd given up everything to keep Lena close to me and get us clear: nothing else had mattered.

This was still true, I reflected, still perfectly true, my intent remained the same, it was my decisions that were questionable.

In our old house in suburban Anchorage—a city where every street was suburban except three or four downtown blocks—I'd kept us warm through several Alaska winters, Lena and myself, I'd cooked soup and stews and lasagna and other hearty foods in a kitchen shining with copper pots and brimming with heat . . . I'd loved it there, I'd arranged all the spaces exactly the way I wanted them. It had been a golden burrow.

All we had now was a small microwave, its walls cool and thin. People we hardly knew, though they were nice enough. The motel's walls were thin too. I *had* no solid walls, I thought. Would a wind rise around us this winter?

A wind *would* rise, I could feel it already, rise off the gray ocean and howl at the thin motel walls.

And then there was my parents' home, far nearer than the house in Anchorage, with its solid brick, wooden floors, and soft throw rugs, vines dormant on their trellises till spring. My mother would welcome us, I thought, if only I could shake this phobia of Ned, if only I could just face Ned and stand up to Ned, if I was willing to call Ned's bluff.

Instead we were living in a room like a cardboard box, with no source of warmth except the wall heater. We were socked in, I thought, perched on the rim of the frigid Atlantic—unknown in a group of other itinerants passing through, their lives as opaque to us as ours must be to them.

This cold, flimsy box was where my irrational impulses had brought us, I thought, my formless certainties.

I HEARD THE YOUNG mogul pacing along the walkway outside the rooms this evening, pacing and talking on his cell phone. Lena was sitting in the bathtub blowing bubbles—she luxuriates in long baths, though without nagging she doesn't bother to ply a washcloth—and I was reading a magazine in one of our two armchairs, the bathroom door cracked open between us. We'd had dinner early because of her bedtime, but most of the other guests were at the café.

The windows of our room weren't open, since the temperature was below freezing; the heater thrummed, so at first I didn't hear his words. But his voice got louder; he grew agitated as the call went on.

"That's not fucking *relevant*," he snapped. "Can we not do this analytical bullshit? If I wanted an analyst I'd lie on a couch and jerk off for two hundred bucks an hour. Hell, put me in a Skinner box. Fix me! . . . I couldn't give a fuck."

I glanced at Lena to see if she was paying attention. But the bathroom was farther away from the door than I was, in my homely armchair backed up to the heater, and bobbing in front of her was a waterproof MP3 speaker shaped like a yellow duck and playing sea shanties. She was impervious to the young mogul's call, dipping a rubber whale toy in and out of the water as it consorted with the duck.

"It has nothing to do with that crap. I'm telling you. My mother was fine. My father was fine. They were both fucking *fine*. They're *still* fucking fine. Everyone should have such fucking decent and doting parents . . . no pervert uncles! Jesus *Christ*."

I swept a drape aside to look out, making a sour mother-face that went unseen. If he moved off before Lena caught on I'd be relieved—and it wasn't so much the swearing that annoyed me as the force of his anger. He stalked by in his elegant leather coat and kicked one of the square wooden posts that was holding up the overhang.

"Well yeah. I told you that already. Not so much now. Before. Doing coke raises your chances of that shit. Plus oxy . . . what? Harvard. Aren't there brain scans? Some other radioactive shit?"

I decided to join Lena in the bathroom, where I shut the door behind us and ran in some fresh water to rinse the shampoo from her hair. I was thinking the young mogul would be bad news for Kay, if she submitted to the sitcom pickup tactics.

I don't know if Kay needs an angry young mogul.

ON TV THERE were numerous "exposés" of small children remembering past lives. One two-year-old boy was born with the memories of a fighter pilot shot down in World War II, they said, and repeatedly enacted scenes of the pilot's fiery cockpit death. He showed a high level of competence at identifying bombers used on the Western Front. A girl of four painted watercolors apparently based on her great-aunt's early life as an orphan in Minneapolis, although the two had never met before the great-aunt perished of cirrhosis.

Their parents had been skeptical at first, the voice-overs told viewers, but over time had clearly seen no other explanation fit the bill.

"Young Alex's parents are highly educated, modern professionals," intoned one narrator. "They did not wish to accept the evidence that past lives are real."

A FEW DAYS before Christmas my car stalled out so I left Lena with the Lindas and got into the cab of a tow truck, where I sat beside a driver who pulled my car into the only car-repair place in town. Imagine my displeased surprise—although I shouldn't have been surprised, since after all the town is small—when I was greeted by the beefy man from the diner.

He was the owner, apparently, since he wore a button-down collar shirt while the other, thinner man behind the counter wore polyester-mesh with the name of the franchise appliquéd. The beefy man—John—reclined with his arms crossed in a posture of managerial ease; I stood across the counter and smiled wanly. I felt the discomfort I always feel in car-repair places, the low-level dread of condescension followed by cost inflation, and wished to call upon my considerable expertise on the workings of internal combustion. Unfortunately I had none.

Waiting for the man to finish typing and Beefy John to finish watching him, I looked around at the walls, at ugly posters for automotive service packages, tires, motor oils.

One poster was markedly different: it was for something called American Family Radio. I peered closely at it, an airbrushed-looking photo of a plump, pink-faced man in headphones, shining smugly. Inscribed beneath his face and what I guessed was the name of his radio show were the smaller words *The AFA Works to: (1) Restrain Evil by Exposing the Works of Darkness* . . .

"Ma'am?" said Beefy John, finally.

I tore myself away from the fine print.

"Hey there, and how's that pretty little girl of yours? What can we do you for today?"

"My car keeps stalling out," I said. "A Honda. It's a Civic hybrid—getting a little old, maybe. But it's always been pretty reliable. I can leave it overnight."

"A Honda, huh? Well sure, we can take a look at that rice burner for you," said Beefy John, and his smile said he was bestowing a favor. "B.Q. here will help you with the paperwork." He smiled again before he clapped the underling on the shoulder, tapped his forehead in my direction in a mock salute and disappeared into the back office.

"B.Q.?" I asked.

"'At's me," said the underling, typing.

"What does the Q stand for? If you don't mind the question."

"Quiet," he said.

"Quiet?"

"Be Quiet. Always saying that to me when I was a kid."

B.Q. looked up from the keyboard and grimaced. His teeth were a rotting brown from the gums up, old-bone yellow and tobacco brown.

Handing over my keys I realized Don wasn't due to pick me up for almost half an hour; it was bitterly cold outside and I needed to be warm while I waited. But Beefy John in his satisfied recline, his crossed arms, the words *that pretty little girl of yours*, the jagged mossy teeth of B.Q.—they made me uncomfortable. The words *land shark* came to me as I signed the work order, B.Q. leaning forward unnecessarily from the other side of the counter, so close that I could smell the residue of cigarettes. B.Q. wasn't a shark, surely, he seemed more ruined than fierce, but the teeth . . . I considered whether his meth use was current or past, whether teeth ravaged by meth could be reclaimed. Then I pivoted and walked out into the winter, pretending to have a goal.

Once I was on the sidewalk I slowed down and ambled, watching my breath fog and feeling the cold on my cheeks until I fetched up in front of the library and went in. I hadn't had that goal in mind, of all the thousands of possibilities offered by libraries no single one presented itself to me, but there, right away, was the librarian I was attracted to. I had nothing to say as he looked up from the front desk, nothing at all. And yet I felt better already.

"Sorry, just coming in from the cold," I blurted.

"What we're here for," he said.

I couldn't think of any more small talk so I wandered along the shelves looking at titles, plucking out books at random. I seemed to be in a section either for children or for adults who were childlike: true-life accounts of balloonists, explorers. Pictures of famous caves. Prehistoric animals turned to fossil—trilobites that looked like beetles, ammonites that looked like snails. *Real-life Monsters. Haunted Houses of New Orleans.* The more I looked at the variety of subjects, the more hopeful I felt.

Maybe we could travel, I thought. Not just in my small car—across the world. To the Himalayas, say, jungles, dormant volcanoes with crater lakes, those acid lakes that shimmer turquoise in the sun . . . we stood on the decks of ships, rode camels over Saharan dunes toward the pyramids, wandered the Prado, the Great Wall of China, treaded the paths of picturesque ruins. What, in the end, would keep us from the world? I'd planned to give her a solid, settled childhood, where she could have the same friends for years and run through the same backyards, a childhood much like my own. But maybe she didn't need that. Maybe we could sail away, out of this chill into a summer country.

I hadn't thought of the voice in a while, I thought (suddenly thinking of it). These days a memory of it will flash through me and what I notice is myself forgetting, the rarity of that flash. It's like sickness—the whole world when you're in its grips, but once gone, quickly dismissed. Within days you take good health for granted once again.

"We only have a fake log," said the librarian, behind me. "It's not as warm as the real thing."

Privately joyful that he'd spoken to me, feeling as though I'd performed a small but neat trick, I followed him to a reading room. In the hearth an electric log glowed orange behind its fiberglass bark. The chairs were overstuffed, the high ceilings dark, but still I noticed, trailing after him, peering with difficulty at the fingers of his left hand, that he wore no ring, and I was pleased. I felt like a cliché noticing, a woman who read glossy, man-pleasing magazines, a member of some predatory horde . . . he had broad shoulders, an elegant posture.

"I'm so glad there *is* a library," I said. "In a town this small. With only one gas station and no fast-food chain."

"The building was a gift from a wealthy benefactor," he said. "He made his fortune in lumber. His wife died young and he never remarried. He died without anyone to inherit his fortune. Brokenhearted, they say."

"Oh."

"So he left his house to the town for a library. In short, his tragedy was our gain," said the librarian.

"Oh," I said again. "Yes!" I couldn't think of anything else to say.

Luckily he smiled at me.

When he went back to his desk I sat gazing into the glowing seams of the artificial wood and wondered whether to ask him out. I wasn't sure I could. It'd be a cold call; I had nothing.

And yet I might be restless enough to do it, I thought, I was bored and agitated at once these days. I was constantly aggravated by the open question of the gathering of motel guests, frustrated by the problem of their continuing presence—and then, bookended with that problem, there were the limitations of my existence and the tedious routine of our schedule. I felt drawn to the librarian but at the same time ambivalent about the prospect of not being alone, that is, not being alone with my daughter, the two of us a capsule . . . the two of us close together after the leave-taking of the voice and our running away from Ned.

Of course it was premature to speculate, I knew nothing about him, but still, I thought, why actually try to know someone if you don't wish to know anyone at all?

Still, in the end you seek out company again. After the noise has passed, after the great clamor's hushed and the crowds have thinned—then a silence descends upon your room.

And though at first the silence is perfect, the silence is thought and peace, after a while the silence passes too.

IT WAS EMBARRASSING to ask him out and I had to buoy myself up with bravado: it didn't matter if he said no. I had nothing to lose. The worst that could happen was that my life would remain the same.

In the few moments after, waiting for him to decline the invitation as I rested my fingertips on the edge of his desk, I thought of a girl from high school: she'd been average-looking and not particularly good-natured—in fact she was manipulative, crude, and often picked on easy scapegoats, the poor kids with hygiene problems, the loners.

Despite this she always had a boyfriend, and her boyfriends were kinder and far better-looking than she. Waiting for rejection, I remembered her clearly.

Years after high school was over, when I was home from college on vacation, I ran into her on the street. We stepped into a nearby bar for a drink. I had an awareness of being only half there, as though the other half of me had continued along the sidewalk without acknowledging her presence. But we *had* caught each other's eyes, we hadn't flinched and glanced away in time—so there we were, perched on adjoining barstools with little in common.

We quickly ran out of old friends to mention and teetered on the brink of leaving, but we eventually succumbed to inertia and ordered more drinks. On the third she told me the key to men was that they always wanted sex but rarely had the luxury of expecting propositions. And they were *tired* of always having to be the ones to ask, she said. From the day they hit puberty they wanted to lay that burden down, so all you had to do, she said, was suggest sex and they would take you up on it. This applied equally with most married men, she said—to be honest, with any of them. Failure was rare, she said, and tipped back her glass all the way.

It was admirable, the ease with which she approached the question. It didn't change my own behavior, however, which in that arena was passive; possibly this was part of why I found myself married to Ned.

In fact, looking back, you could say my passivity in that arena was the start of my greatest failure.

But seeing her unremarkable face in the bar mirror, I felt awed by her attitude, part aggression and part simple confidence. I believed someone should shake her hand or pin a medal on her lapel, but that someone would not be me: for I, even as I was impressed, felt a lucid dislike.

Then the librarian said yes, and I was grateful to the girl from high school.

. . . . .

STILL, THOUGH, EVEN if the bogus exposés and hair-sprayed New Age gurus hawking their bestselling books about past lives had a point, there was no explanation I could find for *my* having heard the voice. There was no reason I should have had to hear anything at all, if little Lena had contained a reborn soul.

It wasn't as though she herself had spoken, like the little boy with his encyclopedic knowledge of Mosquitos and Messerschmitts. She'd painted no old-fashioned watercolors depicting orphanage memories from 1934.

"I'VE BEEN WONDERING," I said to Don as he drove me back to the motel, his backseat a neat row of paper grocery bags. "I was thinking this place would be quiet over the winter. I don't get the draw for all these people in the off-season. I thought you only ever had a full house in the summer, but now it's almost Christmas. Did you—I mean, just out of—were you planning on all of them arriving?"

Don was silent for a few moments as we ascended the long, slow road that leads up to the bluffs, changing from pavement to gravel as it goes. He reached out a gloved finger and scratched the side of his nose, shrugging lightly as he spun the steering wheel with the other hand.

"I'm trying to help them out," he said.

On the expanse of ground beside the parking lot Lena was playing, wearing her hot-pink earmuffs. She appeared to be piling the previous day's graying snow onto a grim effigy vaguely suggestive of a snowman. Around the dumpy figure was a large impact crater where she'd scraped snow off the dead grass.

Main Linda watched her from the doorway to her room, her hands around a steaming mug, ensconced in a parka with a fur-lined hood like she was Peary at the North Pole.

I realized the light was leaving: a long, knife-thin shadow was fall-

ing toward the sea from the dirty pillar of the snowman, which had
frayed sticks for hands, pieces of trash stuck on its torso for decoration
and what appeared to be a rusty zipper for a mouth.

I didn't like the look of it.

She ran to greet me when I stepped out of Don's car, her nose red
and running profusely above her scarf, bundled-up arms flung wide.
She's always excited to see me again—though if I'm being honest, as
long as she has someone else to talk to, she's almost equally excited to
watch me go.

> Though the U.S. is an overwhelmingly Christian country . . .
> 24% of the public overall and 22% of Christians say they believe
> in reincarnation—that people will be reborn in this world again
> and again. —*Pew Research/www.pewforum.org*

AT DINNER in the motel café I took a census of the guests. Lena was
making the rounds; having lost interest in her food quickly—for her,
food is never the point of a meal—she was stopping at every table,
talking to each guest, leaving me alone to watch her progress and
consider the obliqueness of Don's answer.

There were Burke and Gabe; there were the Lindas, Main and
Big. There was Kay, eating at a table with the angry young mogul
who, less shaven every day, was leaning across the table to talk to her
confidingly. Before long he'd be sporting a full mountain-man beard.
There was Don's father, sharing a large table with Faneesha while Don
cooked and the waitress served, and there were the newest guests of all,
an arty couple from New York, maybe in their early forties, who had
the room right next to Lena's and mine at the far end of the row. They
dressed tastefully and didn't seem to talk to anyone.

And then there were the regulars from town, including a woman
who dressed in multiple shades of blue and always ordered the chicken

pot pie and an old man who, before Don opened the café, had eaten only frozen meals since his wife died, Lena said. But I was interested in the motel guests, the motel guests only and why they were here.

Don couldn't have meant to imply his help consisted of letting friends stay for free—the young mogul needed no such help and the chic couple had arrived in two separate gleaming cars, each of which had to have cost six figures. So that couldn't have been what he meant.

On the other hand Kay was distressed, Burke was distressed, the young mogul was distressed too.

Maybe Don offered some other form of assistance.

IT TOOK ME till this morning to ask the Lindas. I asked while Main Linda was driving me to the auto shop; I asked her with no subterfuge.

"So why are you guys here?"

"My cousin took early retirement after some work-related stress," she said briskly. "Down in Orlando, where she lives. She's on her own, mostly, her ex-husband lives in Vancouver, the sons have grown up and left the nest. I get a long winter break. The two of us have been close since we were ten. I brought her up to make her take a breather."

"But why *here*?" I asked. "Specifically?"

Main Linda cocked her head.

"Our family used to have a house in the area. Not on the beach, inland. Came up every summer. We shared the place with the cousins. There was a candy store, we walked there every Saturday. Jawbreakers. Gobstoppers. You remember those? Giant round hard candies you could barely fit in your mouth, started out black and you went through all the colors as they shrank? Disgusting actually, kids taking the things out of their mouths all the time to look at the different rainbow hues, then sticking them in again. Filthy. Dyed tongues. Saliva. Yeah, we loved it though. Also, there were those Atomic Fireballs."

"We had those."

"Naming a candy after a nuclear mushroom cloud. Only in America, right?"

"Yeah. What I meant, though, was how did you choose this particular motel?"

"Liked Don from the beginning. And heck, the price was right," said Main Linda. "I'm cheap as crap. Always have been, always will be."

"Good to know," I said, but I was disappointed in my weak powers of detection. People revealed little to me, and I couldn't even tell whether they meant to be evasive or were just uninterested in detail.

Maybe Don opened up his motel to those in need. But why disguise it?

I was at a dead end, I realized, falling silent as I sat in Main Linda's heated passenger seat, and how did you get out of a dead end? You had no choice. All you could do was give up, turn around and drive the other way, drive back where you'd come from.

I mean I don't want to leave the motel *or* the town, I want to keep my date with the librarian, for instance, a prospect that pleases me out of keeping with its likely outcome. But the sense I have of failing to understand the motel's gathering has started to disrupt my sleep: I lie awake nights distracted by my ongoing failure to grasp why these people are here. Maybe there's nothing to fathom in the first place but maybe there is, and the uncertainty doesn't sit well with me.

And I'm not so sure anymore I need to be hiding us. Increasingly my past interpretations strike me as arbitrary and I pick through them, second-guessing.

There's a chance I could stand up to Ned, I thought, sitting in the car, a chance he couldn't make Lena and me do anything we didn't want to do. Maybe I'm just a coward, I thought, hunkering here, as I was a coward about divorcing him. The line between cowardice and caution was blurred to me.

For a moment, Ned started to look less like a threat than an inconvenience and the future seemed almost simple.

Sitting in Main Linda's car I lapsed into a daydream of peaceful retreat—retreat to my parents' house, their quiet street where snow fell in pristine layers over the lawns. Only the few residents of the block drove down that street in winter, only the neighbors' footsteps marred the sidewalk; the snow lay pure and gently curved on the bushes and old trees of the neat gardens. There would be no cold cement catwalk stretching between the bedroom and dining room, as there was here— no questions to speak of, either, beyond the mundane questions of the design and order of days.

I didn't relish the part where I, fully grown, would be choosing to live in my parents' house again, but they would be good to me and I could help my mother with my father, when she needed me. In that way I could do my part. We would stay there and Lena would go to school; I could get a new job, though I'd long since fallen off the tenure track—a community college might have me, or maybe a private high school. I could almost believe in a return to routine, an end to stealth.

I felt the wings of the normal touch my shoulders, ready to settle on me with a bland, insulating protection. I felt hopeful.

"Here you go, dear," said Main Linda, and I saw we were already at the auto shop. There weren't many cars in the lot: Saturday. "You want me to wait here till you make sure your car's ready?"

"No, that's fine," I said.

"You sure? It's no problem."

"That's OK. I've wasted enough of your time already. He said it was all done. You go ahead, Linda, and thanks so much. I'll see you back at the motel."

I regret those words.

4

IF I SHOULD DIE BEFORE I WAKE

B.Q. WASN'T IN THE OFFICE; BEEFY JOHN WAS ALONE. HE HUNG UP the phone as I went in stamping slush off my boots, shuffling them back and forth on the black rubber mat and making the electronic doorbell chime.

"Enjoying your weekend?" he asked.

I leaned over and scanned the bill on the counter, trying to pay attention to the line items as he explained what had been wrong with my car's workings.

As usual when a mechanic talks to me I put considerable effort into looking interested, even respectful. I was intent on that effort, though it warred against my instinctive dislike of John, when I detected someone behind me, felt or heard the brush of thick, expensive fabric against itself. I registered that the doorbell hadn't chimed this time and there was a scent, subtle but clear, which I had to identify—much as I wished not to—as a familiar cologne.

Beefy John, still talking about the car, looked steadily over my shoulder; I turned.

"Hey there, honey," said Ned.

THERE WERE THREE thinly padded, black folding chairs along the wall, beside a fake potted plant with dusty leaves. I sat down on one. The fake plant was two times a stand-in, I thought, as a fake plant it stood in for a real one, and then the dust on it, the full neglect, made it seem so purely symbolic that it became an imitation not only of a plant but of an imitation plant.

I wished I could stare at that homely fake plant forever, and never, ever look upon Ned's face.

I was ignoring Beefy John too, or ignoring the blank space left by him, because he must have retreated into the private recesses of the establishment. I felt a vacancy in the space over the counter. Had he given me back my car keys? It was as though I'd lost time, I'd skipped some minutes and found things changed. Instead of looking up I was staring at the fake plant and at myself—but from a great lunar or stellar distance, across a reach of airless space. I might have been a pushpin on a map, a piece on a board game, any tiny, manufactured item on a wide background.

I couldn't choose a direction for my attention. I failed to assimilate.

"Relax, sweetheart, it's all good," said Ned.

His presence and the vapid words were separate—the words, I thought as I gazed at a streak in the plastic leaves' dust, an impressively hollow comfort. In the instant when I turned from the counter I'd caught a flash of his handsome face, enough to register his features; but now I was insanely reluctant to raise my gaze to him again.

It *was* insane, I realized that—some kind of rapid breakdown. But I couldn't change the angle of my head. I sat heavy in the chair, sacklike. After a minute he lowered himself into a squat in front of me.

And even squatting he stayed graceful, not subordinate the way a squat can make you. I kept my head bowed as long as I could, avoiding the solid offense of his beauty. Before me rose an immaculate camelhair coat, unbuttoned; a well-cut dark-blue suit beneath it, complete with downy-white shirt and silver tie; crisp, businesslike wrinkles on each side of his knees where the cloth was stretched taut. Yes: even the wrinkles in his slacks possessed a symbolic efficiency. They bracketed his sculpted knees concisely, minutely telegraphing competence, even mastery.

I remembered being in bed with him, in bed where he'd always been so perfect that it disguised his lack of emotion. It didn't occur to me to wonder about what wasn't given.

Ned was still exactly the man he intended to be.

Inevitably I found myself looking into his face. He had a light and pleasant tan that must have looked as out of place in the Alaskan winter as it did in Maine. I tried to calm myself by picturing him in a sunbed at Planet Beach, slathering lotion onto his body, arranging the little goggles onto his face. I remembered how the fatless musculature of his torso was maintained with daily bouts of grunting resistance training. But it was no use, no matter how hard I tried to belittle him I couldn't reduce the feeling of beauty and threat he imparted.

Except for the anxiety of his nearness, though, I found I was less susceptible to his looks than I remembered being. I could see him impersonally by placing the barrier of my dislike between us. As I did this, his looks became less the features of a living person and more a formal structure—less animal than mineral, transmuted into a polymer that encased him in its petrochemical sheen.

Had he already sent his guys to the motel? *Henchmen*, I repeated silently, *henchmen*, a comical word I'd never thought I'd have a use for. Was Lena already with them? Had her babysitters been pushed aside or persuaded?

I felt a twinge of panic. What should I do? What was the right course of action? Call the Lindas? Don? 911? My cell phone was in my bag, on the counter; there were my car keys beside it. I could grab them and run.

I couldn't decide. I was useless. I tried to stall.

"A suit and *tie*? On Saturday?"

He smiled at me indulgently, as though what was coming from my mouth was empty breath. There was no need for him to acknowledge my speech.

"Look, honey, you and me just need a little face time. We need to put our two heads together and be reasonable here, figure out what's best for everyone."

"I don't know what you mean."

In fact I did not know what *I* meant: he was terrifying me. I shook my head. I wasn't in charge of myself, just flustered and stuck. It was exactly what I'd been afraid of since the day he started pursuing us. He'd never laid a finger on me in anger, Ned had never been violent physically. He'd only been false and cold.

Despite this nonviolent history he chilled me to the bone.

"I know you want to come home," he said.

The arrogance of it flummoxed me—as though he was speaking to a third party, a cameraman, maybe, who was watching and evaluating our performances and knew nothing whatsoever about us.

"I don't want to at *all*," I rushed. "I don't *have* a home with you and I don't *want* a home with you. You know what I want, don't you, Ned? I just want a divorce."

"Oh now. Listen. You're getting yourself all in a bunch, aren't you? Relax! We'll go down the street and get a bite. John here tells me y'all

SWEET LAMB OF HEAVEN   89

have a diner in this town that serves Mexican Coke. All the way up here in the pine-tree state. Go figure. You like that Mexican Co-cola, don't you? Cane sugar, not corn syrup? We need to bring that old-style Coke back to the U. S. of A. I'll put a bill in Congress, on down the road when I get there."

He'd ramped up his Southern accent several notches, the Southern manners of speech he'd partly suppressed in his first flush of adulthood. Maybe he'd raised the good ol' boy quotient for electability—Alaska has a certain kinship with the South, a redneck commonality without the heat or black people. Southern accents may be a bankable asset, I thought. Ned had always considered Alaska a frontier, the main reason he'd asked me to move there in the first place—not that he cared about the wild and scenic aspects, not that he was attracted to the state's unpopulated beauty. It was the mythology of fortune-seeking that he liked, the small but abundant niches in various markets in the state that called to him.

Because while it was true that Alaska had glaciers and polar bears, even if melting and starving/drowning, it was a frontier in other ways too—a colony still in development, into which, therefore, generous moneys pour from oil companies and Washington. Ned had been right, I guessed, to see his future in a place where men loved both their guns and their government and corporate handouts. He liked the *cojones* of Alaskans, was what he always said, the way they swaggered like lone cowboys and professed to hate all vestiges of government but at the same time clung fiercely to the coattails of that government—both to their own small government and its big, rich uncle in D.C.

Anyway he'd rediscovered his Southernness. And he was on a first-name basis with Beefy John.

"How'd you know I was here?" I asked.

All of it hung at the margins, all was fuzzy irrelevance except for Lena—where was she, who had her right at this moment? I struggled to think of anything else, stalling until I saw clearly what I should do.

I expected a decision to come: presently I would render a decision, a decision would descend and land on me.

I waited for it.

"I make friends easy, honey," Ned said smoothly. "You know me."

" 'Fraid I got to close up, folks," interrupted Beefy John, emerging from the back office, grinning broadly. The pink skin on his nose and cheeks shone under the fluorescents. "Don't keep Saturday hours, normally."

That was how I came to scrape my keys toward me on the counter and follow Ned out into the parking lot. Trudging through the slush I considered the fact that Beefy John *had* opened the shop on Saturday and then Ned had been there. Conspiracy, I thought, conspiracy, I'd been stalked, I'd been tracked, I hadn't been paranoid at all.

Could Don help me?

I got into my car and of course couldn't stop Ned from following in his own—a rented SUV driven by someone else, some kind of body-guard or other employee—in a dutiful procession to the diner a block down, a procession that made me feel like a condemned person. The diner served beer and wine, at least . . . and what could Ned do to me there, in broad daylight? I didn't care how early it seemed to be; it was a zero hour for me, the time of reckoning. I had to stay clearheaded for Lena, but also I desperately needed to calm down.

I ordered a beer.

STRANGE THINGS EXIST, astonishing oddities—transparent butter-flies, three-foot-wide parasites that look like orange flowers, babies born pregnant with their own twins. There are fish like sea serpents, fifty-five feet long, lizards whose species are all female; there's the mysterious roar from outer space, the contagiousness of yawns, the origin of continental drift.

What I want to know is whether the unknowns in nature are only unexplained phenomena or whether there are genuine anomalies—whether a true anomaly exists. I doubt that it's possible for an event to occur only once, to one person, and as I look and look for an answer the more it seems to me that what are called anomalies aren't unique but only symptoms of gaps in understanding. Some of them are just exceptions to the systems people have invented, showing the limits and biases of those invented systems. Or, in physics or astronomy, anomalies are names for states or forces that haven't been figured out.

It was always improbable that whatever happened, way back then, happened *only* to Lena and me.

a·nom·a·ly [uh-*nom*-uh-*lee*] noun, plural *a·nom·a·lies.*
1. deviation from the common rule, type, arrangement, or form.
Synonyms: abnormality, exception, peculiarity.

I CAN'T RECALL the pattern of our conversation at the diner. Ned, when he wants to, can have a way of saying nothing specific, conveying only a broad intent. And that intent was exactly what I'd been afraid of: he wanted Lena and me back with him, he wanted us to be his TV family.

His position, as far as I could tell—or his pollster's—was that he was much too good-looking to run as a bachelor or divorced man. And the fact that he was married was already public, so now he had to produce the wife.

No emotions were summoned to build a case for this, no passionate declarations or rhetorical flourishes; Ned simply projected his plan. He has the knack of power, I thought as I drank my beer and picked at the corner of a limp grilled-cheese sandwich, intermittently wiping my fingertips on a napkin. It was undeniable. No wonder he's running for state senate. This first race may be small-time but at some point it'll be a governorship or a senate seat, he's in that forum now, and then probably Congress, just as he'd said.

I wondered how I'd ever become connected with such a man, much less married to him—a person who's mechanistic in his view of others, an individual streamlined to exploit them.

We'd met through a woman I'd only half-liked who had a history at prep schools like Choate and a new, expensive silver-blue car, a brand of car I felt should never be owned by an undergraduate. She'd been a student of mine while I was working toward my PhD, a student in a class I taught as part of my grant package.

This woman had thrown a dinner party the summer I finished grad school, while I was still living in Providence and working as a cashier in a gourmet food store, after the assistant teaching gig had ended. (My family money wasn't given to Solly or me to spend as we saw fit; our parents expected us to work like everyone else. Much of the money Ned took came to us at our wedding, by which time my parents were apparently convinced I wouldn't become a wastrel. Now, of course, I wish they'd never handed it over.) I'd gone to the party because I was lonely and needed to feel like a guest for once instead of a cashier, needed to say something to someone else other than *Did you find everything you were looking for today?*

Ned was at the party too, Ned the frat-boy Boy Scout, and somehow not a year later I married him. It must have been partly the setting that carried the evening: a rambling green garden with flowers on trellises and weeping willows and ponds arranged around a house with a colonial aspect, columns, wraparound porches, shining wood floors and chandeliers. I'd had no one to talk to there while my hostess was busy; I hovered awkwardly on the porch, looking out at the garden with my wine in hand, till Ned approached.

He'd been washed in those August colors, a borrowed glow that took a long time to fade since, unlike him, I harbored romantic delusions—that pre-nostalgic filmmaking of the self that separates events into vignettes and montages, curates time into a gallery of sepia-toned images. What were the chances of meeting someone like Ned, a man with movie-star charisma at large among the civilians?

Even as inexperienced as I was then, I was foolish to overlook the indicators of his mercenary bent, blind not to notice his edge of narcissism—an edge that was leading. I must have been quite stupid, I reflected, sitting across from him over grilled cheese. The selfish stupidity of youth had been upon me.

For a minute I sat listless, not even attempting to remove myself from his slick enchantment. In one corner of the diner was the man who had to be his driver or bodyguard, with nothing in front of him on his own table but a cell phone and a glass of what looked like iced tea. He wore a wire in one ear like a Secret Service officer.

It was laughable, I thought, to have a man like that working for you when all you were doing was running for a Podunk state senate.

Lena. I knew the Lindas would still be looking after her, as long as they could. For an hour or two they wouldn't even wonder where I was.

"Have you sent someone to find her?" I interrupted Ned after a while.

He was talking about television or radio, a program he'd been on or was going to be on, some anecdote to which I was incapable of listening. I wasn't mentioning the motel, of course, in case he didn't know where she was after all—in case the car-repair place had been his only touchstone.

"Did you send some of your guys over to where we're living? Is that what you did?"

Ned raised one arm for the waitress, who had already fawned over him. She smiled hopefully, her lipstick bright as she rushed over to our booth, and this eager subservience allowed me to see her as he would: a worker bee possessing only the slightest shading of utility.

Still, no being with any utility, however slight, was undeserving of Ned's charm when he was on active duty. He made small talk with the waitress while ignoring my question about our daughter. As he did so I weighed the advantages and disadvantages of running outside and jumping in my car and I decided that, on balance, I had little to lose. I had to get back to Lena anyway, sooner or later I would have to go to her and inevitably, if he hadn't already found out where we were living, lead him there. I was impatient to be with her again, to see her and be near.

And so, abruptly—while Ned was holding the middle-aged waitress in thrall to his shining attention and I was hearing her say she'd been married to three different members of the same MC—I rose and hurried out the door, not looking behind me.

There was no flurry of activity back there, Ned didn't ever tend to exhibit undue haste, but still it hadn't been two minutes before I could see his rented car in my rearview mirror.

I let out a breath I hadn't known I was holding: a childish part of me had hoped to lose him by bolting, though realistically I knew better.

I DROVE TO the motel with mounting panic, knowing it wasn't the best move. But I had to be with her. I talked to myself as I drove, tapping the steering wheel restlessly at the lone stoplight between the town and the motel. *Of course he can't take her from me, with all his concern about public relations. Calm down. Calm down, calm down, calm down.*

Glass half-full, I said to myself, now you have to face up to the situation, iron it out. Maybe Ned's not dead wrong after all, there's no need to hyperventilate—be practical. *Next steps.* He said it himself, we just need to sit down and figure out what's best for all of us. *I agree for the most part*, I told myself, nodding as I pressed down on the gas pedal again. *For the most part I agree, right? We need to figure out what's best for all of us.*

Except him.

Ned's election to a position of state power was what *he* wanted, but it wasn't what I wanted—I felt it was against the interests of many, indeed most. It's actually my obligation, I thought, not only to think of Lena and myself but also of how *not* to get Ned elected. He relies on an implicit system of beliefs I think are cold as ice, a system of *assumptions* more than beliefs that has nothing to do with either reason or kindness. Ned's beliefs are like the programmed responses of a computer, I thought, they require no justification, in his view, beyond the fact that he has chosen to embrace them.

Maybe I could accomplish all these goals at once, protect my daughter and myself, try to weigh in against my husband's election: File for divorce on grounds of adultery, as a spurned wife would on TV.

But now the motel sign was up ahead of me, here came the parking lot, and I felt despairing. I'd never gathered evidence while we still lived together because once I knew the marriage was lost I assumed Ned wanted out of it too. So I had no proof of his many affairs. Most likely he was certain of this. I'd known some of their names and faces, but he would have covered his bases and I couldn't believe those women would help me. Of the two of us, Ned is by far the more persuasive. And—except for the one instance I knew of when a woman broke it off with him—he tended to let them down easy. He wasn't a bridge-burner; on the contrary. Even the one who'd been disgruntled had to be in his pocket now.

Don, I thought again. Could Don help me?

I didn't want Lena to see her father yet; I wanted to prepare her. I didn't know what to do. He'd park as soon as I did, he'd be right behind me.

She wasn't in front, anyway, wasn't playing in the snow this time, though her snow effigy remained, lumpish, melting. She might be in the Lindas' room, I figured. Maybe they would help me. Although— what could they even do? Ned wasn't a wife-beater. Ned wasn't a clear and present danger. Ned wore a camelhair coat and shone like the noonday sun.

I couldn't sit in the car thinking, I had to press forward. I'd call and tell them to keep her in the room—so I ran to the lobby, Ned's car somewhere behind me, headed up that long gravel road. I ran to the lobby, but Don wasn't there: the front desk was unattended. I looked behind me, out the glass door, then ducked into the café room and closed its door. It was empty. I took out my phone and dialed Main Linda's cell, butterfingers. I got her outgoing message and left a voicemail. I asked her to keep Lena in her room, not to come out until I called again, could she please do me this favor? Please?

I hung up, still trembling.

Lena could be anywhere, exposed . . . I'd go around the back, look in the picture windows . . . what if the Lindas didn't have their cells with them? I snuck back into the kitchen looking for a back door: EMERGENCY EXIT ONLY, with a metal bar. I pressed the bar and it ka-thunked, no alarm. Then I was outside, crunching along the dead grass and snow behind the building, along the rear windows of the rooms.

But all the curtains were closed.

When I turned the corner of the building I saw Lena walking beside Big Linda, wearing her pink puffer coat—they'd just come up from the beach, because Lena was carrying her basket. And a few feet away from her, leaning relaxedly back against the hood of his parked, black SUV—there stood Ned.

He held a large, gift-wrapped box topped with an explosion of professional ribbons. The wrapping was covered in silver glitter and festooned with candy canes.

"Baby girl," he said, and the teeth had never been whiter in his head.

I TRIED TO appear gracious after that, to the extent I could—that was my tactic, for lack of better. I pretended calm as I reintroduced Lena to her father, then introduced him to Big Linda and Main

Linda when she, too, appeared huffing and puffing at the top of the staircase down the cliff. Lena *did* remember him from two years before, though she'd been four when we left, but she didn't greet him with the exuberance she'd shown her grandparents. She gave him a restrained embrace, clearly struggling to understand his sudden presence in our midst.

"A surprise visit," I said, trying to deliver a cheerful smile.

"You're so big," Ned said to her, and to the Lindas, his Southern drawl in full effect: "She's like a little doll version of her beautiful mama! Isn't she?"

An off-base gambit, since Lena's skin is lighter than mine, her hair gold instead of brown; in fact she looks more like Ned. She didn't preen under this particular praise either, just waited patiently.

"She does have those high cheekbones," said Main Linda politely.

I could tell the Lindas were wary of Ned and felt a rush of gratitude for that.

"Why don't we go inside?" said Ned, looking from me to Lena. "Chilly out here, idn't it? And you can open your present, honeypie! I bet you'll like it a whole lot."

I didn't see a choice: it *was* cold, and getting colder all the time. The damage was done: he already knew where we lived.

"You take this?" he asked, and handed me the unwieldy gift before I could answer. He reached down and grabbed one of Lena's hands, forcing her to struggle with the basket and have to kneel down to pick up fallen shells. The three of us began walking, me lagging beside them, hesitant, Ned moving slowly because, I guess, he didn't know where our room was. After a moment I turned around. The Lindas hadn't moved much; they were watching. I couldn't read their expressions.

"Linda, could you mention to Don that my husband is here?"

It was all I could do. Don was the only one who'd know what it meant to me that Ned had found us.

As we made our way along the walkway to the room Lena began to chatter, as she would with any new guest, telling Ned how the motel worked: how towels and clean linens were organized, that she knew how to slide the keycard into the slot herself. I was following them by then, looking at Ned's back, Lena's face turned sideways to him, and trying to figure out what it meant to her to be holding her father's hand.

"I'll show you, see?" she said, and slid her hand out of Ned's to turn and hold it out to me. "Can I have the key, Mommy?"

Duly I handed it over, circling the gaudy gift with one arm while I rummaged in a pocket. I was too aware of Ned looming, his pheromones, or whatever the fuck, casting over me a vibrant net.

Lena clicked the door open, proud of her competence.

"Whoa," said Ned, when he stepped inside. "Not exactly the Ritz, is it. You can do better, can't you, Anna?"

"Ritz like crackers?" asked Lena.

"It's grown on us," I said lightly.

Ned tried to shut the door after I brushed in past him, but I propped it a few inches open with the rubber wedge.

"Let's let in some fresh air," I said.

"Fresh freezing air," said Ned.

"How come it's a Christmas present?" asked Lena, as I set the box down on our small table. "It isn't Christmas *yet*."

"You know that song, baby?" said Ned, sitting himself in the armchair with magisterial ease, crossing his legs. "'The Twelve Days of Christmas'? On the first day of Christmas, my true love gave to me—you know that one?"

"A partridge in a pear tree," said Lena.

"That's right! Smart girl. But don't worry, this isn't a partridge."

Lena approached the box shyly at first, then began to rip it open chaotically as I started to pour water into the carafe for the in-room coffee. Coffee didn't appeal to me in the least, especially not from that little plastic-wrapped packet. But ours was a small room with not many options for looking busy.

"Look, a new friend for Lucky Duck," said Lena, pulling out a fluffy white sheep. "Is it . . . a goat, Mommy?"

She'd turned to me to ask, instead of asking Ned.

"It's a lamb, baby," he said. "And it's made from real *sheepskin*."

Lena was instantly upset. Ned couldn't have known it was a misstep since he knew nothing of what she ate and didn't eat, of her softheartedness.

She blinked away tears and said nothing, holding the sheep at arm's length.

"Go on, give it a squeeze," said Ned.

Reluctantly she did so, first one way and then another, until the lamb began reciting, in a high-pitched, childish voice, "Now I lay me down to sleep / I pray the Lord my soul to keep / If I should die before I wake / I pray the Lord my soul to take."

"Hey look, Ducky," she said, gamely trying to make the best of a sheepskin tragedy. She picked up her ratty, baggy duck from the bed and pressed the two stuffed animals together. The duck was a dingy gray compared to the snow-white, fleecy lamb. "Be nice to her, Ducky. Her skin got cut off her."

Ned raised an eyebrow.

"I'm not going to make her talk that much, OK?" she asked Ned. "It's babyish. And I don't like what they made her say."

"Bit morbid, isn't it?" I said to Ned. "I've always thought that prayer was cloying."

"Well, that's OK, sweetie," said Ned to Lena, ignoring me. He didn't look pleased, though, which made my spirits lift briefly, then just as soon worried me. "It's yours. You do whatever you want with it. But listen, you didn't read my card yet. I wrote it for you special."

"I can read it. I can read a whole book," said Lena.

Ned plucked a card from beneath the efflorescence of ribbon.

"Will you read it out loud to me, baby doll?" he asked.

He'd already achieved a proprietorial air with Lena, an air of ownership.

She took the card out of its envelope, revealing an airbrushed-looking kitten with eyes the size of saucers.

"Dear Lena, I—missed you—very much," read Lena. "To my best girl ever, love x's and o's Daddy."

I was nervous that Ned was right on the edge of saying something to her I didn't wish him to say.

"That's really nice," I said. "Lena, your father's here for a quick visit." I kept my voice easy as the coffeemaker started to burble. "I'm sure he won't be able to stay for long. It's so nice he brought you the lamb, isn't it?"

"OK. Want me to read to you?" Lena asked him. She'd had a break-through in her reading and liked to perform her favorite book. "Want me to read *Ferdinand*?"

Ned arranged her atop his lap for the purpose, flicking on the lamp beside him. They made a Norman Rockwell picture sitting there, their hair burnished the same shade of gold—you'd think the man cherished the little girl deeply, looking over the top of her small head at the open book with his eyes down, his handsome, almost noble features and form arranged in a cast of paternal protection.

You'd think that unless you were me—or unless, maybe, you caught sight of one of his elegant feet jiggling minutely but rapidly under the armchair as he pretended to listen. He hadn't seen his daughter for years, but there was his foot, shod tastefully in black leather, already impatient.

Lena read slowly and haltingly about the peaceful bull who only wanted to sit and smell the flowers, not travel to the big city and fight the toreador. But the men from the city came and took him away, forcing him into the bullring.

Ned took a leisurely glance at his watch and smiled when he saw me seeing him do it.

Would he go away soon? Please? I couldn't even make a trip to the bathroom while he was here with her, I'd never leave them alone. What was his plan?

When she was done she jumped off his lap and scurried to the bathroom herself, announcing she was going to pee. Ned picked the storybook off his knees as though it was soiled, with two fingers, and deposited it on the table. Then he brushed off his slacks where she'd been sitting.

"That bull was light in the loafers," he said.

"Ned. What are you *doing* right now?" I kept my voice low. "We're not going to come back to you."

"How 'bout a compromise?"

He pointed at the coffeemaker, meaning *Give me a cup*. I turned, feeling cold, and started to pour one. It was better than looking at him.

"I propose this, darlin'. Some photo shoots, interviews. Couple appearances. Then y'all can take a vacation. I'll only need you now and then. It doesn't have to be 24-7, if we manage it right. Anchorage is a big enough city."

"But I don't *want* to support your campaign, Ned." I handed him the cup. "I don't like what you stand for."

"We may have policy differences here or there," he said, shrugging, and sipped. "Now, that's just foul."

"It's really not good," I agreed.

He set down the bad coffee on the storybook. It slopped out and made a ring; I grabbed the book and wiped it.

"Bottom line is, we're family."

"As it turns out, that's not my bottom line at all."

Then Lena was out of the bathroom again, looking at us expectantly.

"Why don't you go play, sweetie?" he said, barely glancing her way. "Let the grownups talk."

"She doesn't play outside by herself," I said. "The motel's on the edge of a cliff."

He slipped his phone from a coat pocket.

"My driver can babysit."

"No thanks," I said firmly. "We don't know him."

"Hello?"

It was Don, knocking at the cracked-open door with perfect timing.

"Come in!" I said, relieved.

He stepped inside, nodded curtly at Ned without smiles or introductions, and held his hand out to Lena.

"I've got a job for you," he said. "You want to help me?"

"I'm the assistant!" crowed Lena.

And Don towed her efficiently out of the room.

I was so grateful to see her go that I felt my shoulders unclench.

"Look, I'm not asking you to give any stump speeches, honeypie," said Ned, stretching out a hand and pushing the door closed behind them. "You don't have to say a word. You can be deaf, dumb and blind. Hell, I like you better that way. Just smile and hold my hand sometimes. And get the girl to do the same. You soldier through till the election, smiling all the time, I'll give you a friendly, neat divorce as your very own victory gift. Plus full custody. With visitation rights, of course. Couldn't be looking like a deadbeat dad."

"And you'd actually put that in writing. Before the fact."

"All official. With confidentiality agreements on the timing and conditions there, of course."

"Even if you lose? You'd sign off beforehand on it, no matter how the election goes?"

"I won't lose. Not with the friends I have and your two pretty faces beside me. But sure, I'll sign."

"Because I know you want more than the state senate. Won't you want a wife and kid when you run for something bigger, too?"

"I'll cross that bridge. Let *me* worry."

I was asking questions, but I wasn't seriously considering the request.

"Don't you think I could get sole custody *now*?" I said. "I mean

Ned. You've come to *one* of her birthday parties. Ever. And that was by accident, if I remember correctly."

"You might could get custody," said Ned, and smiled again. "But maybe not. Running off like you did."

"You wouldn't want that fight," I said. "Publicly. You'd *never* want it. Especially not now."

"You'd be amazed how I can spin things, when I need to. I might decide to play the victim. People do love their victims, in America."

We gazed at each other across the room. That is, I looked past Ned, not wanting to look *at* him, so I don't know if he really looked at me either. I tried to remember another time he'd been so direct, and all I could come up with was when he asked me to get married. It had been at a restaurant with white tablecloths and obsequious waiters—he likes being served by such waiters and I hate it. When waiters are too fawning I hear the falseness they've brought to it, possible snide remarks in the kitchen.

Now he was relaxed in the chair, facing me, while I was in a defensive posture, backed up against the counter of our kitchenette as far from him as I could be. My hands were braced against the edge.

"I need time to think," I said. "And while I think, I need you to not be here. And not spend time with Lena, either."

He shrugged. "The clock's ticking."

"Why? Isn't the election a whole year away?"

"Primary's in August. My party controls the governor's office and the House; the Senate's a 10–10 split, but with redistricting we could take over there too, come November. We've been low-key till now, but it's time for a higher gear."

"You're not going to start campaigning before Christmas, are you?"

He picked up Lena's Lucky Duck from where it lay, studied it for a few moments, and then dropped it.

"Getting my ducks in a nice little row."

There was a knock on the door, so I crossed the room and opened it. The Lindas stood there, smiling pleasantly, waiting. Ned rose from his chair and smiled too, at them first, then at me.

"Well, got to be getting back," he said. "You mull it over, honey. So great to see my girls again. Ladies? A pleasure."

The Lindas moved aside for him, and just like that he was gone.

I DON'T HAVE confidence we can run away again. For one thing it would clearly look illegal, now that he's sought us out. And for another he's obviously better at stealth than I am, and he *does* have friends. Whether Beefy John tipped him off or was only a witness, he has sources of information and I'm clearly not equipped to detect them.

The Lindas told me Lena was helping Don in the café; they sat and listened while I explained. I told them what my position was; they were sympathetic. And I didn't have to persuade them Ned wasn't the charmer people always think he is—maybe, as post-reproductive women, they were outside the field of his pheromones.

Almost as soon as Ned was gone the guests seemed to come out of the woodwork: the motel returned to life, with movement and light in the rooms, people talking and walking between them, breath visible in the cold. Don brought Lena back, and Kay and Burke were with them and made remarks about Ned's shining car, his bodyguard/driver, his tailored coat and even the lamb, which lay abandoned in a corner of the room atop its pile of bright wrapping.

Laughter and conversation echoed from the walkway into our room. The day had passed quickly; before I knew it late afternoon was casting its long shadows.

Burke stayed a while after Don and Kay left, helping Lena tend to her bean plants in the miniature greenhouse. Some of them had sprouted; one was growing fast, already too tall for the container, and this they moved into a small pot he'd brought with him.

Eventually he got up to go and I thanked him for coming by, for all he did for Lena. As he was going out the door he turned and looked at me.

"You know, we have to look after each other," he said quietly. "The people who've heard it."

5

HURT, YOU WERE A CHILD AGAIN

I DIDN'T STOP BURKE FROM LEAVING, DIDN'T DO ANYTHING BUT watch as he headed off down the walkway. When he stepped into his own room I closed the door without noise and sat down on the bed.

Lena had her sheep on her lap and had found a buttoned opening in its stomach. Out of the opening, while I sat looking at her in a daze, she pulled a white-plastic box.

"That's how she talks," she said, and pushed a large, flat button on the box, which obligingly bleated out its eerie, falsetto prayer. "See? When you press the tummy she talks. It's for babies. *Mommy*. I'm *six*. Can I throw away the talking part?"

"Of course," I said feebly.

The strength had been pressed out of me; I was breathless and flat.

She turned a small screw neatly with her fingernail, impressing me, and extracted two batteries, which she placed neatly on her bedside table. She marched over to the trash can and dumped the box without ceremony.

"It's not the lamb's fault," she said. "When she talks it makes me think how they took off her skin."

"Oh, honey," I said, reaching. "Don't worry about that. OK? It's sheepskin. No reason to think it's from a baby. Maybe that sheep lived a long and happy life. Maybe it died of old age."

"Maybe," said Lena doubtfully.

"Can I see her for a minute?" I asked. It was occurring to me that the lamb could be a nanny cam, hold some kind of tracker. I'd been paranoid, *this* was paranoid, but then again in broad strokes I'd also been correct.

I held it and stared into its glass eyes, squeezed the face, inspected the nose and mouth.

With Lena in front of the TV I poured myself the glass of wine I'd been wanting. *The people who've heard it*, I thought. It had to mean what I thought it meant. So this *wasn't* a random selection of winter travelers in Maine.

It was an enclave.

But I'd never told anyone about the voice—no one. That was what made my hands shake as I drank my wine.

"I'm going to take a bath, honey," I told her, and carried my glass into the bathroom with me, leaving the door open. I thought the soak might calm me.

I'd have to ask Don, I thought as the water ran, it was the only course of action, I'd ask him now, and this time he'd have to tell me. Or I'd ask Burke how we came to be here, how it was that someone had known and how they'd summoned me, if that was what had happened.

Probably the voice wasn't anything supernatural, you credulous primitive, I thought. I sat there in the hot water and finally leaned out to set the empty goblet on the floor, heard the slight scratch of its circular base on the tile.

Probably it was sound waves, radio waves, technology: that was the best idea I'd had. I'd been so childish to think of magic when it was likely the product of science—some manipulative brainchild of one of these peripatetic characters.

Maybe it had been one of them all along.

I ALMOST FORGOT Ned that evening, preoccupied by what Burke had said. I debated whether to go to dinner and face that crowd. We could always make food in our kitchenette or even drive to town.

But Lena wanted to go because another child was coming, the boy with the robot. She knew this and planned to sit with him. I was worried about the emotional effects of Ned's sudden appearance, although she seemed to have taken it in stride. I wanted to watch her closely and give her the small assurances she asked for, so I said yes.

And when we entered the café it felt homey. We sat down with the little boy's family, at their invitation, and as I exchanged small talk with his parents I studied my fellow guests, wondering who among them was in Burke's club and who was not. The Lindas? The chic couple? Kay? The angry young mogul?

The mogul, yes. I'd heard him on the telephone that night, yelling; and now I thought, *That's* what it was about. He'd told someone what he'd heard, the person on the other end. I watched him and Kay at their table alongside the wall, leaning close as they confided in each other. Maybe they were discussing it right now, I thought.

The mogul's name was Navid, Kay had told me. It meant good news.

And Kay: Kay with the babies at the NICU. Had she heard it from one of them?

I'd accepted the voice, then gratefully dismissed it when it ceased. Once it had loosed me from my moorings so that I had to tread water in a fluid world; finally, when it fell silent, I'd stepped onto solid ground again. But now there was a new unknown, of how and why I'd got to the motel and how the others had, and the earth was shifting beneath my feet again. How much I hated that jarring movement, the rush of fear! I'd tucked it all behind me and moved on; I'd adapted to it as best I could and concentrated on bringing up my girl.

Surely there was nothing else I could have done.

IT HAPPENED THAT I didn't have to buttonhole Don. With his customary placidness he stopped by our table. The family from town had left and Lena was picking at a berry cobbler. He had a tray of cobbler dishes in his hands, which he set down on the table next to us before he placed his hand on the back of my chair; I studied the waves of whipped cream on top of the pie.

Don's friendly, familiar slump suggested nothing too significant was happening; and yet he knew.

"The others found us through a website," he said. "Call it a support group."

"But I didn't," I said.

Lena wasn't listening but waving her spoon and making faces at Faneesha, who sat across the room making them back at her. I thought of the Hearing Voices Movement; I thought of support groups in general, and how I'd never been drawn to them.

"Well, you needed something else," said Don. "You recovered and they're still struggling. You needed a different kind of assistance."

"That's true," I said. "Thank you so much for today. Your timing was perfect."

"No trouble," said Don. "But we're still worried about you."

"What you just said, though, it doesn't explain how I knew where to come."

"You could think of it like salmon," he said, cocking his head. "Or migrating birds. They know where to go, but no one really knows how they know."

"Ducks fly south in winter," said Lena, who'd put down her fork. She had no idea what we were discussing, but lack of context has never stopped her.

"That's right, Lena," said Don solemnly. "That they do."

"Except Lucky Duck," said Lena. She patted him on the chair next to her. "This guy's lazy."

"But ducks and geese and salmon migrate in groups," I said to Don. "They have other ducks and salmon."

"Mostly. But not always," said Don lightly. "Individuals of many species engage in solitary migrations. Humpback whales, for instance. Young songbirds often make their first trips alone. Scientists say direction and distance are written into their genes."

"They travel for food or breeding, don't they?" I said. "But I didn't travel for those reasons." Because Lena was there, I couldn't be more specific and I wanted to keep it casual.

"Well, I don't know about that," said Don, and took a bowl off his tray before he picked it up to move on. "Have some cobbler. It's on the house."

BACK IN the room I went online briefly.

In some butterfly species, for example the monarch, no single individual completes a migratory journey, which is spread over a number of generations. Instead the animals reproduce and die while underway, and it is left to the next generation to complete the next leg of the journey. —*Wikipedia 2015*

"Are you mad at Don, Mama?" asked Lena when I was putting her to bed.

She clutched both the duck and the sheep.

"What? No, I'm not mad at him," I said.

"Don's too nice to be mad at."

"Don's definitely nice," I said. "And we're getting to know him better, aren't we."

"People ask questions to know each other better," she said.

"Exactly."

"Are you mad at my father?"

"Hmm. Well, that's a good question."

"You don't like him."

"I wouldn't put it that way."

"How would you put it, then."

At that moment she sounded over forty.

"I'd say . . . well, I'd say we turned out not to have as much in common as I first thought we did."

"I don't know if I like him either. I love him, because everyone loves their father."

"Right. Of course you do."

"We used to live with him."

"Yes. We certainly did."

"He never gave me a present before. Even though it's not Christmas. Did he give me a present ever before this?"

"Hmm. He must have, mustn't he?"

"I like my sheep."

"That's good. It's a nice sheep."

"I like living here. With you and me."

"I know you do. I do too."

"We live at Don's motel."

"For now. But not forever, sweetie. You know that."

"I know. One day we have to go. That's why they call it a motel. It's not a house or apartment."

"No."

"One day we have to live in one of those."

"I expect so. We'll have neighbors, I bet. You'll like that, too."

"OK. I'm going to go to sleep now."

"I'm glad to hear it."

I COULDN'T SLEEP, so I wrote down that exchange, figuring it might give me needed insight, further on, into my failings as a parent.

Then I consoled myself by thinking that at least I was a good enough parent to try to keep account of those failings.

I lay in the other bed, letting the TV play muted in front of me, laptop on my knees. Don had to be some kind of counselor, some kind of advisor to those who'd heard . . . but now that I wasn't the only one who spoke of "hearing," the word seemed cultish to me and I didn't like it, not at all. The word *hearing* had an unpleasant ring suddenly—now it was a matter for shame, almost, rather than one of the senses—and "the voice" wasn't the plain and straightforward moniker I'd taken it for but a worshipful honorific.

Now it was the Voice.

I wondered if what the other guests had heard was different from what I had—assuming it wasn't just Burke, of course, assuming he spoke for more of them. Not all of the guests had babies, in fact none of them did. As far as I knew, only Kay had necessarily had regular contact with infants. So maybe they'd encountered it, as she had, in the infants of others.

I went over the guest roster, as on TV a pretty woman was murdered with a knife. I knew the voice's life cycle, or I thought I had. But I knew *nothing*. You don't even remember how this supposed knowledge came to you, I told myself—it was never spelled out. If the voice had brought me here, how? What had driven us from old friends' welcoming houses to these Maine bluffs, with this peculiar group?

Maybe Don was onto something, maybe the migration *was* encoded in my genes.

Many mechanisms have been proposed for animal navigation: there is evidence for a number of them, including orientation by the sun, orientation by the stars and by polarized light, magnetoception, and other senses such as echolocation and hydrodynamic reception . . . investigators have often been forced to discard the simplest hypotheses. —*Wikipedia 2015*

How could the other guests have heard the voice? I tried to recall exactly when they had seemed upset. Burke was the only one who'd showed emotion to me, aside from the angry young man on his cell phone and Kay talking about the NICU.

I picked up my computer and scrolled back in this document to what I'd written about Burke. Talking to Lena about giants and beanstalks: that was when he'd lost it. And now I saw it, and it was obvious. His dismay had been brought on by something he himself had said, that Lena didn't have to worry about giants saying "Fee, fi, fo, fum" from beanstalks—a voice, talking down from the clouds.

There was my evidence, right there.

I heard a text alert on my cell phone and rose from the bed to fumble in my bag. *I missed you tonight,* it read. And then another: *Did I get the date wrong?*

I'd entered his name and number into my contacts list, and there it was: Will Garza. I'd forgotten my first date in almost a decade.

I apologized in a low voice, with the door to the bathroom closed so that I wouldn't wake Lena, and found myself relaxing as I listened to his deep and pleasant tone. I talked a bit about Lena, for whom he'd once suggested a book about a donkey named Sylvester who found a wishing pebble and got turned into a boulder. She liked it almost as much as *Ferdinand*. I told him my husband had followed us here. I told him almost every material fact about our situation, leaving out the part where I used to hear a voice.

He said he had never been married, that he had most often lived alone, that he preferred books to people. His parents had been from Argentina but he had grown up in New York before he moved to Maine and had relocated here when the rest of the family had returned to Argentina. They ran a small bakery there, and his father cultivated oak trees.

But he'd stayed here because this, he said, for better or worse, felt more like his country.

His given name was Guillermo but he'd always gone by the shortest Anglicized version, Will, not liking the initials G.G. as a boy and living among Anglos. He used to be a feral librarian, he said, before he went back to school.

That was what they called them, he said, librarians without a master's degree.

> Olfactory cues may be important for salmon, which return from the ocean to spawn and die in the very streams where they hatched. Some scholars believe they use their magnetic sense to navigate within reach of the stream, then their sense of smell to identify the river at close range. —*Wikipedia 2015*

THIS MORNING I woke up simple-minded, as though a dream had narrowed my focus. I had to ask Don the question, the large question was all I was interested in, and now I would take him by the shoulders and shake him and ask it. *Don! Don! Don! Who was it? Who was speaking to us?*

But the urge passed. I guess I couldn't handle an answer, an answer would be too unsettling. I don't want to be part of some enclave of believers, some marginal sect. I've always avoided joining. I don't even have one of those plastic grocery-store cards that make the food cheaper. I haven't enrolled in any frequent flyer programs; though I can't fix a flat tire I've never paid dues to Triple A; even my friend's book club in East Anchorage, which mostly involved eating and drinking, was of little interest to me.

When I was alone I could accept, with difficulty, having heard what I heard, but to find myself among others who might confess and describe it, impute their own meanings—it makes me claustrophobic. And who *is* Don, even, to hand down high knowledge to me? I like him, I do, but when it comes to the greatest mystery of my life I have no reason to privilege a motel owner's beliefs over my own.

I do want to ask why, if several of them are in on this, they hid it from me until now. Why didn't they let me in before, if this is why we're here? When I asked how they came to be at this motel, why didn't anyone answer me?

Ned called and I let it go to voicemail, to which I listened promptly. He said he needed a decision, and followed this with an amicably phrased threat to show up again if he didn't hear from me right away. He's always been restless; after all, it's why he married me.

I struggled under the pressure of his impatience, trying to shrug it off as I made toast and spooned out yogurt for Lena. I wondered if I could put him off. I wasn't ready to see him again so soon, much less decide my course of action. This might be a subject, I decided, I *could* safely broach with Don, possibly Don would have some solid counsel for me, with his background defending wives under duress.

I'd table the other conversation for now, I'd focus my energies on fending off Ned.

So I called the Lindas, who like any excuse to go for a walk, and asked if one of them had time to take Lena down to the beach. I called the front desk and asked Don if he could meet to discuss my situation. I still needed help, I said.

I met him in his back office.

"You have a few options, as I see it," he said. "One, you can leave the country. But that wouldn't be wise, legally. Two, you can hide somewhere, the way you've been doing, but better. On that choice I could help with logistics. But that's complicated legally too, since you're not alleging abuse. He could use it against you, certainly. Three, you simply file for divorce now. Maybe he makes good on his threat, maybe he doesn't. He could be bluffing."

He stopped.

"That's all?" I said.

"Or four, you can do what he says. Sign the papers first, with your lawyer, and then do what he wants you to."

"Isn't there a five?"

"I don't trust him," said Don. "Four's a more dangerous option than it may seem."

"But so is three," I said. "He could try to get custody. Having her with me trumps everything."

"I know."

Don studied me, waiting.

I CALLED A COUPLE of friends, pacing my room while Lena and the Lindas wandered up and down the beach. You shouldn't be rushed in this decision, they said, tell him you need a week. They were kind, but their support didn't help me, beyond the warmth of reassurance.

It seemed to me I had weak information about my choices, so I made more calls. I asked Don for a family lawyer's number, he had a personal friend who would take my call even today, he said, so back in my room used his name to get her on the phone. But she didn't tell me much more than I already knew, and while I was half-listening another call came in—Ned's voicemail had said he'd love to have lunch with "his girls," it'd be no problem for him to "swing by."

When I called him back my call went to *his* voicemail, which pleased me. I said I'd need till Tuesday, but don't come for lunch. Ease up.

I was wary of calling a lawyer in Anchorage. Ned knew so many people in the city that I couldn't be sure of steering clear of his contacts or friends. When I thought of lawyers there I saw two faces of lawyers he'd slept with, a young blonde and a middle-aged hardbody who ran marathons. A few other lawyers were investors of his. But Juneau, at least, wasn't his territory yet—maybe I could find a lawyer there, one who wasn't beholden to him. So when Lena came back from her walk I assigned her some reading and scanned search results.

Then I remembered Will Garza. He was intelligent, I thought, and kind and easy to talk to. I let Lena watch television, since it generates more background noise than reading, and stepped outside to make my call. We barely knew each other, of course, so I hadn't asked anything of him. But now it struck me that maybe I *could* ask his advice, and he, unlike my distant friends, was here.

We decided to meet; it needed to be someplace warm, someplace Lena would play hard and ignore us. Will remembered an outlet mall in the hinterlands, a mall with an indoor playground you paid for. It sounded to me like the worst place in the world for a first date, but I needed someone to talk to more than I needed to set a scene, at that moment, and I said yes.

The place was full of inflated slides and bouncy houses, with tinny pop music playing and bright lights shining and the red, blue and yellow decor of fast-food restaurants and clowns; it smelled like sweat and dirty socks and off-gassing vinyl. For me there was nothing to like, for Lena there was everything. She'd put her shoes in a cubby before I finished paying and was off climbing, running between the machines, making friends: not two minutes had passed before she was holding hands with an older girl as they tumbled down a wide blue slide.

I sat self-consciously under the fluorescents on a sticky chair and waited, following Lena with my eyes as she pulled the older girl from one puffy structure to the next. I wondered if my face was clean but was too self-conscious to check it in the cell phone's camera. I'd seen that a few times: people trying to look as though they were doing something else on their phones when it was clear from the angle of their head, sometimes a set of pursed lips or a hair toss, that they were studying their faces.

Then he got there, carrying a cardboard tray of drinks—a hot chocolate for Lena and a coffee for me, which he handed over without saying anything. There was a little milk in the fourth cup, he said, did I take my coffee with milk?

He brought with him a microclimate of calm. I was drawn to it, his warm calmness that set the stage for trust.

African ball-rolling dung beetles exploit the sun, the moon, and the celestial polarization pattern to move along straight paths, away from the intense competition at the dung pile . . . this finding represents the first convincing demonstration for the use of the starry sky for orientation in insects and provides the first documented use of the Milky Way for orientation in the animal kingdom. —Abstract, "Dung Beetles Use the Milky Way for Orientation," Dack, Baird et al., Current Biology, Volume 23, Issue 4

I'VE DECIDED TO call Ned's bluff, though I have no idea how he'll react. I'm afraid, but I took a couple of Valiums, dredged up from the bottom of my cosmetics bag, and thought of how he's never had a genuine wish to be in the same room with Lena. He's never wanted to be near her, listen to her, keep her safe—never.

It makes me angry to think of this, makes me feel a burning anger. Remembering his disinterest I can't believe a court will ever side with him when it comes to my little girl, I can't believe it's a realistic possibility. Even if his constituency were to believe him, I think, even if he did successfully paint himself as a victim in the eyes of electors, surely a court would not, I tell myself.

So while Don's family lawyer made up the papers—I could file from Maine, as it turned out—I stalled, putting off Ned's voicemails and texts with short texts of my own. I'd tell him on Tuesday, not a minute before I'd said I would, and meanwhile Lena and I spent time with the others at the motel and with Will; we weren't alone much. We kept busy, went to a movie in the afternoon, to dinner in the motel café.

I envisioned a hard, bad conversation with Ned when the deadline came. Because of that I was constantly nervous, I almost trembled with a brimming anxiety. I picked at my food, I tried to keep busy so that I didn't have time to succumb to fear, and on Sunday night I could barely sleep.

I had dreams of small, furry dogs being mauled by something they couldn't see.

Don suggested Lena and I could switch rooms and stay right off the lobby. We could trade with Burke and Gabe, there was no difference between our room and theirs except for location, and that way we'd be near Don—near help, in other words, in the event that Ned started banging on our door Tuesday night. Lena was jubilant, when we told her about the change, at the thought of trying a new room—it might as well have been a trip to Disneyland. She fantasized about trying all the rooms, one at a time. "Then Don's room, then Kay's room, then the Lindas' . . ."

We would move Tuesday morning, before I called Ned and told him I was filing for divorce; by Monday night, on the momentum of Lena's excitement, we had our small bags neatly packed and waiting just inside the door.

But we didn't move to Gabe and Burke's room the next day, because I woke up Tuesday morning and Lena was gone.

IT WOULD BE futile to try to evoke the desperation I felt when I saw she wasn't there.

My head was pounding—I'd been drugged—sharp pains like nails or tacks in my temples. Still that was nothing to what I felt, nothing, and I picked up the phone as soon as I saw her empty bed, the wrinkled sheets, as soon as I called her name and got silence, and then I sat up and saw her suitcase was gone too, Lucky Duck, her puffer coat. The chain on the door hung in two pieces.

All this took five seconds—less.

And then I was standing and running to the door, I was throwing it open and running up and down on the cement walkway in nothing but underwear and the long T-shirt I slept in, calling her name. Bare feet on ice, on the ridges in the pavement. I tore the pads on my toes, fell in a panic and scraped the skin off my knees, flailing.

I found Don in the lobby and I called Ned, hysterical, but of course he didn't pick up. Don sat me down on a brown-and-orange couch with coarse upholstery, whose pattern I still remember well, how I picked at the threads as I sobbed . . . I'll spare myself writing more about this. The point is she was gone, and the worst time in my life started.

I didn't keep a written record during the days after she was taken, but it's not those days anymore and it helps me to write now.

So Will came, Don was there, Kay and the Lindas, Burke and Gabe, even the well-dressed couple with two expensive cars. Everyone was around me after that, though I only half-noticed them. They were a blur of people who weren't my little girl, the blur of irrelevance.

They said things, they called the police and the police were coming, they said, hovering—we'd stay right here and wait for them. A blanket? A heating pad for my feet? I was in shock, said one of them.

I registered goodwill but I hadn't known what desolation was, before Ned took Lena, I'd never known what it felt like to be destroyed.

THERE CAME A TEXT on my phone while I was still almost catatonic. It was a text from Ned, I understood when Will held the phone up for me, though it didn't have Ned's name beside it, only a string of unfamiliar digits. Don said it was probably a prepaid.

The text bubble read *Call off the lawyer.*

"So he already knew she was filing," I heard Don murmur to Will.

"Surveillance," nodded Will.

"And sedation to make them both sleep through it," said Don. "How? The bottled water in the room? Something *I* cooked?"

He was on edge: everyone was.

There were security cameras, of course, the motel had a camera aimed at the parking lot, one in the lobby, a couple more. But when Don tried to view the footage his software told him the files had been damaged and couldn't be retrieved.

Beside me was an egg-salad sandwich on a paper plate. I remember it distinctly: the pores and craters of the beige whole-wheat bread, the fact that it looked nothing like food. I realized, seeing it, that there *was* no food for me—no food existed, in this world, nothing would ever be eaten.

The sandwich sat beside me, aging. I didn't touch it, and though I did relent about food in general—evidently—to this day the sight of an egg-salad sandwich makes me queasy.

Someone got my laptop and at their request I managed to click through a number of frames, I clicked here and there, tears running down my face, until I was able to bring up a photograph of Ned. Don emailed it to himself, then went back into the motel office and printed it out, though everyone present remembered what Ned looked like.

A new text: *No police.*

"He's got to be kidding," said Will.

We were still in the lobby. I think guests must have been coming and going by then, no longer crowding near. Will and Don and I sat on the couches while Main Linda kept busy making tea in the café. The yellow-beige sandwich had gone away—good riddance to it, unappetizing forever. Instead a coffee cup sat next to me on an end table, the surface of its cold, weak coffee as still as stone.

". . . are there people outside action movies who'd actually agree to that condition?" Will was asking.

"Where are the cops? I'm going to call them again," said Don.

Another text came in.

If you call the cops again [end of text bubble] *I'll call my FBI friends* [end of text bubble] *and make a counterclaim of kidnapping.*

"He can hear us," said Don, and stood up hastily. "Still listening, aren't you?"

Big ears to hear you with.

We gazed at each other, Will and Don and I. They looked round-eyed. I don't think I did. I wasn't surprised. I was on a plateau, the final plane of hell, I thought, a flat, dry place.

"He does know someone in the FBI," I said.

There'd been this asshole from the Anchorage field office. A couple of times he and Ned had driven to a rifle range called Rabbit Creek—I remembered because I thought of small rabbits running scared as the two men fired their weapons. They went for drinks afterward at some sports bar, where Ned stayed sober and the FBI guy got sloppy drunk. I hadn't understood what Ned wanted with him, some kind of "ASAC," Ned had said, assistant special agent—a sullen man with pitted cheeks, a spare tire and a comb-over.

I'd expected him to look like Mulder from *The X-Files*, I realized when they stopped by the house once, Mulder had been my main teenage exposure to an FBI idea and it lingered.

But he didn't look like Mulder at all. Sadly unlike Mulder.

And surely they'd had precisely nothing in common, I thought now, nothing but the FBI guy's future utility. Ned was a bet hedger, a fortifier and consolidator, effective at building networks and circuits. They met at a boxing gym and the FBI guy had apparently been drawn to Ned, as so many people were—as I had been.

Considering this I started to feel a spur of practicality again, my ruined center cauterized for a time so that it stopped infecting the rest of me. I could keep it together as long as I didn't think of Lena being alone or afraid. It was her emotions I feared for when I let myself fear, her trust of the world being damaged, eroded bitterly as I sat there with my hands tied, unable to reach her.

I didn't even consider physical harm. I couldn't stand to: that possibility was walled off in me.

Quickly all of us stood up and started searching for the microphone. There sat the laptop and my cell phone, which seemed the most likely, so Don called in the angry young mogul to inspect my devices. Apparently Navid knew about electronics. He came in, scruffy in his mountain-man beard and plaid shirt, and took my computer apart piece by piece. He seemed attentive, not angry at all, and I felt grateful and guilty for not liking him before; I would like him from now on, I would like anyone who helped me get Lena back, more than that I would love them abjectly, I'd be abject, I thought.

At some point I noticed I was digging my fingernails too deep into the heel of one hand. They were too short to draw blood, but the bruises would be there for weeks.

Navid took apart my phone, making me agitated—it was my only link to Lena, and what if it got broken?—but he put it back together again without finding anything.

Was the mike on my person? I didn't wear jewelry and I had no buttons, even, except for the one on my jeans. Don and Navid inspected my shoes—by this time a pair had been brought to me, along with a pile of clothes, and I'd dragged myself to the bathroom beside the café and put them on, the jeans and woolen socks and a pair of worn sneakers—but they found nothing there either. I didn't have my purse in the lobby so the bug, we figured, had to be elsewhere. We switched to inspecting the furniture.

It was confusing, since Ned wasn't likely to have heard about my plan to file for divorce through a microphone in the lobby.

After a fruitless search we trailed out of there, Don and Will and I, and into Don's office, but I was still nervous, I couldn't know when Ned was listening since we hadn't found the bug. I felt conflicted about calling the police again, we couldn't figure out why they hadn't arrived yet, so I insisted we go analog for a while, talking to each other by writing things down on a pad of lined paper and passing it among us.

Don and Will thought Ned must have got to the local police somehow, they suggested he wouldn't be able to do more than delay them and we should call again, get someone different on the phone. If that failed we should try another jurisdiction—the feds, probably, since none of the Mainers believed Ned's threats about the FBI could possibly amount to much.

He was bluffing, Don said, it was highly unlikely his contacts in Anchorage could strong-arm agents in Boston.

But I still felt overheard. I couldn't even trust my clothes, despite the fact that we'd inspected them: everything was suspect. Back in my room I stripped them all off; I stepped into the bathroom and made another 911 call—they transferred me to the sheriff's office and I reported the kidnapping again—they said they were dispatching a car, they promised two officers would arrive within the half hour.

After I pressed the END button I stepped into the shower and let hot water beat down on my face.

What about those chips people implanted in pets, I thought—what about them? Could I have been implanted with a chip? Could I pick it out from under the skin, as I'd once seen in some otherwise forgettable movie?

Scratch, scratch, blood, and a loosened nub of metal dug out of the flesh.

IF I HAD been guided to the motel by some sense beyond the usual five, some navigational instinct having to do with magnetism or light, I wanted to know what for.

THE STATE POLICE finally got to us hours after we'd first called. It was two officers, polite and attentive in their note taking. We made them sit with us in the back office, where we felt Ned might not be able to hear, and I told them everything I could think of—about Beefy John, B.Q., Ned's driver, his rented SUV. Black and American, was all I could say, and of course he might easily have switched it out. A couple of times I had to stop, and the cops waited patiently, their faces presenting sympathy.

I wrote down the address of our house in Anchorage, where as far as I knew Ned still lived. I had no idea where he'd been staying locally—there weren't other motels nearby, said Don, you had to drive at least half an hour for the closest lodgings open this time of year.

"Or he could be staying with local contacts," said Will. "That mechanic, maybe? John something . . . Pruell, maybe," he told the police.

"Ned—my husband isn't the type to sleep in his car," I mumbled. "He never stays in hotels under four stars."

The policemen looked at each other.

"That narrows it down," said one. "He ain't in Maine."

I had a tin ear. My sense of humor had left with Lena.

We were surprised at how soon the cops went away again. I'd thought they would stay near, I thought there'd be a task force, something—in movies policemen walked around the house or apartment of the kidnapped child's family, tapping phones, watching at windows. But in fact the two policemen left after their brief interview of me and an even briefer search for the concealed microphone (they found nothing). Their expressions were mild.

"We'll do our best to find your daughter, ma'am," said one. But I didn't like how he said it—casually, as though it wasn't life or death.

In the silence after the lobby doors swung shut Don said Ned had to have got to them, that their placid demeanor was unnatural. He said we should assume they weren't going to move quickly and I had to just call the FBI. But I wasn't so sure, I was more afraid of Ned's capabilities than they were, so instead I went online and then I borrowed Will's phone, distrusting my own. I hired a private investigation company based in Portland.

They'd assign a team right away, they said.

I called my parents next. My mother seemed shell-shocked, as though Lena's abduction was a sheer unreality, and offered to help with money. Her voice was so faint that I could barely hear her.

I COULDN'T SIT in the motel, I found, waiting for someone else to look for my daughter. I couldn't stand it. I didn't want to talk to anyone who didn't already know what had happened.

So Will and I got into his truck, a beater with worn Mexican blankets over the seats, and at my request he drove slowly up and down the icy streets, up and down, back and forth, prowling. The streets were fairly empty of traffic, only the silence of blinking Christmas lights on house fronts and in yards. There were teams of reindeer pulling sleighs, yellow outlines of bells.

Now and then someone would honk behind us or angrily pass, swerving to make a point. It felt as bleak as it looked, the houses spread out, the odd signal flashing the white walking figure to an empty corner. But I had it in my head that I needed to drive every street, and

Will was willing to humor me, likely knowing I was on the edge of hysteria.

There was a worn map in the glove box, there was a half-dried-out pink highlighter in the armrest compartment, and Will pulled over and showed me how to mark the route we'd already driven. Even though it signified nothing, since we weren't knocking on doors or looking in windows, I colored furiously. As he drove I stared out the window, checking driveways for black SUVs, trying to imagine the potential of each business or house to be harboring her. I tried to intuit Lena's presence. Would I feel it? Would the other animals' senses come to my aid now—detection of the Earth's magnetic field, navigation by smell?

When we stopped at a stop sign or rare traffic light I'd trail the highlighter down the map, along the road we'd driven, which gave me a brief, businesslike feeling. Then I'd raise my face from the map. *The next moment,* I thought, *the next moment it will be . . .* I willed myself to see a face at the window, to see her small figure in the puffer coat.

"We need to stop now and go home," said Will after a while. He said it bluntly but kindly.

I was a child myself now: as soon as you were a victim, as soon as you were deeply hurt, you were a child again.

Helplessness was the one true fountain of youth.

IT WASN'T CLEAR what Ned wanted to accomplish. He'd ordered me to cancel the divorce filing, sure, but that could easily be restarted once Lena was returned. And any contract would have been signed under duress, and not binding.

After his first texts I heard nothing for days. Christmas passed without anyone seeming to celebrate it. Or if they did, I didn't see. It passed and faded and never was.

I went over and over how my girl must be feeling, alone with someone she barely knew, whether her father loomed as a threatening figure or had made himself charming and likable to reassure her. I worked to craft this kind of picture for myself, Ned as a babysitter, performing an imitation of affection—I sculpted this image painstakingly, smoothing my fingers along the edges, pushing it into a shape I could live with. But it collapsed whenever I wasn't vigilant and I wondered what he was telling her, what particular architecture of lies she was living in and what part of them she believed.

I couldn't help recalling Ned's phone conversation with my mother, his sly undermining of me, whether he was doing the same with Lena. But it was her relation to the whole world I feared for most, the way she might be changed. I got a prescription for tranquilizers the day after she was taken and tried, with Will's help, to make a routine for myself around the investigators' progress reports, which they gave to me twice a day.

Not even the voice had affected me like this, made my whole body weak with terror or my knees buckle whenever the knowledge of it struck me. It was my abject state that took me to Don's meetings. Between the kidnapping and the first meeting I attended there was only one exchange with Don about the hearing of voices—one moment when he bowed his head to me and apologized for having kept me out.

"You've been in recovery longer than most of them," he said. "You've done far better with it. For them it's still new. They didn't bring you in before because they weren't ready."

I said nothing to Will about the meetings, didn't even intend to go myself—I only started to attend them because I'd been by myself in my room and, without Lena, was hit by the lightning bolt that had been striking me constantly since she was taken. It was a stupefaction that refused to diminish: as soon as I had a loose, idle moment I was scorched down the center by remorse, burnt black by the feeling of guilt. *My fault. My fault.*

At those moments I'd do anything for distraction, and so it happened that one time I left my room headed for anywhere—looking for the moving figures of people, the sounds they made, the industry of normal lives—and as I passed through the lobby I saw the café door cracked open.

The tables had been pushed back to the walls, chairs set out in a circle. I'd been to an Al-Anon meeting once keeping a friend company, and this had the same encounter-group feeling. There were baked goods and coffee arrayed on one of the tables, a hot-water container and a basket of tea bags. I settled myself on a chair a bit back from the rest—an outlier, satellite chair—and as the fog of panic receded, I took hold of myself and worked not to think of Lena. One minute, I said to myself, one minute first, then two; one *minute* at a time, one day was an eternity.

Navid wasn't there, but the rest of the guests were accounted for.

"It's been four months since I retired," said Big Linda.

It didn't grow clear to me then where they'd heard their voices or how, only that the content of their perceptions varied. They'd heard different sounds, drawn different conclusions and had different responses. Linda had heard a voice at work, somehow, and told no one until much later; Burke had told Gabe about hearing a voice immediately, and Gabe had believed him schizophrenic . . . but in fact, that first day, I barely heard what was said. I drifted on the back of my Valium, lulled by the drone of voices.

And my fear of a cult, at least, was assuaged by the drabness of the plastic chair edge in front of me and the matter-of-fact trudge of Main Linda over to the snacks table. There was no grim power to be felt amid that mundane scene of guests selecting baked goods beneath the tube fluorescents. Main Linda piled sandwich cookies onto a paper plate printed with rainbows, then returned to her chair licking the powdered sugar off a finger.

Don didn't address a single word to me at that initial meeting, just let me sit there behind the ranks, saying nothing.

Not for the first time I thought how groups of people had a habit of making even the exceptional banal. Was it a national characteristic or a trait of all humanity? Crowds could be grandiose, that was true, but small groups in small rooms . . . it took me back to my parents' church, where I'd sat bored and staring around, looking high and low for any object of interest. More often than not I'd failed to find such an object and ended up gazing at the dirty Kleenex wadded into someone's sleeve. I remembered the backs of my legs sweating on the smooth wood of the pew, heard wet coughs off to one side, saw dandruff on shoulders and, in sandal weather, hoary toenails.

Still: there'd been hymns, and some of them were dull but many were beautiful and sad. Although I hadn't felt that sadness till after, long after we had left the church.

It was remembered music that was beautiful.

6

UNCLEAN SPIRITS ENTERED THE SWINE

THE INVESTIGATORS IMPRESSED ME WITH A SENSE OF COMPETENCE as I looked at their faces on the screen or scanned the neat pdf records of their efforts and expenditures, the rows of line items. I thought how easy I must be to fool—experience had shown this with sparkling transparence.

My questions were lame and I was often sedated. So I made Don and Will, and also the Lindas, ask questions for me. They huddled around and gazed into the laptop's camera. The investigators' clean, concerned faces stared back at us from a gray office only a couple hours' drive away. Were they really present, I wondered, in an office building in Portland? Or were they a shallow illusion of service?

Absurd how all transactions had become talking heads, the whole culture a mass of flat images of heads with mouths moving: we barely needed our bodies. There were hardly even dialogues anymore, rather there were a million monologues a day, each head with its mouth, each mouth with its talk. Still I listened with obsessive attention as the investigators fielded the questions, tried to show us they were pursuing all possible avenues.

Whether or not they were skilled or diligent, they hadn't found Lena by the next time Ned texted me.

He wanted to talk, he wrote.

Four days had gone by, the longest days I had lived.

WILL HAD TO DIAL the unfamiliar, prepaid number for me, my hands were shaking so hard, and when we finally got Ned on the line he wouldn't talk long—maybe in case someone was trying to trace the call. I don't know.

"I'munna need a photo op at the announcement, at least one TV show in Anchorage, down the road. Ads, maybe. Events availability. Magazine profiles, what have you. Like I said. And if I don't get 'em, this is just what happens, honey. Kid's just not *with* you anymore. She's gone. There's no cops out there gonna help you. It's my call what happens. If you want to fix it, I need your full onboarding."

Onboarding, I saw Will mouth silently, gazing down.

"Anything," I said. I could barely breathe—I was taking shallow breaths, quickly, afraid I might hyperventilate. "Give her the phone. Please. Ned. *Please.*"

"She's having a good time with her toys," said Ned. His tone was indifferent.

"I need to hear her voice, Ned, and I need her back, please. I'll do whatever. Today, Ned, please, I need her back *today*. You win. Completely, Ned, you won, you win. Please?"

There was a long silence. With my free hand I grabbed the fabric of my skirt and scrunched my fingernails into it, into the tops of my thighs.

"Some other time, darlin'," said Ned. "I want you to recall exactly how this feels."

"It's *killing* me," I said.

But he'd hung up.

YOU DIDN'T NEED a picture ID to take a six-year-old kid onto a plane, I said to Will, perched on a stool at his kitchen island, a bottle of wine open in front of me. The shaking had stopped and I was self-medicating. There had been a small, odd reassurance in Ned's saying she was playing with her toys, maybe just that I was able to picture her. You didn't even need a birth certificate—nothing. No piece of paper attesting to the child's identity, the child's relationship to you. Unless you were trying to leave the country, they didn't ask for anything. You could walk onto a plane with any kid in the world, as long as that kid didn't open her mouth and give you away.

And the country was endless.

Children have no identity here, I said, no one cares who they are. Although the same could be said of adults, I added. More or less, the only interest our country takes in our identities is as taxpayers, consumers or criminals, I said. They could be anywhere, the investigators had reminded us, anywhere in the country, they could be in Vegas or Boca—they could be back in Anchorage.

I couldn't easily picture Lena standing quietly while Ned checked her in at a flight gate, but it was possible. He might have made threats. He might have threatened her. Or drugged her again.

Or she might be somewhere offshore, I thought. Ned might have a boat. She might be on the ocean.

"Don't think along those lines," said Will, and put his hand over mine. "You have to stop yourself going down that road. There's nothing helpful there."

I looked at him and felt flattened and paralyzed: depression weakened my limbs. My whole body felt inert with the exception of a core of fear that burned with its own perpetual energy like a star being born, born, and reborn.

"Come," said Will.

I stood with difficulty, with lassitude, barely moving until he took my arm. He made me lie down on the couch across from his fireplace, covered me in a blanket.

"But I have to be at the motel," I said. "In case he shows up with her."

Will said nothing, because he didn't need to: I could hear the words *he won't* without anyone saying them. He only lifted the back of my head and set a pillow beneath it, smoothing a lock of hair from my eyes. He turned off the overhead lights, leaving only a table lamp or two, and sat down in an armchair somewhere behind me, where he began reading. I gazed at the fire, absorbed in its abstraction, and listened to the crisp cut of a page turning.

Most women probably wanted a man who acted more like a woman, I considered—more like a mother, even. You wanted to be taken care of. As long as he wasn't *womanish*, I thought, as long as he had central masculine characteristics such as strength and confidence, in most other respects an ideal man was more like a woman.

Later I fell asleep.

MORE THAN BEFORE, with Lena gone I lost myself in research. Whatever was said in the meetings was a catalyst for my searches. There was something necessary in the order that research gave me,

in the finding of lists, the recording of definitions. *This is what* x *is.*
This is what y *is.*

Soothing.

> A recent area of development is the discovery that . . . the abil-
> ity to produce "sentences" is not limited to humans. The first
> good evidence of syntax in nonhumans, reported in 2006, is
> from the greater spot-nosed monkey (*Cercopithecus nictitans*) of
> Nigeria, showing that some animals can take discrete units of
> communication and build them up into a sequence that then
> carries a different meaning from the individual "words." —The
> Times *of London 12.2013*

AT THE SECOND meeting I'd taken twice the usual dosage of my tranquilizers but I'd also been drinking coffee steadily.

I still sat back from the others, mug in hand, but this time I leaned
forward on my chair, almost perched. I succeeded in sealing off my
anxiety over Lena only by pretending that my life with her, my devoted
focus on her, did not exist at all. Fortified in this way, holding an
image in my mind of a wall placed between emotion and me, between
my life and myself—by blocking out my life outside the room—I was
able to listen with a manufactured singularity of purpose.

Regina spoke first. I'd barely heard her talk before but now she
was painfully eager. She has what I guess is a Dutch accent, and what
she said corrected me: it wasn't just preverbal infants. There too my
assumptions had been unfounded.

I listened to what she said and it never struck me to disbelieve. She'd
been exposed through someone named Terence, and though she didn't
describe him he clearly wasn't a baby. She was an ad exec who began
hearing the voice when Terence was with her in her corner office. At

first it spoke to her only in ditties and slogans; whenever she was with Terence, these ditties and slogans were audible, though he didn't seem to hear them. Almost right away it began happening when they were at home, too, she said, so now I assumed Terence was her husband—that they had worked together and gone home together too.

The man she'd come with sat across from her, nodding. But he couldn't be Terence; the way she talked about the absent person was almost patronizing. She'd cycled through various fixed ideas, she said, one of which had to do with wires in the walls, the audio of her TVs, computers, and many other interlinked devices. In service to that idea she'd hired contractors to tear into the walls, looking for speakers, receivers, anything that could be transmitting—she watched the workers like a hawk to determine whether wires existed where they should not. She'd pretended to be opening the walls for other reasons, she'd actually pretended to want to renovate, she said, had her company pay through the nose to renovate her corner office. Then she renovated her home, where, as a pretext for opening the walls and having the electricians carefully inspect all wiring, she paid to install complex systems that controlled the house's appliances, temperature, and lights.

Nothing had been found, the contractors dismissed her as a neurotic rich woman—which she was, she admitted in her tight, well-bred, Dutch voice. She *was* a neurotic rich woman, but so what?

Finally she went online and she found Don, she said: "I found all of you. And it was such a relief."

"She didn't tell me any of it," said her companion, who also had a Dutch accent. "She never told me what she was hearing, why she had taken on these construction projects, until we were on our way here."

"You know," said Regina. "I feared that Reiner would dismiss me. For being mentally ill, you know? People just get dismissed. It's how we get rid of people these days, we throw their opinions in the garbage can by calling them crazy. Whenever a man talks about his ex-wife, he says she's crazy! You notice? Because she must be crazy, right? To want to get a divorce from him."

"Ik wil geen scheiden, schat," said Reiner fondly.

"He says, 'I don't want to get a divorce,'" translated Regina.

Quaking aspen trees make clones of themselves to build colonies, becoming one large organism connected by its root system. They are able to survive forest fires because, although individual trees may burn, the roots underground remain intact. One colony in Utah is 80,000 years old.

Not to *have* to have children, I thought as I read about the aspens in Wikipedia, or at least not to have children that were separate from you—and yet to live throughout history, your family not only close around you for all that time but part of your own body.

Not to have to be alone.

I envied those aspens.

NAVID TOOK A TURN at the next meeting, shuffling his feet on the linoleum and clearing his throat nervously. I felt the attention of the group fasten on him: he must not have talked much before.

He'd been on set, he said, he loved being on set, and even though his job almost never required it, he did it as often as he could. He had one assistant, he said, just out of film school whose job it was to hang around a movie set all day and then, when finally a scene was ready to shoot, to text Navid so he could drive over. Best money he ever spent, he said, best money . . . he trailed off. I saw Kay catch his eye and smile at him, encouraging.

When he had started hearing, he said, it was a period of hard work and, he admitted, chronic drug use, and so his assumption was that what he heard was a cocaine artifact. Well, also crack, he said, because sex on crack, you know, was really excellent, he added awkwardly. "Or maybe you don't know, ha ha," and he looked around at the room of non-crack-users and emitted a nervous laugh.

No one else laughed.

His problem was, he said, he didn't know where the voice was coming from—there were so many people on the soundstage that he couldn't isolate it. He'd gone home to his house in the Hills when the shoot was over and hadn't heard it there; the house was empty except for his housekeeper cook and one other staff and the big rooms hung heavy with quiet. But as soon as he was on set again—the same movie, but there was a large cast, there was a massive crew, it was a big movie—the voice started up.

It drove him crazy, he said, because visiting the set was the only real perk of his job. He'd never cared much about the money, he liked to be there seeing movies get made, it was the whole *reason* for his career, and this movie, *this* movie in particular was his baby, he'd nurtured it from the cradle, it was *his* project. He even tried *not* doing drugs, but that didn't help (he smiled, self-mocking) so he went back off the wagon a couple of days later.

The voice performed speeches, he said, as far as he could tell it was speeches from hundreds of different films, scripted monologues and dialogues—not all of which he recognized. It might as well have been making its way through the AFI Catalog.

"I mean, I guess—" he interrupted himself, and looked at Don. "I guess I'm wanting to know what we're all doing, like, what *is* this? Why *me*? I just wanted to do my thing, make the pictures and sell them, you know, stay on trajectory. I was making, like, this almost perfect arc. And then there was this—it was pretty much *noise*, like static, like really fucking annoying, I mean I'd punch walls, man, I put a hole in drywall once—which—and cracked a Lexus window—anyway. So this is what I'm saying—assuming it *is* some kind of higher power or whatever, then what's the goddamn point of it? It fucks us over, and for fucking what?"

Instead of answering, though, when all of us turned and looked at him, Don just nodded.

"Go on," he said gently, as though Navid hadn't asked him a question.

"We come here, we talk, we tell our stories and whatever, say what we heard or felt, what our perception was. We have this—with the cookies and the donuts and that shit. Group therapy. But it's, like, circles. Around and around. Are there answers? Will anyone ever fucking tell me why and how this shit happened to me?"

Don kept nodding solemnly.

We sat there in an uncomfortable silence. But Don was waiting too, clearly, as though he didn't get that he was being directly asked—as though he didn't feel the pregnancy of the pause. Still no one wanted to say anything. There was a force field around Don, it seemed.

"He means, Don, do you have an explanation for us," said Kay softly.

The group seemed embarrassed, people fiddling with coffee cups or adjusting their positions on the hard chairs.

"Basically I'm one of you," said Don, after a few seconds. "They don't offer degrees in this, I'm afraid. I need you to understand that I try to be here for you, I want to do everything I can to help, but I'm not a credentialed expert."

There were a couple of nods, but faces went slack and shoulders sank with a disappointment so tangible I could feel it even from the cheap seats, sitting behind a row of backs. They'd wanted him to explain in simple terms what had happened to them, they'd thought he might really have the key.

I had too. I was no different.

Someone's cell phone rang from a bag under a chair and around the circle the guests shuffled their feet, started to pull on gloves and wrap scarves around their necks. I noticed they'd come bundled in full winter gear, even though most had only twenty feet to walk from their rooms.

"One thing," said Don. "Navid. When you say *why us*, it's not that we're the only ones. We're a subset—we heard more clearly than most. But we're not the only ones by a long shot. None of you are alone."

"'My name is legion, for we are many,'" said Gabe.

There was a glazed look in his eyes.

Listless, wanting something to occupy me when I got back to my room, I searched for the quote online.

It was from Mark 5, when Jesus cast demons out of a man and into a herd of pigs.

> He said to him, "Come out of the man, unclean spirit!"
> Then He asked him, "What *is* your name?"
> And he answered, saying, "My name *is* Legion; for we are many."
> The unclean spirits entered the swine; and the herd rushed down the steep bank into the sea, about two thousand of them; and they drowned.

IN A SUDDEN acceleration they started holding the meetings twice a day. I built the meetings into my routine, though I always had my cell phone ringer on high waiting for Ned to call. Part of me lived only for the second when he'd call again, or even better—a perfect ending— the investigators would call and tell me everything was solved, Lena was there with them, safe and sound and beyond excited to see me.

My limbic brain waited for that, the call that would effect reanimation, while the rest of the neural circuits were dedicated to not feeling alone while Will worked, marking time as I listened and watched at the meetings. I abandoned this journal. I had no wish to think, I had no wish to record. Until I found her I would distract myself with whatever this was, some talk-therapy hunt for God or even more ominous possibilities—none of it frightened me anymore. That was the difference: the second-worst thing (not the worst: I blocked the worst) had already happened. Whatever phenomenon they were pain-stakingly trying to uncover, there in the cafeteria beside the folding table of cookies, it was easier to consider than Lena.

Once I would have paid through the nose for a cogent explana-tion of the voice; now I sought that understanding mostly to stop agonizing over what I couldn't do or was not doing to find her. Part of me stubbornly refused to believe I couldn't just walk until I found her—treading through snow, knocking at doors—and felt a rotten guilt. Part of me couldn't believe she wasn't still neatly indicated, as I was, by a small blue dot on the map on my phone, moving as I did, going where I went.

I grilled myself over my incompetence, how I had come to let myself be roofied. Nights when I wasn't with Will were the worst, but I couldn't ask him to take care of me every minute so I pretended to need "time alone" some nights, whenever I could stand to. I often passed the time by retracing my steps in the hours before she was taken, seeing a simple blueprint of our room from above. In bird's-eye view I moved around performing mundane actions, the oval of my head between the knobs of my shoulders, the tips of my shoes beneath. There was Lena, a smaller oval, the same shapes in miniature.

I tried to reframe each movement to determine how the drug was introduced, think of myself brushing my teeth—was it in the toothpaste?—or brushing my hair. Maybe it hadn't been a pill at all, maybe it was some kind of narcotic that was absorbed through the skin. I played back that hour before I went to bed, when Lena was already sleeping. It couldn't have been the toothpaste because she uses a different one—a children's flavor called *Silly Strawberry*—and she must have been sedated, as I was, otherwise she would have woken up as they carried her out, she would have kicked and screamed.

Sedated or not, I told myself, I would have been woken by a scream. Since she was a year old I've jerked awake at the slightest sound, a murmur or one-word whisper of sleep talk.

The cops had taken away the half-empty wine bottle and the plastic motel cup I'd drunk from, claiming they were going to test them; the wine was all I remembered eating or drinking, after our restaurant dinner one town over.

But they didn't report any results. They were useless, Don said, they've been bought off or distracted or co-opted, he had no idea how but it seemed to be the case.

There was also the possibility of a needle, that I was injected while I slept and never found the pinprick hole. I couldn't figure it out no matter how many times I set up that blueprint in my mind's eye. No matter how often I took us through the paces, I could never narrow it down.

We never found Ned's recording device, and together the two unknowns obsessed me.

WHAT IF ONE of the aspen trees was cut down, while the rest of the organism remained? Did the remainder grieve?

TRYING TO AVOID images of how Lena was living in that moment I lay on top of the neatly made motel bed and stared at the ceiling. I thought how, in our normal, middle-class circumstance, we almost relish the idea of dark forces that lurk in the shadows. We watch movies, read books made glamorous by black-and-red palettes of horror, the hint of an otherworldly malice running like quicksilver through the marrow of our bones. We like to call the dark rumors demonic, like to have monsters to fear instead of time, aging, the falling away of companions.

Even people who scoff at the supernatural can embrace the demonic with a gothic fervor, hold in themselves an abiding fascination with that beauty of darkness and blood.

. . . . .

BIG LINDA HAD been working, she said—her work for decades had been training orcas like Shamu. She's pursued that vocation for most of her adult life.

She hadn't been doing the shows for a while, though, she'd gotten middle-aged and taken on more of a supervisory role, because to get in the pool with the animals you had to be in peak physical form. There'd been human deaths, of course, she said, maybe you read about them, saw them in the news, and trainers knew the real story, that it wasn't trainer error that caused those deaths but rather psychosis, because the great, predatory whales lived captive lives of aching, maddening frustration, shut up in their small cement tanks.

Some were more aggressive than others. Tilikum, she said. *Blackfish*.

Of course killer whales aren't whales in the sense of *baleen* whales, the kind of whales that cruise gently through the deep, slowly straining millions of krill and copepod through large maws full of white comb-like structures (she told us). The orcas were toothed whales, big dolphins really, though also apex predators, if we were familiar with the term. They were so highly intelligent that parts of their brain appeared a good deal more complex than our own—the part that processes emotion, she said, was so highly developed that some neurologists believe orcas' emotional lives are more complex than those of humans.

We know so little about them, she said, even the scientists, but they have language, even different dialects. They have culture. There are three kinds of orcas in the wild, all with their different cultures.

"They are astonishing creatures," she said, her voice trembling. "Some peoples hold them to be sacred."

I think I wasn't the only one to feel how much she cared, in the moment when she said that—how palpable her passion was—and how also, on this large, horse-faced older woman, passion like that looked almost pitiable.

Anyway, her favorite whale was a youngster who'd been bred and born in captivity, which is still fairly rare, she said, they die off more quickly than they can reproduce, the captive ones. His mother and father were popular with the crowds who visited the aquarium-amusement park where she worked (swiftly I shut down the mental link *children*, blocked an image of children laughing, splashed by the orca's leap).

Big Linda was alone one morning at the pool—the pools they live in, she added, only have to be twice the length of an orca's body. Main Linda cleared her throat, jerking Big Linda out of her sad reverie.

There was a silence, a pleasant tranquillity, said Big Linda. This was Florida in summer; there were palm trees overhead, the smell of heating pavement.

"I can't say what it was like, exactly," she went on, shaking her head and staring at the floor in front of her. The others also looked at the floor, as though listening to the shameful confessions of an addict. "I don't know how to describe it."

I saw Burke nodding slowly, pensive, also not lifting his eyes from the linoleum. I had no idea what Linda was getting at, couldn't make sense of it in the least, and was gazing distractedly at the side table, thinking about eating a cookie—they had some that were an unnatural shade of pink, those long rectangular wafers stamped with a waffle pattern that seem like play food. Lena had play food—she had fruit and vegetables made of wood that you could slice and put back together with Velcro. She had berry pie slices made of plastic. *No! Stop.*

"First I thought I was making it up," said Linda, "truth is I'd been real unhappy there lately, I don't like how we keep the animals—you have to understand, we only stay, most of the trainers stay because we're sorry for them, deeply sorry. We stay to do what we can for these creatures. For years I couldn't leave because of that, I'm so attached to them, you know, the little guy especially. Not *that* little, of course, since he's fourteen feet long." She laughed nervously.

I got up, telling myself to block out the lingering image of Lena at play, and gingerly approached the snack table; I put one of the waffle cookies on the tip of my tongue. Like balsa wood with sugar, I thought, and sawdust between the layers—sawdust with sugar. Still I chewed it, studiously not letting my thoughts stray back to Lena with her toys.

"Point is I was stressed out. Still. I finally had to admit to myself that something was there. I mean not the clicks and whistles and chirps, the usual elements of calls that we occasionally hear, you know, the vocalizing . . . it wasn't that."

I stopped mechanically chewing the balsa wood/sawdust wafer and turned toward the circle, where others were also gazing at her, their faces unreadable to me. She meant she'd heard the *killer whale*, I thought, and had an abrupt urge to laugh.

Instead I swallowed the mouthful and sat down on my chair again, careful to make no noise. I wanted to be very polite. It was Big Linda, I thought, who'd always been so kind to us—to think of ridiculing her made me wince. I would be unfailingly polite, I would be more attentive than I had been before, and I would suppress the instinct to laugh. It'd be hysterical laughter anyway, I told myself: again I had signs of incipient hysteria, as I had after Ned heard the voice. Both euphoria and hysteria had risen in me as I jogged along our street in the dark. Now they threatened to rise in me again.

But I was still a wretch. My misery came crashing back. I felt no lightheartedness at all; I was as heavy as lead.

"I always heard it, whenever I was at the tank, and I couldn't tell you how I got anything from it, but I knew—something about the way it was, somehow the rhythms were linked, how he'd be moving around and I'd be hearing it. I knew it was connected to him. He'd just been separated from his mother, you know, he'd just been weaned, but in the wild the male orcas stay at their mothers' sides for their whole lives. He'd been taken away from her, you could tell he was lost, basically, and then there was this—it was a kind of wall of sound, I guess, a wall of sound that also felt like a wall of feeling."

In the end—to me at least—a baby, a whale, there was nothing more nonsensical there than anywhere else.

Male humpback whales have been described by biologists as "inveterate composers" of songs that are "strikingly similar" to the products of human musical tradition. —*Wikipedia 2015*

I TRIED TEXTING Ned's various numbers, the temporary cell phones he'd used recently as well as his old number, the one he'd had for years. I repeatedly typed messages such as *I'll do anything you want me to, I accept your terms, Give her back and I'll do whatever you say.* For several nights there was no amount of abjection I wouldn't stoop to.

Finally I pulled up short and pretended to be made of granite, went from spineless to fossilized. There wasn't a middle ground. I knew it wouldn't last, either, the rock-like immobility, the erasure of my real life.

It was unbearable to submit to my profound weakness and so the only choice was to shore up surface strength.

Plants might be able to eavesdrop on their neighbors and use the sounds they "hear" to guide their own growth, according to a new study that suggests plants use acoustic signaling to communicate with one another. Findings published in the journal *BMC Ecology* suggest that plants can not only "smell" the chemicals and "see" the reflected light of their neighbors, they may also "listen" to the plants around them. —*National Geographic News*

ONE EVENING AROUND dusk there was a call from a new number, and when I picked it up after one ring, as I picked up all calls—instantly, slavishly—I heard her.

"Mommy?" said Lena, on the brink of tears.

"I'm here! I'm here!" is all I remember saying.

The phone was passed from Lena to someone else, an adult voice I didn't recognize. A contract was being faxed, it said, and I would have to sign it in front of a notary. We both understood, technically, that it wasn't binding, wouldn't hold up in court since it was being signed under duress, etc., but Ned also knew *I* knew that if I didn't stick to its terms this would simply happen again.

"But worse," said the person, inflectionless.

After I signed the contracts and they were delivered, Lena would be brought back to me.

These events unrolled quickly. The contracts were received and signed, Will and Don read them, as well as Reiner, who turned out to be a corporate lawyer. Will drove me to a notary at the fire station that stayed open all night, and after that a messenger took the packet from me. Then we went back to the motel and waited.

I took no pill and drank no wine, determined to be sober as a judge. Instead of drinking I walked around and around the outside of the motel, my heart beating fast, my cheeks hot, until my calves burned and the soles of my feet were sore. Freezing, I walked for hours. Every brief headlight near the end of the road made me breathless.

It was after midnight when the car pulled up and two men got out, two men I didn't know, though I wondered in passing if I recognized one of them as a cop.

Then Lena was here, I had her with me again, and the motel guests were close, and Don and Will, Don's father smiling widely as he leaned on his wavering cane. Everyone was hugging Lena or patting her, congratulating me, whatever. We were in the warm lobby without having walked there—we'd floated, I think now, and when I finally looked up there were no men and there was no car. Vanished.

SO NED HAS BECOME a condition again, a feature of life. Our end date is still the election, contractually, after which Lena and I should be released—but for now we're indentured. We're flying to Alaska next week for the official candidacy announcement, to do our duty as mannequins.

Ned's staff booked the tickets; Ned's staff booked the rental car. We're staying in our old house for almost a week. Without speaking to me at all, only sending me emails containing flight confirmation numbers and the rental car details, Ned's staff took charge of the arrangements.

Lena's still saying little about her time in kidnapping—I can't tell how deep the injury may go, though Don found us a counselor forty-five minutes away and we drive to see her three days a week. It doesn't seem to be the case that anything of substance occurred while she was in Ned's hands. That is, as long as she hasn't blocked a trauma. All that happened, apparently—once the initial violation had occurred when she was drugged and taken from me—was that she stayed in a hotel suite with a babysitter. And of course she was frightened because they told her I was sick.

It sounds like it was one of those big chain hotels, more like apartments in an office park, possibly in Massachusetts somewhere, the PIs say, with generic but pleasant enough bedrooms off a central living room and kitchen. The babysitter had her own room, and so did Lena, between which the doors were left open.

Apparently she only saw Ned once. The first morning he stayed away and had the babysitter tell her that she was safe, I was safe, the illness wasn't life-threatening. Everyone was safe, but she was staying there for her own protection in case the sickness was contagious. He made his single in-person appearance that evening, bearing ice cream and an expensive, wholesome-looking doll wearing a red-velvet ice-skating outfit. After that he sent her toys daily through the caregiver: animated movies, books, doll clothes.

She kept the doll for longest, toward which she felt a parental responsibility, but finally she asked me to take it to the same donation bin in the grocery-store parking lot where we'd taken the other items he'd sent. The gifts must have left a sour taste in her mouth.

The babysitter, a kindly, bland-sounding woman, prepared their meals: whatever Lena wanted, up to and including large ice-cream sundaes, chocolate layer cake, and piles of frosted cookies. For exercise she was taken to the indoor hotel pool, which, to hear Lena tell it, was always deserted, except for the babysitter and her. She liked the hot tub, which kids weren't allowed to go in: she had received the babysitter's special permission.

She watched a lot of TV.

Now that she's back I can stand to hear about it, I want to know every detail she imparts. Her experience has taken her sense of security and consistency from her—her exuberance has been curtailed. She doesn't sob or clutch at me, but she moves more cautiously than she used to, she's more measured.

One afternoon a guest checked in—a tired man from Quebec who didn't appear to hear any voices; he was so tired he barely even heard ours—and Don asked if she wanted to offer him a tour. She was polite and dutiful, mainly, I think, to protect Don's feelings. She didn't want to seem ungrateful. Yet the tour was subdued. She skipped the ice machine entirely.

I'm so angry at Ned for taking it from her, that free, unreasonable joy that was her greatest possession.

. . . . .

SO MY FEAR has turned mostly to anger, which is much easier to live with—I see now why it's popular.

But I continue to need distraction so to expend my nervous energy, maybe dispel the rage, I scroll and scroll and click and click once she's tucked in at night.

I've been going to the meetings faithfully, knowing we're leaving, trying to absorb as much as I can before I say goodbye to this strange circle. I can't take Lena with me to the meetings and there's no one I trust to watch her when I'm occupied except Will, so I've been vague about the meetings, implying only that they're about "recovery"—my own therapy, as she has hers. Fifteen minutes before they start I drop Lena at the library.

I've been trying to learn if anything unites the motel guests beyond the fact of having heard—whether, for instance, a message was conveyed to anyone. For me there hadn't seemed to be a message, as I've written, for me the voice had been like weather, but I shared Navid's questions, we all did: they were basic. I wanted to know if the voice had carried portents for others—if they'd felt like the Maid of Orleans, if any had believed they were receiving instructions or prophecies. It was a whale that spoke to Big Linda; well, whales have often figured in myths and stories. It seems well within the standard imaginative canon.

And just yesterday Burke spoke to the group at length.

"Chinese native," he mumbled, looking down at his feet. Burke has the bearing of an absentminded professor. "*Acer griseum*. Paperbark maple. Beautiful, peeling red bark, this great, faded red I've never seen anywhere else. I remember having the impression that it was melodies made by the flow of cellular division, the phloem and xylem. The movement of sugar in the trunk."

For him the voice—something like humming or singing, he said, a pure music sometimes like a chorale, sometimes like a Glass symphony—seemed to issue from a certain tree in the arboretum where he worked. The tree sang and its music was holy.

"But you know. Maybe it wasn't really *coming* from the maple tree or Shamu," said Navid. "Maybe they were both sort of like one of those ventriloquist's dummies—like the sound or the song were being thrown *onto* them."

I spoke for the first time. I said I'd been quite sure, when I was hearing the voice, that it was closely associated with Lena. It was either part of her or attached to her, but she was no ventriloquist's dummy. I said how its monologues would follow the movements of her eyes, at times, commenting on what those eyes beheld.

"Assuming it's not technology or communications from extraterrestrials," said Big Linda, "maybe it can have many kinds of living hosts."

"ET, really?" said Navid. "Hadn't gone *there*. But now that you mention it."

It seemed we were almost considering levity, or at least some of us were, and others were resisting and disapproving, at least that was how I interpreted the silence.

Kay spoke, softly as always.

"I know something," she said.

Heads turned.

"I mean—I don't have all the answers, I don't mean that," she went on carefully. "But I know part of it. I thought everyone did, until this meeting, hearing what Linda said, what all of you have, I thought we all knew that part of it, but now I think maybe that, with us hearing things, maybe I have this particular piece, and others have other pieces. I guess?"

Kay has that insecure person's mannerism of ending her statements with question marks.

"What piece?" asked Navid.

"It—so what we heard is, how can I put it," she said nervously. She was looking down at her hands in her lap, as though embarrassed by her claim to knowledge. "It exists in most things that live. It's language, or the innate capacity for language, is a better way to put it. You could say it's the language of sentience."

"Trees don't have language. Trees don't have *opinions*," objected Navid, kicking the floor with his toes.

Kay looked up at him. It was a different look from those she usually gave him, I realized. It was sympathy.

"It's not that we're the only ones who have it, or hear it, or *are* it," she went on, so quiet that I had to strain to hear. "What's different about *us*, different from how it is with the other animals and even the plants—what happened with Lena and Anna and in my case with Infant Vasquez? What's different is that we're the only ones it *leaves*."

> Communication is observed within the plant organism, i.e. within plant cells and between plant cells, between plants of the same or related species, and between plants and non-plant organisms, especially in the root zone . . . plant roots communicate with rhizome bacteria, fungi and insects in the soil. These interactions . . . are possible because of the decentralized "nervous system" of plants. —*Wikipedia 2016*

IT WAS A LONG meeting, a meeting that went on for three hours instead of one, and by the time we dispersed afterward it seemed that Kay had always had a clearer understanding than any of the rest of us—Kay's hospital infant, an infant with a hole in its heart that lived for only three days, had somehow imparted more to her than the voice had told the rest of us in months. Even years.

Kay had heard more. Or Kay had listened with a greater aptitude for hearing.

I hadn't thought I was special, just equal. Equal, at least, I always assumed. But by the time I left the meeting I was unsure, unsure and diminished.

After the meeting I suspected I wasn't equal, and more, that there *was* no equality. Our idea of equality is a fiction useful mostly for the purposes of fairness, for law and economics. Elsewhere it's an empty husk, a costume we put on when we get up in the morning. In the length of our legs and arms, the breadth of our shoulders, the tendons that give us strength or weakness, our beauty or lack of it, sharp or dull intelligence—we aren't equal at all, and we never have been.

7

SOUL IS A UNIVERSAL FEATURE

NOT MANY TOURISTS FLY INTO ANCHORAGE IN WINTER. IN SUMMER there are backpackers galore: the small airport is full of tower-like packs with attachments dangling from them and duffel bags lumped on the floor in archipelagos of nylon and canvas. Among them you see hippies milling, hikers, hunters, fishermen, naturalists and wilderness fans of all stripes, talking excitedly about their planned itineraries as they wait for their car rides or small-plane connections. They crowd beneath the terminal's fluorescents in a fug of B.O. and patchouli and bug spray, headed for Denali and other points west or north.

But January is quiet in Alaska. When we flew in, the airport was almost deserted. It had that peculiar desolation of an empty public space, and in the silence our roller-bags squeaked and our footsteps rang out. Lena squealed at the sight of a rearing grizzly in a glass cage, which a placard claims is the largest bear ever shot. Paws raised, it looms over the polished expanse of floor in a perfect embodiment of overkill. She stood beside me and gripped my hand as she read aloud the sign at the bottom of the case: WORLD RECORD KODIAK BROWN BEAR. The bear's reared-up stance was upright, almost gentlemanly.

Ned wasn't there to meet us, happily, only a driver at the curb. Everything had been choreographed by his staff; there was a schedule with places, times, and tasks listed: *4:30 p.m. Consultant Appt. 1: Wardrobe.* He's as disinclined to be in my company as I am to be in his. No good words will ever pass between us now.

We had an appointment with his lead media person right off, in his campaign office; we were instructed today, before the first press conference tomorrow. There are even clothes I have to wear, looks custom-designed for me as though I'm Sarah Palin. Clothes have been picked for Lena, too, apparently. *Really?* I thought. *Even for the small time?*

Ned has to do everything with corporate shine, he needs to be at the top of his game from the start. And he requires similar performances from his associates.

So we met with them and tried on the clothes. It was tedious standing around as they recorded our sizes and made adjustments, trying to keep Lena in one place. A hair and makeup person came and practiced painting our faces, taking pictures of us colored in different palettes. Lena was turned out like Shirley Temple at first and looked like a beauty pageant contestant, so I said no. The media consultant trotted out a second outfit, slightly less frilly, and agreed not to curl her hair into ringlets.

I know I won't be able to stand Ned's platforms and opinions, much less concur with them, so I'm doing my best to learn nothing more than I have to about what I'm shilling for. This is a farce I'm acting in. Except for one dinner with some women's church group, I don't have any conversations on my to-do list. I hold Lena's hand whenever I feel doubt, press her to my side when I find I'm quizzing myself on how I could have been so easily brought to heel.

But I'm not willing to take risks: I stay close to her all the time. I was given a second chance, I was rescued after a shipwreck, and my goal isn't ambitious. It's just to keep our heads above water.

After the meeting with the wardrobe consultant we were driven to the house, once our home. I felt anxious walking in, not sad or nostalgic; the abduction had erased even the vestigial possibility of that. But I did feel off-kilter entering the place. Lena was merely intrigued and ran around trying to identify what she remembered.

Ned has a housekeeper so everything is neat, and he's replaced the furniture I chose with items that are new and more generic. There's beige upholstery and beige drapes, a bland beige background everywhere; there are cut flowers on mantels and tables, as though the premises are being kept at the ready for a meet-and-greet. Behind shining cabinet doors there's a huge flat-screen TV, and photographs of snow-covered mountains have been placed on the white walls, no doubt by a decorator connected to his media team. They're Alaskan mountains, of course—discreetly labeled at the bottom lest anyone doubt Ned's loyalties. *Chugach Range. 2008. Wrangell-St. Elias National Park.*

Wrangell-St. Elias, I remembered telling Ned once, was larger than Switzerland. He'd shrugged: to him national parks were a waste of rich mineral and timberland.

But now he has pictures of them.

"Where'd my room used to be?" asked Lena. "Did I have my own room?"

"You did," I said. "But mostly you slept in the bed with me."

We stood at the door of the very small room that had been the nursery, which now contains an exercise bike and free weights.

"It doesn't *look* like my room," objected Lena.

"Your daddy likes to stay fit," I said.

THE NEXT CONSULTANT made her practice standing beside me in front of a video camera. She showed us the footage on her laptop, showed Lena how she was fidgeting and playing with her hair. Lena should stand still and smile and keep her hands clasped together, she said, or at least let them hang by her sides. She shouldn't move around, said the consultant, because it would distract from Ned.

"Your daddy's going to make a little speech, and then he'll answer questions."

"What if I have an itch?" asked Lena.

The consultant smiled and said the whole thing would be over before she even knew it.

The initial response to an anomaly is typically to ignore it; this is how the scientific community has responded to the seeming anomaly of consciousness.

Then, when the anomaly ceases to be ignored, the common reaction is to try to explain it within the current paradigm . . . to date, no such effort in any discipline—be it chemistry, quantum physics, chaos theory, or computing—has proved fruitful.

No matter what theory is put forward, the central question remains: How can immaterial consciousness ever arise from matter?

When it comes to consciousness itself, science falls curiously silent. There is nothing in physics, chemistry, biology, or any other science that can account for our having an interior world.

—*Peter Russell, huffingtonpost.com 12.2013*

I DON'T WANT to see my Anchorage friends, because to see them again now would bring them into this queasy distortion of my life, the fake alliance with Ned. It makes me ashamed, even though I'm looking down the barrel of his gun.

Some know about the kidnapping, some don't; others know about how it resolved, others don't. I can't stand to do the mental accounting of who knows what, can't bear to revisit the ordeal—it was hard enough writing it down for myself. I don't need to listen to sympathy or indignation on my behalf.

And from the few calls I made while I was panicking, I have the lingering feeling that most of them don't believe I was trapped into making this deal with Ned. None of my friends here seem to understand the urgency of my fear. They live in a personal world where rules are followed and fairness reigns; they're mostly white and mostly middle-class, meaning they feel entitled to justice for themselves and expect it for all the other people in their lives. Corruption belongs elsewhere, other countries, Wall Street or Congress, lobbyists.

They tried to be sympathetic when I talked to them, as people have to in the face of a missing child, but I felt, behind their commitment to sympathy, a steady seep of disbelief as though they suspected I was exaggerating or dramatizing. I was failing to stay normal, so either my perceptions were biased or I'd mistaken the facts of the case.

Because their take is that Ned's a good guy, basically. Too handsome and too charming, one of my friends wrote me, and sometimes you resent him for that. But as soon as you see him again you forget the resentment—you like him again the moment he speaks to you. *He's maybe a bit of a playa,* she wrote. *There've always been rumors, but there are always going to be rumors when a man's that HOT-HOT-HOT* [sic]. Men aren't monogamous anyway, they're just not *built* that way, and *I'm sure it was hard to live in the shadow of the light he sheds . . .*

That was the kind of email I got from my Anchorage friends about Ned. He's not a credible kidnapper to them. They figure he probably just missed his kid. Maybe he missed her desperately.

The first time we saw him was an hour before the press conference to announce he was running. We sat in his campaign office, waiting to go into the room with the small stage and podium where the reporters were going to be; Lena was in modified pageant gear, only half as gaudy as the outfit they'd first put her in, and no ringlets. I was in a suit that made me look like a first lady, and they shellacked my hair with spray so that it was big on top and swooped up at the bottom. The makeup artist gave me pink lips.

Ned came in while they were working on us, making his usual pretense of jocular fatherhood—bending to hug Lena, then grab her face and say "Got your nose!" (She jerked back at this, banging into the hairdresser standing behind her.) He acted as though he'd already greeted me, as though we'd spent hours together earlier that day—for the benefit of the staff, possibly, he squeezed my arm as he passed—preparing himself, maybe, for the public embraces we'd been asked to perform.

We hadn't seen each other since the day he showed up in Maine. Since before he took my daughter.

"My girls ready?" he asked.

My girls triggered my gag reflex, surprising me, and I fled to the bathroom. I didn't throw up, in that closet-sized half bath full of rolled-up campaign posters and yard signs, but it was close.

Once we were up in front of the flashbulbs and digital recorders, my nausea turned to a stunned thoughtlessness. When Ned spoke I barely registered the content of what he was saying. Everything but

Lena, who held my hand, was scenery, and when I embraced that I felt less nervous.

When people say "scenery" they can mean either a stage set or the beauty of the natural world—the two are interchangeable, in the word *scenery*. In that strange word the entire landscape, up to and including mountains and the moon, is only a background, probably two-dimensional, for the human figures in front of it. But it helped me, in those minutes, to think we were just playacting.

The press didn't ask many political questions; mostly the reporters there were interested in giving Ned opportunities to talk about his success at business, to brag about his companies, of which the room seemed to be full of boosters. There was one timid question from someone at the back about a drillship that had almost run aground in Unalaska Bay, but the other reporters moved on quickly when Ned waved that one away. The room was stacked with his allies.

Just when I thought we'd got off scot-free and things were winding down, a reporter waved at Lena.

"What do you have to say about your daddy running for office, honey?"

Lena blinked and said nothing, and then, as the silence lingered: "He's my daddy."

Her tone was confused, almost questioning, but because she's a kid and her voice is high and thin, this bland remark gave the room an excuse for aw-shucks laughter. People shuffled out, grinning and shooting the breeze.

WE NEEDED TO be seen out on the town together, so Ned made reservations at upscale restaurants for all our dinners on this trip, except for the very first night when he took us to a pizza place that's a local favorite.

The "narrative," as he calls it, meaning the group of fabrications we give out for public consumption, is that I have a dying parent back East, and Lena and I are staying there to help my mother suffer through the time of decline and hospice. My father gets to be the one who's dying.

"Lymphoma on top of the ol' dementia," Ned said.

I hope my mother or Solly don't see any of the coverage of Ned's campaign, that none of it makes its way onto YouTube. I imagine how their faces would crumple, seeing my father used that way.

At dinner I had to talk directly to him at close quarters. I had to look closely at his smooth features, his deep-blue eyes that glance off me now, never resting for long, straying around whatever space we're in as though even a table leg is more compelling than my face. I welcome it in practice, but it hits me how he used to work those eyes so hard to make me believe he was earnest.

The Moose's Tooth was crowded as usual—there are always lines there—and our booth was sandwiched close between two others. Ned's fake-Secret Service bodyguards took the nearest two-top, but still we were back to back with other diners and I could tell Ned felt everyone must be watching him, so the fake cheer of our conversation had to pass muster. It was surprisingly difficult to smile and nod and be a wifely mainstay.

I found I couldn't eat. The restaurant's pizza, which I used to love, reminded me of egg salad. So I drank my one glass of white wine, picked at a salad and listened to Ned rattle off his campaign reports. My single glass of white wine was mandated by his staff, as it didn't look feminine to drink beer, it didn't look Christian to have a second glass, and red might stain my teeth. I drank my quota slowly, savoring it as I watched Lena doodle on a child's menu and Ned reeled off a list of coming events, repeated sound bites about his exchanges with campaign donors, why they believed in him and his values "in their own words." There were the usual anecdotes about small-town Americans, a farmer named Milt, a grandma named Pearl. He seemed to be running lines, rehearsing his material with a very small focus group.

After a while I looked up from Lena's artwork and found myself staring at elements of his face and carefully detesting each. You'd think a facial feature in itself would tend to be inoffensive, particularly a well-formed one, but I discovered that if I concentrated even an earlobe could be invested with spite.

Lena spoke quietly, softly about the plot of a Disney movie while I stared at the earlobe and savored my distaste. There were a couple of moments when I felt deranged looking at him, considering my loathing, but mostly I relished it.

I couldn't believe we'd make it out of the restaurant without running into someone I knew. Ned had instructed me to prepare my Anchorage friends on the specifics of the narrative even if I didn't plan to see them; he'd sent me a list of talking points as an attachment to one of his blank emails, including a timeline: when my father became terminally ill, when we were notified of the diagnosis, when we left Anchorage to help my mother take care of him.

The timeline projected forward, even stipulating when my father would enter hospice. These would all occur, of course, in the months before the election, explaining our absences from Alaska.

So I'd emailed my friends and bcc'd Ned as he instructed, putting the talking points into a "personalized letter." Partly because of this, the prospect of actual in-person encounters dismayed me. As we were rising to go—Ned had, to my relief, spent half the meal talking into his phone's headset—we were intercepted by a group of people from city government, civil servant types who were mainly Ned's contacts but whom I'd spoken to a few times at parties. Their faces betrayed a certain hesitation at my presence, which made me wonder who Ned was sleeping with these days, whether these people knew the marriage was a sham. I wondered how it was possible that everyone didn't know, since Lena and I had been away two full years. Yet they acted

as though nothing was out of the ordinary and I reminded myself that
Ned took care of business, Ned kept his ducks in a row. For the past
few months we'd been staying with my terminally ill father . . . the
narrative, unbeknownst to me, has been in place for some time.

I made my excuses and led Lena away, Ned grabbing his jacket and
glad-handing behind us.

WHILE LENA AND I sleep in the house that used to be ours, Ned's
supposedly staying at a B&B tucked away in the foothills of east
Anchorage. He thought we'd be noticed coming and going from a
hotel, whereas he can move around discreetly. I'm not sure why, since
he's the public figure with the striking face and still lives full-time in
the city. On the other hand, so far no one *has* found out that we're
sleeping separately, so maybe he's correct in his calculations.

He has a "house," these days, not a house, much as he has a "family."
His car, driven by the chauffeur, had dropped us off and pulled away
quietly in the dark: entering the building I felt stealthy, though it's
hard to feel stealthy in puffer coats and mukluks.

Lena and I have been sharing the master bedroom, which feels
like a hotel room—as though no one familiar has slept there before,
certainly not me. Along with the rest of the place, its redecoration was
drastic. There's the skin of a polar bear on the wall—Ned must have
bought it from a native, I thought, or possibly on the black market—a
bold choice, given the politics. Maybe it signals his radicalism; in the
bedroom, maybe he reveals his radical anti-government core. But it
doesn't quite ring true, since the king bed's piled high with satiny
showroom cushions that only his interior decorator could have chosen.
They do feature masculine colors.

Lena fell right to sleep despite the bearskin, curled up with Lucky
Duck, and I went back to the living room, where I flicked on the gas
fire in the fireplace. I took a bottle of wine out of Ned's new wine

refrigerator, poured myself a glass, and sat on the sofa with a blanket, feet tucked under me, to call Main Linda.

She said the mood among the motel guests has changed, it's gone from a support group to the scene of a dispute. Navid and Kay were a couple, and now they're estranged. Navid says Kay kept her understanding of the voice from him—"intentionally, privately kept her knowledge to herself," as he apparently put it, like a "hoarder of information." Kay's hurt by this and says she never hid anything.

Meanwhile Burke and Gabe argue that Kay's assertion that the voice is language, the language of sentience, is unimportant. *Of course it's language, that's a truism,* Burke wrote in an email to me. *Words. Yeah. We know. The question is where that language is coming from.*

"Do you realize how *Regina* heard?" said Main Linda in her gruff voice. "The whole time I thought she was talking about a kid, when she talked about Terence, I honestly thought it was a retarded kid, sorry, developmentally disabled. Turns out that Terence was one of those little, yappy dogs. Probably wore ribbons. And miniature vests. She heard the voice of God from a Pomeranian! Or maybe a shih tzu. She showed us a picture on her phone. She used to carry him around in a Fendi handbag."

I couldn't help it, I laughed. I thought of a curly dog trotting around at Regina's heels, speaking the way the voice had spoken to me.

"It died," added Main Linda.

A linguistics scholar had been called in, she said, an expert who'd been talking to Kay. He seemed, said Main Linda, to be somewhat outside the mainstream of linguistic studies, though still (she'd looked it up) fairly well published in peer-reviewed journals. He had theories about grammar genes, about animal communication systems.

"The FOXP2 gene," said Linda. "This English family, I guess, has this speech defect down through the generations? And it ends up they have a defective copy of one gene. Or maybe it's a protein, but anyway, I guess the idea is language is maybe genetic. I only half-listened. Don reached out to this linguistics guy because Kay, I guess, does a speaking-in-tongues thing. Like, she can spew out a bunch of languages she isn't supposed to know. Stuff she supposedly heard from Vasquez. Plus she can do insanely complicated chemistry diagrams. Idiot savant shit. All Greek to me. Hey. Can we talk about normal crap?"

"We have consultants who pick out our clothes for us," I told her lightly. "And there's a family photo shoot for some glossy local rag, basically a real-estate brochure. Tomorrow. Ned's using someone else's *dog.* Can you believe it? A dog-for-hire!"

"That's low," said Main Linda. "A trophy dog? Is that even legal?"

"A golden retriever."

"Hope God doesn't talk through it."

"Do you believe Don knows more than he says?" I asked, pouring my second glass of wine.

I'd gotten restless sitting and was cruising through the rooms, taking a closer tour of Ned's model home. There was a picture of him fishing, the standard fishing photo with a giant salmon dangling from one hand. *Kenai Peninsula,* read the caption. Ned never fished. He hated the smell of fish and never ate it. A guide must have taken him and he must have learned some lingo to be able to shoot the shit with other fishers and hunters. Everyone fished in Alaska, practically, in season salmon falls from the skies here like rain and everyone has a smoker in their backyard, but Ned hadn't allowed fish in our kitchen.

"Don wants to keep things friendly, that seems to be his role, you know?" said Main Linda. "Moderator."

"I don't see how any of this can be proved or not proved," I said. "It was a phenomenon. But it's not as though any of us were given instructions. It's not like we have a task to do. Is it?"

I stopped in the hallway. Beyond the standard fishing photo, the standard hunting photo (deer on truck), the photo of Ned in crampons hiking up a glacier (looking down from the heights, smiling), there were numerous family photos. Some of them looked like upscale versions of mall shots while some were "candid" action shots: Ned, me, and Lena. All of us together, in different variations. Lena was a baby on a rug, Lena was a toddler in Ned's arms, all three of us stood beside a Christmas tree; there we were cross-country skiing, with Lena standing on a pair of junior skis, poles held in snowflake-mittened hands.

Except that none of the scenes, with the exception of Lena sitting on the rug all by herself, were real.

Ned had never done any of those things with us.

"Oh my God," I said.

I set my wineglass down on a table and flicked on the overhead light, leaned in to look closely. The pictures looked authentic. They were carefully framed and artfully staggered on the wall. Some seemed recent; they featured Lena's face pretty much the way she looked now. Ned must have taken the photos from my phone and used those images.

While I was sleeping a drugged sleep, when he was taking Lena.

Or he had open access to my phone.

"There's a whole wall of family pictures," I said. "They never happened at all. Family vacations, skiing—there's us on matching snowmobiles and us fishing. There's Ned with a dead buck and a truck and rifle. Redneck wholesome. They've been messed with to put us together when we never were. I don't *believe* it."

"Brazen," said Main Linda. "That guy's got some big ones on him, you gotta admit."

After we hung up I took pictures of the pictures, sat on the couch and scrolled through looking at them, comparing the faces in them to the faces already on my phone's camera roll: Lena with her snowman, Lena on the beach, Lena with Faneesha the UPS driver. I texted a couple of matches to Will, nearing the bottom of the wine bottle, and then called him.

He communicated his reserve with few words. He wasn't happy

that we'd gone up to Alaska, wasn't happy with anything concerning contact between Ned and us. Ned is probably sociopathic, he has suggested. *He feels no empathy.*

And I have to admit, when I find a list on some website of the behavioral characteristics of a sociopath, there's only one box I wouldn't check for my husband.

- ✓ Superficial charm and good intelligence
- ✓ Absence of delusions
- ✓ Absence of nervousness or neurotic manifestations
- ✓ Unreliability, untruthfulness, and insincerity
- ✓ Lack of remorse and shame
- ✓ Inadequately motivated antisocial behavior
- ✓ Pathologic egocentricity and incapacity for love
- ✓ General poverty in major affective reactions
- ✓ Unresponsiveness in general interpersonal relations
- ✓ Sex life impersonal and poorly integrated
- ~~Failure to follow any life plan~~

We have no control over his actions, Will reminds me, no one does, possibly not even him. Much of a sociopath's game is aimed at controlling people and outcomes, Will says. All you can do about a sociopath is steer clear of him. Ned's a time bomb, Will has insisted since the abduction, and we don't know that it's finished exploding.

Still, neither of us was able to come up with another course of action for me—not one that wouldn't risk Lena being taken again or hinge on police cooperation.

So here I am.

Now almost every piece of information I give Will about Ned seems to escalate his anxiety, so I find myself trying to avoid mentions—from thousands of miles away there's no use alarming him. He's done too much to help already: I'm confused about why he has time for all this for us, for me. I wonder what I've ever done for him other than need his help.

There's an imbalance of generosity.

Panpsychism is one of the oldest philosophical theories, the view that mind or soul (Greek: ψυχή) is a universal feature of all things, and the primordial feature from which all others are derived. —*Wikipedia 2016*

ON THE WAY to our potluck dinner with the church group Lena sat bolt upright in the back of Ned's Town Car holding Lucky Duck. She doesn't relax around her father since the kidnapping—her rigid stance stops just short of afraid, bespeaks reserve and attentiveness.

In what I felt was an egregious lapse in taste on the part of the consultants, we were made to wear matching dresses. Sitting there in the Town Car in my dress that was the same as a six-year-old's, I felt beyond foolish but hadn't bothered to protest. Also it was too cold for dresses by far; there was slushy snow on the ground; dresses don't look too good with puffer coats atop them.

But of course Ned couldn't have cared less about my discomfort or opinion. And Lena was pleased, saying the twin dresses reminded her of dolls you can order from a catalog in "look-alike" form, with features custom-selected to mimic your own hair and eyes and skin. It was one of those dolls that Ned had offered her during the kidnapped period.

"You didn't bring the lamb I gave you?" he asked from the passenger seat, texting rapidly, not bothering to turn.

"Lamb got sick," said Lena gravely, a doctor delivering the bad news. "She had to go in koranteen."

"Quarantine," I said.

"Quarantine," said Lena. "She got a cancer in her tail."

"Sounds serious," said Ned.

"Uh-huh. She's almost dead," said Lena.

Ned did turn and look at her. I was surprised too.

"I see," he said.

It piqued his interest for a second, but then he went back to pushing buttons. He was holding the phone at a different angle now, and I could see he wasn't texting about business or the campaign; no, he was playing Angry Birds.

Once we pulled up at the church, though—it was a potluck in the basement—he snapped into his public mode, his face suddenly animated. The light of Ned's personality has an ON/OFF button, which when he's alone with us now is typically set on OFF. It's fine with me, in fact I prefer it since he's nearly a robot when the switch is off, far easier to tolerate shut down. The ON switch makes me anxious with its vibrant, fizzing current.

When he's switched off I can almost ignore him.

"Hey Mom. Lamb's *not* dying," she whispered to me, as Ned was getting out of the front seat. "Lamb's *fine*."

My instructions for this more fluid assignment were to avoid all topics of conversation except the shortlist Ned had specifically allowed: food, weather, his qualities as a good husband, and, if additional content was absolutely needed, I could reminisce about the times when Lena "did cute things. IE u can take out phone, show Haloween bunny fotos" [sic].

Only Lena made any waves, as it turned out, and even those were small ones.

"Do you like my dress?" she asked, as she and I stood awkwardly near a food line, trying to be nice to some middle-aged ladies in the congregation after Ned pronounced a blessing that was also a stump speech.

"Why yes! I do!" said the woman.

"My daddy made me wear it."

"I see!"

"My mommy doesn't like matching dresses," she said.

"Oh?"

"*I* do. They have them in a catalog. You can order your own doll to look like you and even order the same dress. Like not in doll size but for a real person. My mom said matching outfits might be OK for dolls but not for real people."

The women eyeballed each other, smiles faltering.

"Oh, now, I like the dress fine," I hurried. "I just think it looks better on *you*, honey."

I set a hand on her shoulder as I turned to the ladies. *The penalty for poor performance will be,* Ned had written in an email, and left the sentence unfinished.

"She's very fond of those dolls," I made myself say, trying to pass. "She studies the catalogs as though they're the greatest story ever told."

"My daughter had one of those dolls, too," said the first lady. "I still have it in her bedroom! In a little bitty chair."

"Girls just *love* them," agreed a second.

"I don't know," said a third, shaking her head. "I think that company's *liberal*. Don't they sell Jew dolls too?"

Lena gazed at her.

"You must be *starving*, sweetie. Let's go and scoop you up a plate of food," I said, as smoothly as I could.

"What's Jewdolls?" said Lena as I steered her away.

"Honey, these people aren't your daddy's *friends*," I said in an undertone as I plunked potato salad she'd never eat onto a paper plate. Technically it was true, after all. "They're more like people he needs to impress. And it's our job to help him because we're his family. It's not for long. For now we have to just smile, OK?"

"I think that lady might be mean," said Lena.

"We can talk about all of it later," I said. "We'll talk it through. For now, though, would you do me a favor? Just try to smile and be friendly?"

"If you're nice to mean people, Faneesha says you're mean too."

All in all I was surprised at how down-homey the church event was, with its paper tablecloths and deviled eggs whose yoke-ridges had gone crusty. There must have been someone in the congregation to whom Ned owed a personal favor. We got away finally with Lena sulking, face screwed up into a mask of resentment, but no open conflict.

Her father talked about sports to his driver as we headed over to the magazine shoot, where, in high-tech outdoor gear, he would run and throw a Frisbee across a field of snow to be caught by the dog he had rented.

LENA LOVES VIDEO chats and I'd promised her she could do one with our Maine friends, so we opened my laptop in Ned's living room and hooked up to my cell phone's hotspot. She talked first to Kay and then the Lindas and Don.

When she got tired of talking and settled down with a TV show I carried the open laptop into the bedroom, panning around at the dead polar bear and the pictures of snow-covered mountains.

"Why don't you take that outside?" said Don.

"It's freezing," I said. "Are you kidding?"

"You don't have privacy in the house. Which you'd do well to keep in mind—I hear you had a sensitive conversation with Linda recently. And possibly Will?"

I'd registered when we first walked in that the house was probably set up for surveillance, I had no reason to think otherwise, but then I'd conveniently forgotten. I still have the habit from my old life of not feeling watched, somehow, a habit that's been hard to cast off even after I was roofed and had my child stolen—I can be paranoid one minute and the next relapse into my lifelong, previous routine of feeling unwatched.

But my conversation with Linda hadn't been too revealing, I told myself: the part about the voice would have been of no interest to Ned, at least, though he or his proxy would have heard me exclaiming over the faked pictures.

"OK," I said.

I stepped onto the small back patio, gloves on, a blanket over my shoulders. It was getting dark, the sky indigo already and not overcast at all. A few stars were out. If I turned to my left I could see through a large picture window into the living room, where Lena sat on the couch watching her TV show, her face small and expressionless in profile. The scenes of the television screen flashed their varying colors over the room.

I grabbed the laptop and strolled away from the building, into the expanse of dried grass.

"So it turns out your husband's bankrolled by a major PAC," Don said. "This isn't going to be a local or state career, if he succeeds. It'll be the governor's race next or a Senate seat. He's going national."

"I'm not surprised at all," I said. "That's what he has to want. He's always been ambitious."

"I have a friend with D.C. connections. He said big plans may be in the works for your man Ned."

"I'm not surprised at all," I repeated.

The angle of the picture changed, with Don's head sliding beneath the bottom frame and jumping back into view. Behind him I could see Will.

"So are you thinking that after the election he'll smile and let you walk away into the sunset?" said Will. "Is that what you're hoping?"

"I mean, there's a contract. Don, your lawyer read it."

"The contract lays out the terms of the divorce, custody and so forth," said Don. "But it's only a piece of paper. It's not a guarantee of a happy ending."

"What do you mean?"

"We're not feeling so great about your safety."

It was hard to see their faces, both of their features in shadow. The tops of their heads were blurred in front of a sconce that haloed white light.

"There are plenty of ways to make a contract irrelevant," went on Don. "Say after the election you had an accident. Then Ned could be a grieving widower and loving father rolled into one. He'd have Lena as a permanent prop. It would look *very* nice on him, in terms of electability."

"But I'm *not* going to die after the election. That's . . ."

"It's really easy to die."

"Don. I was *married* to this guy."

"Look," said Will urgently. "You don't think, once he's elected, that he'll want to be a divorced guy, do you? That title won't be his first choice."

"Well—"

"And he likes to have his first choice. He *really* likes it. Right? We know that about him."

"But you're—but he's not physically violent. He never even hit—"

"He drugged you. And Lena. No reason to assume he's not capable. He wouldn't have to do it personally."

"You don't have any—I mean, there's no proof of any of this, though, right?"

"Clearly we don't have Ned bugged," said Don. "He has *you* bugged. All we have for evidence is our familiarity with him. His record."

"Life's not a TV procedural," said Will. He sounded stiff and almost condescending—unusual for him. "We don't live in a place with instant forensic identification of every killer. It's common for murders to go unsolved."

I didn't know them that well, I thought, I barely knew them. Don seemed more than ever to have entered my life under a guise, leaked into it through a minor opening I hadn't known was there. This slumping man with his womanly hips, I thought. I still didn't understand him. Was I even *supposed* to know him, was it even right that we were familiar, or was it part of some dimly occluded design that might hurt Lena or me? Indeed, had it already? And Will—there I felt soft-centered, the pull of attraction and fondness and gratitude, but he was new, and I hadn't shown good judgment in the past.

Pointedly *I* should be the last person to trust someone because I wanted to sleep with him.

But maybe they weren't the sketchy ones after all—I was the one who'd married a man devoid of emotion. I might be the one who couldn't be trusted. I'd caved to Ned, and in my weakness I'd brought them in too—into something that shouldn't involve them at all.

"You need to get away from him," said Don.

After the blobby icon replaced their faces on the screen I walked back to my former patio and stood there shivering, imagining the dark shapes of bears in the woods behind the house. Many times in the past I'd spotted them there, humped figures barely distinct under the interwoven shadows of branches—except for once when a mother and cub lumbered into the backyard looking for garbage scraps. They must be hibernating now.

Around me on the patio were some plants that used to be mine, shriveled brown threads I couldn't identify anymore, though I remembered picking out their pots in a big box store. I remembered patting down the soil around the green seedlings. I should have taken them inside or given them away . . . they'd lived for years while I was in this house, growing, flowering, then suddenly been abandoned out here on the flagstones when I left. They would have died in the first frost.

I thought of all the green surrounding the house in summer, the green in the woods, long trailing banks of green, great oval storms of leaves, how despite that huge green outside I'd pored over and tended these small green outcroppings. But then I'd walked away from them.

What *could* I take care of?

I went inside the house, annoyed.

But despite my annoyance—*he's never been physically violent,* I repeated to myself several times, walking around the house in my sock feet—I found myself hesitating as I took a fresh bottle out of the brushed-stainless wine cellar, letting the heavy glass-and-stainless door close with its small suck.

I don't know that much about Ned's life before me, actually. I know he started working at age twelve, I know the story of that: he ran errands for petty criminals, then not so petty. At last he scammed his way into a prestigious university, but dropped out after two years, switching to a business school with a degree he finished online. All that was the tip of the iceberg, the part he pretty much had to tell me, but the rest of it was a blank.

He'd always been closemouthed. No matter how gently I asked, he wasn't interested in *rehashing ancient history.*

It occurred to me, looking at the bottle, that he'd never been a wine drinker. He'd only ever accepted a glass of wine when there was no liquor or beer available. And wine wasn't likely to be part of his image makeover; it was too bourgeois for the image he was cultivating, bearing rumors of Europe or at least California. This was Alaska, where Europeans were fags and Californians were too. He might as well drink espresso and drive a Volvo instead of his hulking Ford truck.

Maybe the wine had been selected for me.

I'd drunk one before, so far with no ill effects, but still.

I put the bottle back.

> Some cultural and religious traditions see mind as a property exclusive to humans, whereas others ascribe properties of mind to animals and deities. —*Wikipedia 2016*

OUR LAST COMMITMENT was today, a dinner with some of the donors and staff. We leave tomorrow and don't have to come back till spring.

I've been torn since the call with Will and Don. Their theory of Ned as a murderer has set me half-against them. It's irrational but I can't help it—I'm set off at a new distance. Their conviction seems to skew them to outlier status. On one hand there's Ned, for whom I feel fear and loathing, and on the other there are these men who've been kind enough to help me, given me time and care. But their murder thesis is an awkward weight on my shoulders I have to shrug off.

I float in isolation between Ned and them, not touching either of the shores.

In the morning I pulled my old belongings from storage, lugged them to the post office and sent them to my parents' house, Lena tagging along with her face in a picture book. In the afternoon I visited my closest friend here, the only one who didn't seem to think the reported kidnapping, or its poor resolution, was the result of my own weakness. Charley, who taught with me at the university and is soon to retire, has disliked Ned from the start, much as Solly did, and it relaxed me to be with someone I didn't have to convince of anything—Charley has a serene bearing and little surprises her. From the trees in her garden hang bamboo wind chimes and homemade birdfeeders.

We sat in her sprawling house full of natural light and drank tea, watching out the big bay window as Lena made snow angels in the backyard.

It was during the snow angels that Ned showed up: his driver had dropped us at Charley's, our whereabouts weren't secret, but I hadn't expected him to take an interest. He'd always dismissed Charley with her hand-knit sweaters, her chunky necklaces made of shell and rock; yet now he rang the doorbell and when she let him in he was with a beautiful girl, doe-eyed and long-limbed, draped in furs and wearing giant, shaggy boots that gave an impression of an adorable yeti.

She might have been twenty-two, she might have been nineteen. She would have been more usual in SoHo or Milan.

Trying to be polite, I think, she pointed at a sculpture on Charley's mantel and asked if it was "done by an Eskimo." When Charley said no, it was a Chinese Buddha, she went on to say *Oh* with a round, pretty mouth, frozen in wonder. The words were blank as paper: that lovely child was so slow to make connections that it almost hurt to listen to her talk. Maybe she was *sixteen*, not nineteen or twenty-two, I thought, and it was simple childishness.

Ned bringing her was of course, given his PR focus, his obsessive commitment to the slick campaign, startling. It seemed needlessly risky and certainly meant to be needling. He may have thought I was still capable of jealousy. But I felt only pity for her as she sat, nestled into his side on Charley's deep sofa, long legs drawn up.

Charley, who cared as little for what Ned thought as he cared for her, asked her outright how old the girl was at one point, but Ned intercepted the question and asked Charley how old she *thought* the girl was.

When Charley said "Too young for *you*," he smiled and trailed his fingers along the gazelle's spaghetti-thin upper arm. With her furs off she wore only a tight dress sparkling with gold flecks, and the arms were full of holes made to look like knife slashes.

They didn't stay long, only long enough to accept Charley's offer of coffee with disinterested shrugs and then leave before it was finished brewing. The two of them stood briefly at the big bay window, from which Ned—one arm strung over the young gazelle's shoulders— watched Lena run across the snow for a few seconds while his girlfriend looked down at her phone, texting with lightning speed. When it came to texting she wasn't slow at all.

"Place hasn't changed one little bit," he said to Charley as they were leaving, in a clearly insulting tone. He turned, smirked and pointed at me. "We'll pick you up at six. Cocktail dress in the master bed."

Charley looked at me for a long time after the door closed, shaking her head. Meanwhile Lena was still playing in the back by herself; she'd never noticed they were there.

8

BONES THAT FED OUT THEIR COLD

My brother's apartment is small. He makes decent money for a young guy working at a start-up, but this is Manhattan—where he was lucky to get five hundred square feet in a building with roof access.

So he sleeps on the couch and Lena and I take the bedroom. He wakes us up by coming in to open his closet; Solly's a sluggish awakener and every morning he stands there tousled and half-asleep, swaying faintly and staring at his row of shirts on their hangers. The shirt indecision paralyzes him.

I promised we wouldn't stay for long, this is a quick visit, but he waved away that promise when we arrived and said we could stay forever, if we wanted to. Lena nodded solemnly.

"For*ever*, Uncle Solly," she agreed.

Forever means two weeks. I feel safe in this prewar ziggurat with its thick walls and overheated air. I don't love the city at this time of year—the way white snow turns to gray slush, how the freeze of the sidewalk reaches right through your boot soles. But it's good to see Solly, and I need a break before we go back to Maine.

Whenever I call Will he brings up his worry about Ned, his fear that Ned's going to have me hurt or killed. It makes the conversations strained. I was so pleased by his quiet bearing when I first met him, his calmness that had an almost mystical quality. But now that quality is gone, its glassy surface has been broken and doesn't seem to be smoothing out again. He's still soft-spoken and kind, but there's wariness when he talks to me. I know he feels he should be here—whether he wants to or not, he believes he should be near enough to guard me, that it's somehow his responsibility, which is preposterous.

Conspiracy theories are a mostly male hysteria, it seems to me. That style of paranoia isn't my own—it has a self-importance I don't relate to. Even now, when I know for a fact I've been conspired against, it's hard for me to believe in conspiracies.

Ned acted against me not because of who I am but because of who he is—I'm just the one he happened to marry. And the kidnapping was only a conspiracy in that he hired some people and used others.

Without Will in front of me, though, the attraction is more abstract. Was it only a wishful idea? It was *my* idea, I know that, I asked him out and brought him in—but the newness of knowing him and Don makes them feel less like fixtures in my life and more like bystanders. Only the Lindas, with their earthiness, seem concrete and reliable.

Lena and I need relief from the closeness of the small apartment, so we do her lessons in a coffee shop. After the morning rush has subsided the place is colonized by mothers and their goggle-eyed toddlers, who stagger around banging plastic toys on the backs of chairs and gumming them; the women chatter to each other, brooding on nests of scarves and coats. Lena takes the roaming toddlers under her wing, holding their hands and showing them colorful objects. She's popular with the mothers for this.

Most days when Solly gets home from work the two of them go out to a nearby playground; she doesn't mind the creaking freeze of the swings, the burn of the icy slide. Sometimes I walk out of the lobby with them, wave goodbye as they cross eastward to the park and then veer west myself. I walk to the Hudson River, past a bagel shop, bodegas, some kind of pretentious cigar lounge, and an opaque window whose neon sign reads HYPNOSIS. QUIT SMOKING / LOSE WEIGHT / MANAGE GRIEF.

YESTERDAY IT WAS the Lindas first on Skype, then Kay. When Lena and Kay had finished singing together, a tuneless song about a mermaid, she ran off to build a LEGO castle and I slid into Solly's desk chair in her place.

I was dismayed at how Kay looked. She had the same hollow-eyed face she'd had when she first arrived at the motel—ghostly pale. She and Navid hadn't reconciled; after her meeting with the linguistics scholar Navid had spun off, his behavior erratic. He said he couldn't trust her again because she had concealed too much.

But we don't *know* how much we know, she said unsteadily, or we don't know how *little* other people know. None of us ever possess this knowledge. We can't know what others are thinking.

"It's like a kind of instinct we go on, right? After we get reassured we're not crazy. You know what Don told me?" she asked.

It was hard to hear her so I raised the volume on the laptop's speakers.

"He told me there are crowds of people who never get to that point, they never cross that barrier. People who hear and never stop thinking they're just insane, spend their whole lives on Thorazine or getting ECT. Living their lives all alone. And sad. We're just this small fraction of people who, basically, refused to believe in our insanity."

She hadn't meant to keep secrets, she just hadn't talked enough, she guessed. And now Navid was gone, flown back to Los Angeles. If all this was, he'd said, was some kind of off-brand encounter group, he might as well bite the bullet and do the real twelve steps. And when it came to AA, he had said, or NA or GA or CA, L.A. was the nation's capital.

"I'm sorry," I said, watching her cock her head to one side in the jittery connection. I had the fleeting illusion that she was preparing to keel over sideways in slow motion.

But she didn't say anything, just gazed at me, so I kept on talking.

"I don't think you were holding out on us, but I still want to know everything you know."

"There are so many words for it," she said.

I felt alarmed as I gazed at the fuzzy image of her face, the brown half-moons beneath her eyes. She always looks pretty, with the waifish delicacy of a ballet dancer, but there was a distraction to her expression.

She's not paying attention to her own welfare and no one else is, either. She has no one to take care of her yet I suspect she needs help. I want to call her mother; I wish I had her mother's telephone number.

It can't be my job, though, to look after Kay as well as Lena—not now, especially, when I've failed so dismally with my own daughter. I'm not equipped.

"It *is* language," she said. "The same kind that makes your body work without you telling it to. You know how the brain runs your kidneys, say, or tells an embryo how to grow in a pregnant woman? What's the difference between that kind of implicit, like, limbic OS for our biology—and for the biology of all animals—and just a miracle?"

"I don't know," I said.

"It's part of deep language that runs these operating systems for us. You see? It's not the language we *speak*. I mean our language comes from it, like all language, but our own specific language is like the surface of the ocean, the very top line of the water. Just the *line*. Deep language—I mean I happen to call it that, but there are other names—it's the rest of the ocean beneath, see, Anna? It's the rest of the water below, and it's everything the rest of the ocean holds, that makes that thin line of surface possible."

She was doing something with her hands behind her head—scooping her hair into a ponytail as wings of the hair fell forward around her face. She kept talking faster and faster and shook her head as she did this, making it hard for me to hear; the volume was already at maximum. I wondered if she was manic.

That has to be it.

"See Western medicine doesn't come close to understanding the body, that's part of what I learned in med school and my residency, for doctors, we have to act like we know things, 'project an air of competence,' is what they said to me"—here she used air quotes—"but let's be serious, it's a crapshoot, with anything in the least rare, whether you can get to a diagnosis that works and maybe jury-rig a cure for it. Medicine's more guesswork than the AMA wants patients to even *think* about, if they knew how much of a gray area there is they wouldn't believe a thing we said—"

"Mama," said Lena, behind me. "I can't *find* it."

"Shh, honey. Just for a minute. I'm trying to hear Kay."

"We'd never be able to tell our brains how to manage the body's systems, so much more sophisticated than our self-awareness," went on Kay, and now she was fiddling with an earring and in the process turning her face away from the computer's microphone. ". . . colonies of microbes—billions! Not to save our lives! What I got from Infant Vasquez, what I didn't have time to tell Navid, is *that* system . . . one aspect of deep language . . . the other—"

"*Mama*," repeated Lena, apparently deciding Kay's desperate monologue was background noise. "I can't find the *bottom LEGO piece*, you know the one you make into the floor? I can't find that big flat green piece to even *build* them on, *Mom*. I swear, I looked *everywhere*!"

"In a minute, honey, just a minute, OK?" I said, flapping a hand at her impatiently, but I'd already missed what Kay was saying.

Then Solly and his new girlfriend burst in the door stamping snow off their feet, his girlfriend whom I'd never met before was smiling at me expectantly, so I made my excuses to Kay and got up from the computer.

> Language extinction has occurred quite slowly throughout human history, but is now happening at a breakneck pace due to globalization and neocolonialism—so rapidly that, by 2100, 50 to 90 percent of languages spoken in today's world are expected to be extinct. —*Wikipedia 2016*

LUISA WAS SITTING with Solly and me in his kitchen/dining room/living room (Lena had gone to bed) when we got the call from my mother.

Solly put her on speakerphone.

Our father had been losing weight and sweating at night, she said—so much that he soaked the sheets. They'd gone in to see the family doctor and the doctor had sent them to a specialist, where he'd been biopsied.

"Why didn't she tell us this before?" asked Solly, after punching the mute button. "A biopsy?"

"I didn't want to bother you, in case it wasn't anything," she said.

I guess the mute button doesn't work.

"Sorry," muttered Solly, but he was already distracted by the import of that.

"I'm afraid it did come back positive," she said. "A fairly common cancer of the blood. 'Hematological malignancy,' they said. We don't have the staging on it yet, but we should know soon and I don't want you to get too worried just yet. OK? It's not necessarily a dire prognosis, depending on the staging, of course, whether it's metastasized—it doesn't have too low a five-year survival rate. More than half of all patients pull through. Maybe even three-quarters, we'll see. So your father's chances aren't so bad."

Luisa squeezed Solly's hand, her dark eyes glittering. Solly and I looked at each other steadily.

"Do they have a treatment plan yet?" asked Solly.

"There *will* probably be chemo," said my mother. "Possibly radiation, possibly surgery. I'll share all of that with you as soon as I know more, dear."

"Blood cancer," I said, after a silence. I'd begun to feel uneasy—beyond even the facts of the case I felt a creeping apprehension. "That's where . . . isn't that . . ."

"It's where the white blood cells divide faster than normal cells, or live longer than they're supposed to," said my mother. "He has at least a couple of primary tumors, which they tell me is a common presentation. With this kind of a lymphoma."

AFTER WE HUNG UP I told Solly what Ned had said to me before: lymphoma. I described it to him before he left for Luisa's place for the night, right before I took out my laptop and began typing this.

But he shrugged it off as though the detail either wasn't accurate or wasn't relevant. Our father has a disease, our father has a potentially terminal illness of the kind we all fear for the insidious poison of its medicine, the emaciation of bodies, shedding of hair, desiccating of bones and aging of skin. That was all Solly had room for, and I can't blame him.

And our father will have to endure all that without ever understanding his illness. He'll be like a child throughout the suffering, confused and blinking as my mother herds him gently on.

I think of those scenes to come and I also think of my father when we were young and he was middle-aged instead of old—how he read us stories using different voices, some deep, some squeaky, here a quaking mouse, here a growling lion. I think of how he carried us on his shoulders—"so you can pretend to be giants."

He had so much dignity back then, but he was willing to cast it off to entertain his children. He tickled us until we grew out of being tickled, he made corny jokes until we grew out of those too.

Now I feel an ache of remorse when I think how we stopped laughing at his jokes. I would laugh so hard, if I could have a do-over. I can see that to Solly we're only losing my father now, where to me we lost him some time ago—or maybe it's fairer to say that Solly seems to be able to lose him twice, while for me once was all I could do.

Still Ned's casual assertion a few weeks ago, his matter-of-fact statement that my father would get sick with lymphoma—which at that time I assumed was just a fictional element of the so-called narrative—vibrates so hard I almost get a headache. I've actually been taking painkillers when the thought of it starts to make my temples send out their thin flashes of pain.

But Ned's foreknowledge vies with the diagnosis for my attention and I can't let it go. It may be coincidence—or maybe it's information gleaned from surveillance. Could he be surveilling them as well as me, tracking my father's diagnosis? Observed by Ned or his consultants, did my mother find out weeks ago and only tell us now? And what use would it be for Ned to spy on my parents anymore, when he already has my cooperation, when I've already done what he wanted me to do?

I'm going to ask my mother tomorrow when she heard the diagnosis. I'll reassure her that it's not a problem if she decided to delay telling us—we understand completely. But I need to know when she heard.

. . . . .

YESTERDAY, she said.

> And the whole earth was of one language, and of one speech
> . . . And the Lord said, Behold: The people is one, and they
> have all one language . . . and now nothing will be restrained
> from them . . . Let us go down, and there confound their
> language, that they may not understand one another's speech.
> —*Genesis 11:1–7*

I HAVE IT—I have it here on my desktop, a written record.

It's in the "templates," as he and his staff call them: the schedule for the narrative, with our travel dates; the list of his positions on issues, which I'm supposed to know even though I won't parrot them, and a partial list of planned public appearances, both with Lena and me and without us; the breakdown of campaign employees by job description, plus key volunteers. All this is supposed to be memorized before our next stint in Alaska.

It's so repellent that I hadn't looked at it after a cursory glance, but here it is. The templates are connected to my laptop's calendar, which I don't use for anything else, with events assigned to months or weeks or days. The events pop up, color-coded, and I can't take them off again—I tried once and it gave me a message about contacting the administrator.

Apparently I don't have permission.

The developments connected to my father, and therefore my extended absences from Anchorage and Ned's campaign, are lime-green bars extending across several different blocks of days on the calendar.

They're labeled like this, on various dates:

LYMPHOMA STAGE 3. DIAGNOSIS, PROCESSING

TREATMENT MODULE 1: SURGERY, CHEMOTHERAPY

TREATMENT MODULE 2: RADIATION

METASTASIS: BONE MARROW, CEREBROSPINAL FLUID

And there's one I didn't notice before, a little further on.

PALLIATIVE CARE/MEMORIAL SERVICE

"Lymphoma Stage 3" is assigned to this month, the month we're in right now: February.

I called Ned, I left a voicemail for him asking how he knew, but I strongly doubt he'll tell me anything at all.

He typically has his staff email me when information needs to be exchanged; he and I don't communicate.

"STAGE 3," said my mother, on the phone again.

I'M PASTING IN an email I got from Kay, strange and dense. I think she may be bipolar.

You said you wanted to hear everything I know. So OK. So I have trouble explaining how I know it & what it is—writing isn't my thing. I mean I was more the organic chem type!!! I used to get visions of like resonance structures & chair conformations & stuff, when I was holdig Infant V. But so. You know how I told you we r the only ones it leaves, what I meant was, it doesn't leave the whales or the crocodiles, it doesn't leave the plants &

the trees, & that's not because, like, theyre dumb. Theyre not. Deep language is in all living things but all the others, it stays with. Only not humans. Its because the other things, apes, cats, even the grasses in a field, don't live just for themselves. They live for the group. They live for all, this whole of being. We used to be like that to, once a long time ago, once in our evolution, I don't know when but once. But slowly it chaged & now we live for ourselves. So the deep language does'nt stay with us when we get our own, our surface language, you coud call it. We split off from it then & are forever alone. God leaves us Anna.

God leaves us.

I can't tell how much is rumination or fabrication, whether some is intuition, how much she was given to know. In short I'm not sure if she has much authority.

But I'm keeping her message. I read it over in quiet times.

MORE GUESTS ARE leaving the motel, Big Linda reports, all vowing to keep in touch—I've started to check in on the Listserv, where so far Navid's the only one absent. Regina and Reiner have gone back to their professions in the city, and Gabe has decamped too. He cited the needs of a lonely Bedlington terrier, pining away under the care of a neighbor back at the condo he shares with Burke, who's soon to follow him home.

And what did they accomplish with the meetings? I get Navid's impatience, though I wish he'd been nicer to Kay. Unlike me, the rest of the guests knew about each other before they came—they had an earlier version of the Listserv. They'd already exchanged messages containing much of what they'd say later, alongside the table of watery coffee and stale cookies. So I was the only new element. And they can't have got much from me.

I never illuminated anything.

I account, on my fingers, for all the elements of these events I keep failing to understand. I wish I had an abacus—confusion like this calls for a deliberate, manual counting, a ritual of organization. Digits or beads, bones or a rosary. Even assuming there does exist an ambient language that underlies life, what some people call God, others possibly photosynthesis or humpback song or the opinions of a dog, I have the same questions that I always did. I want to know why I heard it, and why through Lena; why it fell silent when she slept; why it departed when she said her first word. I want to know not only its rules but its purpose, but all of that remains opaque to me.

There are the practical questions, too: How did I know to go to the motel? How was Ned able to find me? How did John know to contact him, when I took my car in to his shop?

And how did Ned know my father's diagnosis?

On the face of it my questions about Ned are in a different category. And yet there's the lymphoma diagnosis. This is new, this introduces a fresh mystery, and it counts just as fluidly on my fingers as the questions that came before.

It was recorded digitally, "Lymphoma Stage 3," a number of weeks, not days but weeks, before the doctors even biopsied my father. It was set in stone then, it has a path, a history that can be verified—the fact that he had that information, or at least that he acted as though he had it.

Lymphoma Stage 3.

I WAS ALONE in the subway today, coming back from getting my hair cut, during which appointment Lena had stayed at home with Solly and Luisa. I was on a crowded platform at Columbus Circle with my bag over my shoulder and a book in my other hand—I must have been standing distractedly at the front hem of the crowd, my paperback curled back on itself in my hand as I read.

Then there were the lights and roar of the train. I felt a push behind

me like a head butting against the small of my back and suddenly I
was teetering, one of my legs over the edge, before someone grabbed
my arm and my book flew out of my hand and I was jerked back, my
neck strained and one shoulder wrenched.

With a rush the train was screeching to a stop, people surging past
me as the doors opened, jostling me and turning me around. I felt a
weird heat prickle where my scalp meets my face, was breathless and
seeing spots of light. Somehow I found my way to a bench, newly
vacated and still ass-warm.

I never knew who pushed me or if it had been an accident, or who
caught my arm and saved me either—maybe the push was just the
movement of the crowd, that's the likeliest explanation. Right? But as
the train pulled away I noticed a child staring at me through a train
door, a dark-hooded child with a white face, and the child's head turned
as the train moved, the child was staring at me fixedly . . . it had been a
forceful push, so forceful it seemed it must have been purposeful.

Or so I felt as I sat there.

As soon as I got over the shock a wave of gratitude washed over me, a
pure beam of gratitude struck out toward my unknown rescuer—how
impossible it always is, I thought intently, to remember how lucky we
are each second we remain alive.

When the train was long gone and the platform bare, I got up shakily and walked back to the edge. On the tracks was my book, ripped up
and streaked with gray, its pages spread over the black. I gazed down
at it for a while and then sat down again to wait for the next train. I
wanted to call someone, maybe Will, maybe Solly, but of course there
was no signal in the tunnel. And what had happened, anyway?

When the next train finally came rushing in I found I was trembling. I had to press my back against the cool, grimy tile of the wall.
Presently I left and hailed a taxi.

Since then my day has been cast in a fractured light. I go back and
forth between telling myself it was pure accident and wondering if
Don and Will's fears deserve more serious consideration.

· · · · ·

I SENT AN EMAIL to Navid. Can I find out online, I asked him, who's financing Ned's campaign? I wouldn't mind knowing who Ned's backers are, what interests they represent and how deeply embedded their money is in institutions. Maybe one of them has connections to hospital records, who knows, some shadowy X-rays that were interpreted before the biopsy without my parents' knowledge— some link that would provide an explanation for that premature diagnosis.

Ned left his family of origin when he was in his teens, left and never looked back. His father had disappeared when he was an infant, his mother was strung out or drunk all the time, and there were no others. He lived outside the house anyway, from when he was twelve or thirteen, only returning to sleep. This was what I had gleaned, anyway, from the couple of times he'd talked about it to me.

But somewhere, now, he has another family. I want to know who his new family is.

WALKING BY MYSELF to get a carton of milk, I suddenly spun on my heel and entered the business with the HYPNOSIS sign. I hadn't planned it.

There was no receptionist, only a counter with a fiber-optic lamp sitting on it, an abstract medley of colored lights pulsing. I wondered how a hypnosis business made the street-level storefront rent in this neighborhood; I rang a push-button bell on the counter and heard an electronic chime. After a minute a woman came in from the back, a woman with a soft, homely face and wavy hair. She was about to close up for the evening, she said, could she help me?

There was a voice, an auditory hallucination I used to have, when my child was a baby, I told her. I wanted to remember it now—wanted to hear it again to see if I could figure out what it had said. Could that kind of memory retrieval occur through hypnosis?

She asked me if the voice had issued instructions, had told me to do anything I didn't want to do.

I said no. No instructions.

She asked me a couple more questions I guessed were supposed to screen for mental illness, then hemmed and hawed briefly. She said there were no guarantees, that it was up to me, in a sense, what was accessed, but sure, she was willing to give it a shot. She could implant a suggestion that this "voice" return, she said; she could invite my mind to generate the "voice" again.

She had me sign a waiver and I made an appointment.

NAVID WROTE BACK saying he'd research Ned's funding. He was good at following money trails, he said. Somehow he doesn't seem to blame me as he blames Kay and Don; with me he doesn't seem to have a bone to pick. Or maybe, because of what happened to Lena, he's just sorry for me.

USING VACATION TIME, Solly's going to visit my parents and taking Luisa with him. He wants to be there to help out, as he puts it, but has urged Lena and me to stay here in the apartment without him. All four of us descending on my parents would be a burden and not what the doctor ordered.

> It is possible that all languages spoken today are related through direct or indirect descent from a single ancestral tongue.
> —*Wikipedia 2016*

THE PRACTICE OF HYPNOTISM seems to hover in the alt-medicine gray area, near chiropractors and acupuncturists. It's viewed as sporadically

effective in treating certain bad habits and disorders, but tarnished by
its history of showmanship.

The hypnotherapist had me lie down on a huge, brown recliner with
wide arms—my arms had to be stretched out, hands laid flat, feet
raised. She dimmed the lights, put on music, and asked me if the
room's temperature was comfortable.

And I had to admit the temperature *was* comfortable. The air felt
like a soft extension of my skin, without too much moisture or too
much aridity. I could stay here, I thought.

A person could remain.

"Remember, I can't make you do anything you don't want to do,"
she said. "This is a completely safe space."

She had me close my eyes and listen to her voice describing a wooden
rowboat over a deep blue lake. Out we went into the lake, rowing,
rowing. Maybe I dove off the side of the boat or sank into the water,
deeper, deeper, deeper; or maybe I was just looking down, looking into
the water from the dry bench of the boat. I recall the color blue, the
clarity of the lake water.

During this tranquil immersion a jellyfish floated up from the
depths. I don't know whether it was associated with the therapist's
words or only with my thoughts, but I gazed at it—a pink-white
bulb with tendrils rippling. Although I wasn't asleep or dreaming
I knew in the way of dreams, the passing of information that happens there where one thing is simultaneously another, that the jelly,
having no place in fresh water, was an emissary from the ocean Kay
had spoken of.

There was something to know here, something to discover. So when
I left I made another appointment.

AROUND LUNCHTIME YESTERDAY we got a call from downstairs: Will
was in the lobby.

We went down in the elevator to meet him and there he stood, talking to the doorman.

Lena ran to him and hugged him and then turned her attention to the doorman, her friend. Will stepped away from them and turned to me, a woolen cap in his hands, the shoulders of his coat sparkling with melting snowflakes, and I was so happy to feel my stomach flip, to know how much I still liked him. More, even. His eyes, skin, mouth.

"I brought your car," he said.

I'd been selfish. I'd given him nothing, and I'd added insult to injury by doubting him. Yet here he was.

He didn't ask to stay with us, in fact he had a friend's place lined up, but then he did stay.

It was good but curious, after so long a time—like walking through a forgotten wood. Like wandering beneath old trees, whose faint smell reminds you of a person you may once have been.

NOT ONLY DOES Will know *now* about the motel's Hearing Voices Movement—as I've come to call it privately—but he's known about it all along.

He knows the backstory of the motel guests; he's familiar with our group pathology. And he *has* known about it all, he says, since a couple of years after he got to know Don, when he first moved to Maine. Don has always lived there, as far as Will knows, like his father before him. He's a feature of the landscape and has never seemed to do anything but what he does now.

"But that's the thing. What *does* he do?" I asked.

Will shrugged.

"He's a host."

We were in bed. I was so glad to be there, though at first it took me a while to relax about Lena, who was fast asleep in the bedroom and still too near for my sense of propriety.

"So confused people who hear voices have been coming there for years," I said. "All of us with that same complaint."

"You don't all seem the same to me," he said.

The only unity I'd found in the guests was economic: none of them were poor. There were men and women, young and old, white, Asian and Iranian and Dutch Americans, straight and gay. We had no profession or other clear trait in common save money—everyone was at least middle-class, no one was on food stamps. I'm a former academic, Kay's a med student, Navid a producer; Burke is a botanist and between them the Lindas have three master's and a PhD.

"That's true," said Will. "Because the poor don't weigh in on the channels Don uses to bring his guests together. He can't find them because he can't separate them in the social-service world from the population with schizoid conditions. They may be institutionalized or on the streets or just toiling, but they don't tend to be online so much. He doesn't have a way to get to them."

But Don never found me online, or if he did I didn't know of it. I wondered if Will knew that too.

"Why does he *want* to bring them in?" I asked.

Maybe it was just group therapy, as Navid had alleged, I was thinking.

"He says it's just his role," said Will.

After breakfast we sat on Solly's cheap, caving-in couch, which pushed us together comfortably in the middle, as Lena played with a magic coloring book Will had brought for her. Depending on how you flip through the book, its pages are blank or black-and-white or startling full color. Lena had wanted to do the trick in our coffee shop, but only a one-year-old had been present, on whom the trick was wasted. Babies think magic is normal, she said.

She flipped through the book as Will and I sat against each other, my laptop on my knees, his arm around my shoulders. Then I brought up the schedule and stared at it. Where before it had annoyed me, now the bristling field of white seemed ominous. Onscreen it didn't seem inert, as any other file would, but almost radioactive: it bore the weight of grim prediction.

By Ned's reckoning, it appears—or the reckoning of his aide or campaign runner or secretary, whoever created this schedule—my father will begin hospice in June and die before Independence Day.

NAVID CALLED ME on the phone Will just bought me, his face popping up on the screen. I'd never bothered to use my cell that way before. He was wearing a headset and seemed to be sitting in a car: I saw the curves of a headrest behind him.

"Are you alone?"

I was trying to figure out how to hold the phone so that he didn't see the inside of my nose or ear. "Lena and Will are here. Can we just talk normally?"

"Yeah. I wanted to see it was you," he said. "Now I've seen."

"Did you find out anything?"

"So his donors fall into two categories. Industry kingmakers, the ones that run the politicians, first. Then there are others—also rich but not *as* rich, one or two have as much as half a billion in revenue, sometimes their wealth is shared among smaller entities or they're hidden behind so-called educational groups, these 501(c)4s—a big corporate entity of biblical literalists that owns hundreds of radio channels, for example. Those guys are his other backers."

"It's not so surprising," I said. "He's been talking the talk."

"It's how he found you," said Navid. "Turns out these guys have citizen networks. I wouldn't call it grassroots, there's too much money moving around for that. Or let me put it another way: there's money at the top and blue-collars at the bottom. Far's I can tell, the money at

SWEET LAMB OF HEAVEN   197

the top talks about ending the separation of church and state, making biblical law the law of the country. Like sharia, right? But Christian. End-times bringers. They use this shit to get the blue-collars to do their dirty work. It's cynical. So your husband's friends put out their version of an APB, you go down as a threat on the list they give out to their little-guy helpers across the country, and you're a target. I'm guessing it was your VIN that tipped them off. You took your car into the shop, right?"

"My VIN," I repeated slowly.

I thought of Beefy John and the radio poster on his wall.

"Ned knew my father's cancer diagnosis before the doctors told my mother. Before there was even a biopsy. So I'm thinking maybe there was a scan or something, maybe the doctors knew earlier but just needed the biopsy to confirm to the family. Maybe someone connected to him had access and knew the probability."

"I couldn't tell you for sure," said Navid. "I can't get into hospital records. There are people who can, but it's not my bailiwick."

It struck me after I hung up with him that he'd spoken faster than he used to when he was staying at the motel, he was energetic and focused but without the anger. High.

WHEN I PASSED along Navid's discoveries Will gave me a look like *I told you so*—why I'm not sure, since there was nothing in what Navid had said that would link Ned to murder.

I keep trying to see clearly. There *are* clear signs out there, I feel sure, but all I can make out are the blurred edges. I feel a ghost of pressure on my lower back, the push that felt like the crown of a head. I remember a hooded child with a white face. Male or female, I don't know, but whatever it was stared out at me from a window of the subway train.

Either it was a simple accident or it was Ned's agency, no matter who was acting on his behalf. If it wasn't connected to Ned it shouldn't matter, since in that case it must have been pure accident. And it's a characteristic of accidents that they don't often identically repeat.

A programming language is an artificial language used to com- municate instructions to a machine . . . thousands have been created rapidly in the computer field, and still many more are being created every year. —*Wikipedia 2016*

ALONE IN HER SMALL walk-up apartment, Kay took an overdose of sleeping pills last night. She lived but they had to resuscitate her, and now she's in a coma.

There *was* a bipolar diagnosis, as it turns out.

I can't bring myself to tell Lena. I should have been there to look out for Kay, should have done what I could: something. I seem to plod along in my own tracks, following footsteps I made before; this is always how I proceed, I don't look sideways, I'm not willing to stop. I was inside my own concern, walled up in it—worried about abstractions, worried about the future when for so many people, Kay for instance, the present is already a state of emergency.

I overlooked my duty for the sake of my convenience.

Will tries to tell me it's not my fault. I know I didn't cause it, but I didn't stop it either. I see what he's doing and I know it comes from affection, but listen: This is what we do for the people we're close to, all in the name of comforting. We ease the path for them to excuse their own failings.

We let them off the hook and call it love.

The truth is bare—I abandoned her, that tall, sad girl.

WHEN I WENT back to the hypnotist I was like an addict. I rushed out of the apartment with the usual weight of guilt clutched to myself. The sessions are the only times I've left Lena with Will. And I do trust him, but he's not family.

I saw a city, mile upon mile of buildings, a cluster of tall commercial ones at the center and then, moving outward, the residential blocks, the tree-lined streets. The buildings were dilapidated but elegant, there was a detail of ornament to them like the tiny lines on an engraving, the careful, hair-thin lines of pictures on paper money.

The cave-in began in the distance, with the smallest, farthest buildings disappearing first, only visible as yellow clouds of dust billowed up and curled in. Like puffy hands clenching, I thought: beneath the furls of dust buildings were collapsing. Above them something dark raked down from a cloudbank, fouling the air.

I was standing in sand, sand that used to be an ocean and would be ocean again. I stood on the edge of the city as dust rose from the falling buildings. But these buildings were made out of words, locked into each other like bricks and beams—small words, minuscule words, inscrutable as seams.

Ned was coming, flying in from the west. His advent turned the distant sky black. Before him he whipped up a slave army, a crowd of gruesome flying things that drove billions of insects before them, clearing a path. The cloud was made of words too but the words were deformed, they meant confusion or blankness or insidious poison. What light filtered through them was cadmium yellow and leaked a slow disease.

I HAVEN'T SLEPT well lately; I often sit staring at the screen of my laptop while Lena and Will are sleeping. I sit there and stare as the screen resolves into dull letters or right angles of light and fades into disinterest again. It was open to my inbox and at some point I noticed, on the left panel of the page, that my spam folder said 172. I clicked on it and was about to Delete all spam messages now when I saw, buried between an Enlarge Your Manhood and Hot Women in Your Neighborhood, another email from Kay.

I felt sick for a second, scared it was a suicide note or a goodbye letter—so sure I sat there for a long time gazing out Solly's window at the yellow and white squares in the buildings, tall rows of windows rising into the night sky. It's a sight I've always loved, assumed everyone loves: columns of lights in tall buildings at night in the city. Beneath them was the irregular black solid of the park's treetops.

Finally I looked back at the screen and it wasn't as dire as I'd thought. The date and timestamp were there as always, on the right: Kay's message hadn't been sent the day she took the pills; it had gone into my spam folder two days before.

Still, five more minutes passed before I was willing to click on it. I sat on and on at Solly's desk, counting the rows of yellow squares hovering midair, wondering what forms of life moved in the darkness of the park below.

The problem is, now, were going to be nothing BUT surface language. & no safeties, no backups, no checks & balances. The future is nothing **but** language, see, not languageS but language. Monolithic. The little ones are dying off @lightning speed. Programming Language, ad talk, 1 speech for all, a juggernot, that's where we're going Anna. All the native languages dead, all we'l have left is shells & false things & tongues spoken for profit &/or by machines. Don't u c Anna **this** is the tru end of God. When everything that lives the deep language dies. This is the end of God and not the fake god made up to look like us, not that fake god anna, the **real** god, the god tht IS evolution & speciation & Life, a god that did make the world, u see?—b/c this god **is** the beautiful unconscious, it is billion processes & intuitions under all of biology & personality & art, the thousands and millions of cultures of both Man and Beast. We're killing that deep god ana,

the speakers of false language are suffocating the deep, they are
the oil on the water beneath which all suffocates & dies
Satan is God weaponized
God weaponized by man
Now is the point of danger b/c true language is the Soul Anna,
tru deep language the soul & the soul can be **ruined**. God needs
us Anna, as much as we need god

I WONDER IF Ned's allies are mostly true believers or, like him, mere
opportunists.

Will believes, like Don with his geese and songbird migrations, that
I found my way to them via some kind of homing instinct, since a
couple of others over the years have showed up without prior contact.
He thinks it's part of the background orchestration of the deeper
language, an urge that underlies our patterns of survival.

It isn't that I learned nothing at the motel, only that as soon as
I learned it I seemed to always have known it, yet still feel I know
nothing at all. Burke with his speaking tree, Linda with her theme-
park whale, Kay with Infant Vasquez—I picture Burke's maple in its
arboretum, planted halfway across the world from where it evolved,
a lone specimen with a plaque in front of it bearing its names, both
Latin and common. So unlike the aspen that grew not far away from
that arboretum—those cloned aspen, connected underneath the earth,
that lived as one for what could be millennia . . . I watch a pigeon strut
around on Solly's windowsill, dirty but free, and wonder about the
orca in its pool, its home only twice the length of its body.

They did have something in common, all those the voice spoke
through: they were captives. Even Infant Vasquez, who quickly died,
or Lena, who lived on and spoke. All infants are kept creatures, after
all. I remember how snatches of poetry were given out to unfortunates
when we passed them; I think of prisoners and victims and martyrs,

the persistent notion of their closeness to God. I think of how a tinge of the divine rests on the hurt or unfortunate, how so many of them wear a kind of halo of gilded pity.

But if the injured and wretched *are* closer, what does it point to? Likely we give the poor and weak and sick their halos reflexively, I think, to make it easier to detach from them and not have to do fuck all. We give them sympathy in the place of help. We say they're not like us, they're sanctified and only half-human. They might as well be on a cross.

I recall acutely how abjection makes you a part of a herd. The kidnapping left me feeling robbed, not just of my assumptions about freedom but of my personality—no one has personality when their leg's being amputated, no one has personality when their eye's being poked out. You don't have any selfhood when you're suffering extremely: in suffering you could be anyone. Whether that makes you *everyone*, though, is a different question.

And I don't like the proposition that suffering puts us closer to each other. That suffering isolates the sufferer—this is equally valid.

So Will has comforted me over Kay. He's trying to be kind, of course, and I'd do the same if our positions were reversed, you don't question the rightness of trying to comfort someone. As behaviors go, it's universally acclaimed. Yet he told me there wasn't anything I could have done, when in fact there was: I could have done more than nothing.

I think of the duress that can be brought to bear on a soul, how selfhood, which we depend on so completely, is a luxury good.

I turn my palms up reflexively, thinking of those who suffer their whole lives. As though the gesture would make me one of them.

WE LEAVE SOON, after one last hypnosis session. Kay has been moved to a hospital in Boston, near where her parents live. We will visit her there on the way to see my parents.

. . . . .

LYING IN THE RECLINER I found myself walking along an institutional hallway, following green footsteps on the white floor—the footsteps were color-coded to the different wings and there were colored lines along the ceilings, too. I walked with deliberate steps until I came to a room.

An older woman sat in a chair, knitting with blue-gray yarn. The nightstand was crowded with propped-open cards. But instead of lying inert in her coma, Kay hovered above the bed. Her levitation had a Buddhist quality—though her posture was comfortable, not a straight-backed, cross-legged stance as in meditation or yoga. She slumped a bit, relaxed, and remained in the air smiling down at me, with a serene quality that's rare inside the confines of real life.

I wanted to rise to where she was, but I couldn't, so at an angle from each other, she high and me low, we gazed out the window. Out there was the crumbling city of words, much as I'd seen it before, though farther in the distance, dust rising from its slow-motion collapse. Kay nodded and stared. Her face had a kind of shining, imperturbable sadness like a bronze statue in a park, somehow civic.

I followed her gaze back to the window again and saw it wasn't a window after all but a computer screen.

She wouldn't explain at first, though her face kept on gleaming with a smooth and oddly official grief: yes, her grief seemed ceremonial. It was a stately mourning, like a dignitary presiding over a state funeral.

Expository words scrolled quickly along the windowsill.

IF Our symbols are corrupt. IF Our tools are made of symbols. IF We are made of our tools. ∴ We are made of our symbols. ∴ WE ARE CORRUPT WE ARE CORRUPT WE ARE CORRUPT WE ARE CORRUPT WE

The last sentence ran on repeating forever, scrolling across the bottom of the screen like a stock-market ticker tape.

"Think of social-media websites," said Kay.

For some reason she insisted on speaking silently, using a comic-book speech bubble.

"Are you kidding?" I asked.

"Think of all those sites, all those apps, the billions of selfies. Now we filter ourselves through them. Sometimes it's our whole presentation of ourselves to the world. That's all that enters the social sphere—that imprint of our ego is all that ever meets up with the collective."

"Seriously?"

I was sorely disappointed that here, under hypnosis, an oracle appeared and spoke to me, and the subject turned out to be *social media*.

The oracle had actually said the word *apps*.

"Lena will be all symbols, by the time she's grown up," said Kay. "I'm sorry to inform you. It's a fact. Nothing but symbols, your little girl."

The lights dimmed in her room, and in the corners dark beings flitted. I couldn't see them but I knew they were only half-alive, hybrids of flesh and machine, and they moved through the pipes in the walls, among the wires and conduits. Those too, the long tubes and threads that were supposed to be inanimate, moved sluggishly behind the drywall. Between the girders they pulled themselves in. Closer and closer they approached.

"Why do you pretend to know everything?" I asked her. "Are you right about it all? Or are you just sick?"

Kay's face kept on shining, turned away from me, but the knitting mother looked up from her bedside chair. Now the hands in her lap, holding a panel of blue-gray yarn that might have been a scarf, were made of metal: robot hands, with clicking needles. Her face was contorted with rage.

"This isn't a dream, Kay. It's more like a horror movie," I said.

She was supposed to be trustworthy—she'd watched over my

daughter's sleep, cried to me and told me about her life. But telling a feeling isn't the same as knowing someone, I thought regretfully. We think it is. A piece of the Freudian inheritance. People tell their emotions, tell their *emotional story*, and think that equates to knowing each other.

The pipes in the walls turned from ducts or sacks to the old bones of patients, bones that fed out their cold onto me so that the hairs rose on the back of my neck and my forearms. Yet when I tilted my head back the ceiling hadn't gone brittle at all but was warm and rotten, like pink foam breathing.

Kay turned her head slowly and looked at me, and when she smiled I saw her teeth were gray, not regular teeth but some kind of ugly digital code that shifted and moved in her mouth.

It looked a bit like hieroglyphs, a bit like 1's and 0's.

I thought: *What have they done to her?*

Suddenly her mouth opened wide, wider and wider, far too wide. And something ugly streamed out.

"Your little girl won't even need her face," she said.

9

TO THE WHITE CASTLE

FOR A WHILE LENA AND I ARE GOING TO STAY WITH WILL. I DON'T want to move back into the motel—memories of the kidnapping give the place an edge of chilled hardness for me, replacing the clean sea air, the pine needles I loved for their scent and sharpness, with an atmosphere of dread.

Will wants to be my bodyguard, and if he had his way I'd never be out of his sight. This has a cloying aspect, but more and more, during our last days in New York, I found myself hugging the sides of the buildings as I hurried down the sidewalk. I'd catch myself glancing around to make sure that no one was following me, no one was looking at me too purposefully.

I may not be any safer in Maine, but I want to see trees again that weren't planted by city planners. I'd like to take Lena sledding. I remember Will's house as neat and tasteful, floor lamps instead of fluorescents, old rugs and a lot of bookshelves. And next to Solly's apartment it's the Taj Mahal.

I'VE FOUND a replacement for the hypnosis sessions and this afternoon, our first of three days with my parents in Providence, tried it for the first time. Lena was sitting at my father's feet putting on a show with puppets she'd made out of paper bags; Will was fixing a broken step on the porch. So I retreated to my childhood bedroom, which still bore the dusty traces of my teenage self—the pocked bulletin board that had held printouts of pop-star faces, snapshots of me with my arms around friends, a stray ribbon or two.

One ribbon that's been pinned to my corkboard for twenty years says just PARTICIPANT.

I lay down carefully on the bed on my back, stuck in my earbuds, and cued up a twenty-minute hypnosis track downloaded from a website: "Goodbye to Stress."

All it did was put me to sleep, but I'll try again tonight.

Later Will and my mother cornered me in the kitchen; she plied me with peppermint tea and announced she wanted to have a serious talk about "personal security."

Somehow Will had convinced her I need protection. At least, she said, I could agree that there was a risk and humor her by letting Will install a home security system. Then she could rest easy, she said (and here she looked careworn and shaky—more elderly, I realized, than she ever had before). She already had my father to worry about; she didn't want to have to worry about Lena and me too.

I pictured a couple of sluggish rent-a-cops pulling up fifteen minutes too late, shooting the breeze about their personal lives as they casually dismounted from a company car whose doors were emblazoned with a bogus-looking shield. I don't like the idea of being guarded by electronics, of being sealed off from the world outside. More surveillance, I was thinking—all it's done in the past is harm us. It was surveillance that allowed my daughter to be taken from me.

But my mother looked drained. Resistance was futile.

"It's already being set up," said Will gravely.

Panic welled up: I'd done everything Ned asked, everything I could possibly do to meet his demands, and still maybe it wasn't enough.

My mother advised me to carry mace whenever I go out.

"Or maybe pepper spray, dear," she amended. "I think it's better. For their health. The criminals', I mean."

> Hypnosis is ". . . a special psychological state with certain physiological attributes, resembling sleep only superficially and marked by a functioning of the individual at a level of awareness other than the ordinary conscious state." —*Encyclopædia Britannica, 2004*

It was a quiet and uneventful visit to Kay, who lay, much as you'd expect, motionless on a stainless-steel bed hooked up to machines. We had her to ourselves, as her parents had just gone to get lunch, a nurse told me. Kay's face was a ghostly shell, but Lena sat beside her bravely and held her hand. She only cried later, as we were walking out. I'd told her Kay took too much medicine by mistake.

The private room didn't bear much resemblance to the one I'd envisioned under hypnosis—no surprise there—but one thing struck me as we were leaving: a pile of knitting, two needles sticking out of it, on a low shelf on her beside table.

The yarn was blue-gray.

WE HAD a car accident today.

Or almost had an accident, I should say. We avoided an accident, but it was close.

We were maybe half an hour northeast of Boston on the freeway. It was my turn to drive and I was fiddling a bit with the radio when abruptly the car started weaving back and forth across the lanes, fishtailing. My right hand flew back to the wheel as I felt the loss of control in the pit of my stomach and tried to keep the car straight. I almost hit someone on my left but veered away just in time, and then the car almost crashed into a guardrail on our right.

In the end we veered away from that too, luckily, and somehow I steered us onto the first off-ramp, pulling over onto a wide shoulder without any more near-collisions.

It happened too fast for Lena—startled out of a nap by the car's fishtailing motion—even to get frightened. When I'd pulled up the emergency brake I turned to look at her; she smiled at me uncertainly and rubbed her eyes.

Will and I got out and walked around the car: *all four* of the tires were flat.

The three of us rode in the tow truck to the car-repair place, where we hung around in a brown-tiled lounge area that smelled of disinfectant while they sprayed foam on the tires, performed some other tests. We were sure I'd driven over a spilled cargo of nails or other sharp objects—what else could have caused four same-time flats?—but finally they seemed to have exhausted their diagnostic tools.

Never seen anything like it, they said. There were no holes or slits, no punctures at all: the tires were perfectly good except for the fact that the treads on the rear ones were a bit too worn for comfort.

They wanted to sell us two new tires.

"Maybe these mechanics are in league with Ned too," I said nervously. Lena was feeding coins into a vending machine, out of earshot, and I watched her as I spoke.

"I thought I was the paranoid one," said Will. "Still. Maybe we *should* replace all four tires, huh?"

"I don't want to be chickenshit," I said. "But OK."

Will drove after that while I tried to play a word game with Lena, thinking of animals whose names started with the last letter of the animal before. But she soon tired of it and asked to use my tablet for a game, making hairstyles on cartoon people whose faces looked like square potatoes.

When we got to his house I was relieved. I'd sat in the passenger seat with the muscles in my stomach clenched—sat forward the whole way, strained, unable to relax enough to lean back in the seat. The guy who'd installed the alarm system was waiting for us, his van idling in the driveway behind Will's truck, now covered in drifts of hardened snow. Will warned me as we were driving into town, so I wouldn't take fright, I guess—that's what I've come to, apparently. I have to be warned about the presence of men in vans.

We all went up to the door, rubbing our gloved hands together in the cold, the installer chugging along beside us, a drunk-nosed man with a beard. He let us in and walked us through the system, whose electronic display looked out of place amid the weathered wood trim and old furniture. Lena was puzzled by the setup, asking why we needed to touch a display to come in. We hadn't needed to before.

"It's like Doug," said Will. "Solly's apartment building has a doorman to watch over it, right? But we don't have Doug in my house so we're using this little guy right here." He rested his hand on the console.

She'd loved Doorman Doug, of course, who brought her puzzle books that featured the Mario Brothers, with a few of their yellowing pages scrawled over long ago by his now-teenage sons. Lena did not prefer the Mario Brothers. They were strangers to her.

But she liked Will's explanation and named the alarm console New Doug.

ON OUR FOURTH afternoon back in Maine, while Will was off at the library, Lena wanted a nap; I was tired too so I lay down beside her on the double bed in Will's guest room, which he'd given her for our time here. The walls, covered in antique wallpaper of faded but regal-looking lions, were festooned with her taped-up decorations, drawings she'd done of fairies and princesses, photos of Kay, Faneesha, Solly, herself standing with both Lindas beside her snow effigy, its head already half-melted.

I dozed off not long after she did and was only woken by a wrong smell. It was familiar, but still I took a minute to put a name to it: smoke. And it was too warm in the room, I realized—sweat had beaded on my forehead and under my arms.

Had I left something on the stove, maybe a kettle? I left Lena sleeping and started down the stairs.

But there was smoke at the bottom, enough of it to hide the view below, and a block of hot air hit me. I turned around again to get Lena—and where was my phone? Downstairs, damn it, somewhere past the smoke, I'd left it charging down there. Will's landline was on the first floor too.

I shook her awake and bundled her into a thick sweater and we ran to the bedroom where Will and I slept, which had French doors that opened onto a balcony. I wrenched the doors open and stepped out onto the rickety wooden platform, which hung over the back of the house. The view was of the large and unkempt yard, brown grass mostly covered in thin patches of ice and crusts of snow. At the back of it were trees, over which rooftops were faintly visible, but not close enough to yell at.

Most of the neighbors were probably at work, I thought, since it was the middle of a weekday.

"Honey, I think we have to climb down," I said.

"It's too slippery!" cried Lena, her voice squeaking. She touched the ice along the wooden rail.

But Lena's a much better climber than I am, a climber who shimmies up to the canopy of trees and freely climbs rock faces I'd never try, and we got out safely, she first, me after, though I fell the last couple of feet. I twisted my ankle, scraped my elbows a bit. We went around to the front yard and still saw no fire, just smoke leaking out the crack at the bottom of the front door. We ran next door, knocking and waiting, and just as the neighbor's door opened we watched the roof cave in.

THE HOUSE ISN'T a total loss. A fire engine pulled up not long after the neighbor called 911, siren shrieking, and we stood by shivering as the firemen plied the hoses, stood with our eyes smarting as smoke billowed out of a broken front window.

I picked up Lena and held her on my hip the whole time—she's old for holding like that, but still light at forty-some pounds. She didn't cry. She was openmouthed but not outwardly frightened.

Other than the section of roof that collapsed, only the kitchen and living room are badly damaged. Mostly they're waterlogged. Will's homeowner's insurance will cover the repairs, but those repairs will take a while. It was an electrical fire, the cops told us when we met with them at the station. There's no evidence of arson, they said.

I assumed it was Ned, somehow this too was Ned's doing. But the firemen shrugged and said the house is old, its wiring is pre-code. One of them brought me an informational brochure, nodding helpfully as though the handout would fully explain everything.

On the front it has a picture of a fifties-style couple in their kitchen—she beside the stove, he sitting straight-backed at the table, wearing a suit and tie, with a cup of coffee and a plate of eggs in front of him. The man and woman are both slim and attractive, and smile at each other in a satisfied fashion. But sticking through the open door behind their backs, as though to peer in and wave, are plump, decorative tongues of flame, apparently unseen.

Each year, household wiring and lighting cause an estimated average of 32,000 home fires in the United States. On average, these fires result in 950 injuries and 220 deaths. They cause more than $670 million in property damage.

Even the insurance forensics guys who came to inspect the house shook their heads as though the fire had been inevitable—we'd been asking for it by being so brash as to live in the house at all.

So it's back to The Wind and Pines, where Don has set us up with two adjoining rooms close to the lobby. He keeps the security system updated since the kidnapping: he gave himself a crash course in the software after it happened. So we're still surveilled, and the homeowners' insurance is paying for our rooms until the repairs are done.

There are other motels in driving distance, of course, but Don is Will's friend and Lena's so fond of him, and besides the Lindas are still here, the sole holdouts of the group, still setting out on their beach-combing walks every morning, still not ready to part ways from each other and go home.

In the end, coming back here, it seems we didn't have much choice.

WE ALL ATE in the motel café tonight, Will and Don and the Lindas and Lena and I. Somehow it felt like we were trying too hard to have a regular meal. No one from town was there; the café's first emptiness had returned.

Don and I were left alone together after dinner, when the Lindas went to show Lena some video clips of kittens who were friends with tortoises; Will headed back to our rooms to unpack. We'd maybe had a couple too many glasses of wine, Don and I. Or at least I had. Don was drinking whiskey.

"At first, when it began," he said, "I *did* worry. I knew there were antagonists who might also be attracted, antagonists like your husband. We're a magnet for them."

"You mean—a magnet? How?" I asked.

"Some people, historically, have heard the voice when—let's say when danger is already near. But after a while, this year, I relaxed my vigilance because no one showed up. No one to worry about. And then they did. I'm sorry I wasn't better prepared, Anna."

"You did your best," I said.

We sat in silence, likely both wondering if that was true.

"Kay sent you some emails," said Don after a minute. "Didn't she?"

"She was so upset. And with her diagnosis—I didn't know what to make of them," I said.

"You can credit them. She knew," said Don softly.

I met his gaze for a moment, but there was something too plain or too frank there and I had to look away.

"She *knows*," I corrected, a little halfhearted.

"If you pay attention to the culture," said Don, "you can see these threads of recognition. There are interferences and smokescreens all over, but the threads are perceptible if you know where to find them. Kay was right. And she's sick, yes. She suffers from an illness of long standing. She's struggled very hard against it. But she also has rare insight. These years are decisive, Anna. We're in the midst of a great acceleration and a great implosion. These years are our last chance."

I sat there sipping my wine and wondering if Don *was*, finally, a crank. I think like that when bold pronouncements are made; I wonder if both sides are nothing but cranks, with one simply more powerful than the other. Ned's Bible-thumping friends think they're right and all others are wrong—their powerful fear of other groups that turns to hatred and plays into the hands of the profiteers. But the profiteers themselves, with their millions of tentacles sunk deep into every crack in the earth, don't give a shit about being right. They're powerful. When you have enough power, right or wrong is for kids. Then there's

Don, with just us, this small crowd of overeducated, confused liberals who also believe the other side is dead wrong, his small stable of adherents to the Hearing Voices Movement.

"No," Don said into the silence.

I guess I'd spoken out loud, though I could have sworn I hadn't. But I was drunk enough not to worry about it.

I probably still am.

And I did know what he was talking about, I knew what he meant by *last chance*. He meant what Kay had written to me in her rambling and half-coherent email. He meant the world that had evolved over millions of years, the mass of living things through which all forms of intelligence cycle, through which a billion variations move and express themselves, the ark of creation over eras and eons. He meant the spirit and expression of all creatures and all people, their cultures and tongues and arts and musics, from the vaunted to the unknown; he meant what was organic and alive, the broad, branching tree of evolution that was history and biology and all kinds of astonishing bodies full of ancient knowledge.

He meant that it was on its way out.

THE PUSH IN FRONT of the subway train, all four tires going out on a fast road, the house fire while we were fast asleep—they seem too multiple for sheer coincidence, but they don't add up to an understandable pattern. Also, after the subway push someone had grabbed me and pulled me back. That was the first attempt, if I want to see it that way. The second: our tires went out on the Interstate, but in the end we hit no other cars—not the car so close on our left, not the dinged-up, rusting gray guardrail on the right. And the third: Will's house burning. But I woke up and I smelled the smoke, and ten minutes later Lena and I were standing safely outside in the snow, watching an empty building burn.

Will barely believed in the fire when I called him at work. He's seemed to be in a mild state of shock ever since, a man who's been pushed too far: many of his dear old books were destroyed, all the books on his living room shelves.

I want to tell him: *Really, Will. You don't have to be in this with me. I'm grateful. And I don't know the difference anymore between gratitude and love. But I'm willing to cut you loose.*

I know he wouldn't go.

I wonder what's more important, the fact that all these events occurred in the first place or the fact that they were only close calls, that in each case none of us have succumbed.

So far.

Since the fire I'm obsessed with when the next "accident" will occur, when the new onslaught will begin.

The subway episode was ten days ago. The car accident was less than a week. The fire was the day before yesterday. They fall closer together now.

I lie awake thinking of Lena, of what will become of her if something happens to me, or if she is also a target. She was there two out of three times, after all. I harbor wild thoughts, such as: Maybe I *should* have fallen in front of the subway train, because at least then I was alone. At least she might be safe right now. But I fear what would become of her if I die, so there's cold comfort there.

I lie awake worrying about Ned having custody. It's Solly I'd want to raise her, I guess, but since Ned and I aren't even divorced I'm pretty sure there's no way to legally exclude him. If he wanted guardianship, regardless of his craven reasons, he would get it. And I lie awake berating myself for my lack of leverage. I've brought this down on our heads, but I cast bitterness in Ned's direction too. I blame myself but I also know hatred.

I never knew it before him.

. . . . .

I TOLD WILL I was going to turn in with Lena last night, that I was exhausted—because I was—and then I lay in bed wearing Lena's earphones, which are large and shiny plastic discs in the shape of monkey faces. I thought of what Don had said to me, what Kay had written, of how I'd seen a city crumble beneath a cloud of dust.

Lena rolled away from me as I prepared to say Goodbye to Stress, and before long fell asleep clutching her duck.

The images didn't feel like a dream. I was aware of the room as I lay there, the shape of the TV cabinet, the bathroom door slightly ajar, the mirror on the dresser showing glints in the dark. I lay in an indoor twilight holding those dim motel-room shapes in front of me as I began to sink under. Did I keep my eyes open?

Into the dark room came a thin, stooped man. My impulse was to fling my body over Lena, shielding her and keeping her safe with me forever. But I couldn't move.

The thin man turned to look at me, and I recognized him. With his bloodshot eyes and tobacco-stained mouth, his gray, grubby mechanic's workshirt with the franchise logo on the pocket, I recognized him instantly: B.Q.

I felt repulsion, then fear; I knew I couldn't turn onto my side or cover her with my arms, I knew I had to lie just as I was, belly up and exposed. And she was exposed beside me. That was the worst of it.

But next I understood he was a weak and broken person. He had never been a threat to us. He worked for Beefy John, that was all—he drew a paycheck.

"She told you herself," he said sadly. "But you didn't listen, Mrs. Mrs., she sent me with a message because she can't bring it. She can't say anything anymore. So here it is. True language is the deep magic. As old as time. God of the hills and water. God of the sun and trees."

He stood at the foot of the bed looking down at Lena, and as he reached out toward her I felt I had to stop him—but instead of touching her he swooped farther down and grabbed something else: Hurt Sheep, which had fallen off the bed and onto the floor.

He picked up the stuffed animal and kept on walking across the motel room, headed toward the window now, where he stood and drew the drapes open.

In the night sky there was a deep-blue light, a kind of royal blue out over the ocean, and stars twinkled in it, the four-pointed stars you might see in paintings. They made me think of the three kings, of the Nativity.

I turned my head and watched him leave by the window. After a couple of seconds I could see quite well, almost as though I was standing at the window myself. He walked out through the glass and into the air and kept going, the sheep tucked under one arm, to where Kay waited, standing on the furling crest of a wave.

"HEY. MAMA. WHERE'S Hurt Sheep?" asked Lena in the morning. "Hurt Sheep was right exactly here!"

"Maybe under the bed. There's lots of space down there. Remember to check *beneath* things, when you're looking," I said, brushing my teeth.

Later I helped her and we looked everywhere.

No, I thought, no no no. Come on now.

"Maybe she's gone. Oh! Yeah. I guess she went with Kay," said Lena, and shrugged, cocking her head.

"What do you mean, love?"

"It's a good place for Hurt Sheep. That's OK, Mom. She went with Kay. I told you before. Remember? In the boat, to the white castle."

We are sending this message to our daughter Kay's friends, her fellow medical professionals and students, and others who knew her. This is to let you know with our deep sadness, that in the evening of this past Friday, we authorized the medical staff of Brigham and Women's Hospital, to remove, Kay from her ventilator and other support equipment. This was the most difficult decision, a parent can ever make, but as she left a "Living Will" document on her Computer, we know for certain, that it is what she wished.

Please do not reply to this Email, because neither Kay's father, nor I, will continue to use Kay's Email address, which we would view as a violation, of her personal privacy. We used it only to access her many Contacts, which we could not find, in another way. Neither of us uses an Email, and this is the only time, we will send a message with Kay's Email Account. However, regular mail can be sent to us at the address below.

Also below, is listed a charity that was close to Kay's heart, for any gifts made in her memory.

Our deepest thanks to all of you for your visits, cards, flowers, and for the love, you also held for our beloved daughter.

10

I WASN'T MYSELF, BUT
THE IMAGE OF ME

IT'S LATER NOW—MUCH, MUCH LATER.

I was in the shower one evening before Lena's bedtime, just after Kay's death. One of the two rooms we were renting off the lobby—the room that used to be Burke and Gabe's—had a shower curtain in its small bathroom that Lena had pointed out right away. Where our old curtain had borne a pattern of blue flowers, this one had golden sheaves of wheat repeating on a background of creamy white.

I remember noticing, as I stood there letting the water drum down onto my shoulders, the cleanness and freshness of this new shower curtain with its sheaves of wheat. I noticed the sparkling-white quality of the small tiles on the shower walls, how they contrasted with the worn and grimy tiles of our previous motel-room shower stall, frankly a sorry bathroom feature. We were living the high life now, I recall saying to myself.

I washed my hair with plenty of shampoo. I saw no need to rush, since Lena was safe in the room next door with Will, reading to him from her bedtime books. I'd just rinsed out the lather and was looking around for my razor—had I left it on the sink counter?—when I felt a scratch at my ankle and glanced down to see a thin trickle of blood. What had cut me? I must have rubbed my other foot across the ankle—my big toe, on the other foot, had a freakishly long toenail.

Unattractive. I didn't like it. How had it gotten so long without me noticing? I felt embarrassed, despite being alone. I'd clip it right now, as soon as I shaved my legs and stepped out and toweled off.

But wait, the other toenails were long too—they all were, on both feet. They were almost obscene; they looked like a bird's talons, like bird claws stuck onto a mammal. How could Will not have noticed, either? Maybe he'd been too polite to say anything. The front edges of the nails had to be nearly a centimeter long. Beyond disgusting.

I'll get out right away and grab the clippers from the bag next to the sink, I thought. It was both strange and vile: my toenails had never been so long in my life. *Must be because it's winter,* I told myself, *you wear thick socks all the time, even to bed usually, hating to have cold feet—that must be how you missed it.* I was about to turn off the water when I caught sight of my ankles, my calves. The hairs on them were as long as the toenails, practically. *Jesus,* I thought. How could that have happened?

My gaze hit the wall tiles. I'd thought they were so clean, but now I saw some of the cracks between them contained lines of mildew. I'd get the maids in here first thing tomorrow, I'd get down on my own hands and knees . . . wait. My fingernails were almost as long as the toes. Hard to believe I hadn't cut up my scalp with them while I was lathering. My gaze flicked back to the wall tiles and I saw a line of mildew was *creeping up the grout.*

It was visibly extending itself before my eyes, indeed all over the white surface of miniature tiles on the shower wall mildew was creeping. In a grid of right angles a black mold was spiking out farther and farther along the network of tiles, straight angles in every direction.

"What is this," I said, "what *is* this," and tore the curtain back without even turning the water off. Wait—the water had flooded, the floor was soaked, and everything was damp. A lightbulb flickered above the vanity. In passing I noticed the tub was full, backed up, the water a sludgy gray, and a rim of scum ran around the tub over the waterline. I panicked, throwing a towel around my middle, tying it over my chest—it too smelled stale, possibly moldy. I pulled the door open and ran out into the room: there were Will and Lena reading on the bed, pillows propped behind them, with a picture book open across their laps.

Relief: she was there. She was safe.

But all around us the room seemed to be changing, though I couldn't put my finger on it at first.

"Goodnight, little house. Goodnight, mouse," read Lena. Her voice was muffled.

"Goodnight, comb. Goodnight, brush," read Will. His voice, too, sounded like it was coming through a barrier.

They looked relaxed, as I'd left them, but around the bed they lay on other features shifted and altered. The desk lamp turned off and on rapidly, at irregular intervals; dust piled on surfaces and then seemed to go away, as though either blown or wiped; an object vanished and reappeared somewhere else, a toy on the round table, a glass. They didn't take notice. Through a chink in the drapes I saw flashes of light outside. But it was night, and there shouldn't have been light on that ocean side—so I ran past the foot of the bed to pull the drapes open where the big picture window looked over the cliffs and sea.

And I saw it was day. But then it was night, again, night in the sky and rapidly back to day. Boats appeared on the surface of the water, both far and nearer, then disappeared in an eye-blink, only to reappear elsewhere; the sky switched from morning to midday to evening to night within the space of seconds, and then did it again—this time with different cloud formations, other ships.

"Will, Will! What's happening?" I shrieked, turning to look at him and Lena where they sat with their backs against the headboard, their legs stretched out on the bedspread.

But they seemed to be walled off. When I leaned over the bed to reach out to them something in the air resisted me. I couldn't punch through the space around them, though I tried, increasingly desperate. Lena and Will looked the same as ever but I could see my hair growing in front of my eyes, my hair was getting longer and longer on my shoulders, inch by inch it moved down the front of my shirt, my hairs were visibly lengthening.

My little girl was looking calmly at her picture book, touching the drawings. She looked so normal, just here, just the way she should be. But I—I looked up at myself in the mirror. There was an ominous element to the growth of my hair, the choppy, almost digital-looking growth of the ends, so fast it was visible to the naked eye. There was something badly wrong. I wasn't myself, but the image of me.

Lena's fingernails were normal where they lay on the bottom edge of the pages of her book, bitten off a bit but normal: *Goodnight, nobody,* said the text on the page.

Beneath my own lengthening fingernails a line of dirt crept, growing along with the keratin.

I'd seen this somewhere, I thought, seen this somewhere before.

"OK," I said, and made myself take deep breaths, count slowly. One of the hypnotic visions or a vivid nightmare—in any case noth-

ing physically real, that was clear from the nails, from the hair—
impossibility. I had to figure out the rules of the nightmare; possibly
I could control it and wake myself up. I turned my back on Will and
Lena and walked to the window again, where birds appeared on the
cliff edge and then flicked away. The grass was greener, yes, the ice
melted and springtime was here, even the color of the ocean changed
from gray to a bluer hue, even the color of the sky.

I heard a voice in the other bedroom and went back through the
interior door, reluctant to let Lena and Will out of my sight but pulled
there somehow—still, all this was an effect, wasn't it? *An effect,* I
remember telling myself as the light kept changing up around me,
lights shifted and went from dark to dim to bright. It was disorienting. But part of me also worried that I'd been drugged again and this
would turn out to be another kidnapping, so I made sure the chain
was on the room door. *Dream or not, lock the door,* I said as I went.
Dream or not, lock the door.

The voice was coming from my laptop, open on the bed where
I'd left it during my shower. I came up beside it and I could see the
screen: Ned's face. It was a video call, his head in a window on the
screen—talking to someone else as I came up, his face in profile, but
he turned and looked at me.

"A little fast-forwarding," he said.

"What? What do you mean?"

"I hit the fast-forward button," he repeated. "Didn't you see? The
kid. Your boy in there. They're not going so fast, are they? You're all
alone."

They were at regular speed, I realized. But I was sped up.

"You're growing old," said Ned, and smiled again. "See?"

I looked down: new wrinkles on my hands. Old hands. Somehow
I'd moved through time alone—and yet still I spoke at normal speed,
or else I couldn't have talked to Ned; I still *thought* normally. Didn't I?

"It's impossible," I said, more to myself than him. "It's just a bad dream."

"That's what you do with losers, right? Isolate them. You're one of the losers, wifey."

"But how—why are you doing this? I was cooperating, Ned. I did what you asked, didn't I? I don't get it."

"I've got the primaries in a few weeks and I need my pretty wife where I want her. A mental case, alone and needy. Makes them do what they're told. Obedient. And a nice little bereavement in the family. Sympathy vote's the icing on the cake. I look good in black. Well. I look good in everything."

"A bereavement?"

"I took your time from you. You've missed a whole lot. Just take a look."

Outside the picture window the sun was bright. Gnats and flies hung in the air. There were bunches of grass near the edge of the cliff and they were full green, bowing and dancing in the breeze.

"Ain't we got fun?" said Ned.

Doris Day was singing it in the background. *Not much money, oh but honey, ain't we got fun . . . There's nothing surer: the rich get rich and the poor get children . . .*

I had a cold feeling. I was brittle as bone.

Had he made me a ghost?

I'd disappeared—I'd gone, slipped out of being like water down a drain. Was my girl alone now? Was Will looking after her?

"Like I said, we're going out today," he said. "We have a public appearance. Believe me, darlin', it's easier if you don't fight it. Don't get yourself all bothered. You won't get anywhere, I promise. You're confused, sure. You're a sick woman. You're weak. But it won't be forever. You don't have to go on that much longer like this. Just do what I say. OK? Put on the gown."

I looked behind me and saw a black dress laid out on the second bed.

"I'll see you outside," he said. "Be on your good behavior, now. You see what I can do."

His face went gray and for some reason I reached out and touched the screen softly. But it wasn't warm, and fine dust came off on my fingertips. The laptop wasn't even on. I raised my face: Lena and Will were standing in the doorway. Will wore a suit and Lena's eyes were puffy.

We weren't in the motel at all but in my parents' house; I stood in my old bedroom. There was a rush of confusion that was almost a thrill, almost velocity. Then it stilled. Here was my corkboard with its colored pushpins and ribbons. PARTICIPANT. The air was humid and close; my parents had never had central air. I heard my father's voice: they never "held with it." I was wearing the black dress now, I saw, glancing down—no memory of changing into it—and toe-pinching black shoes with heels so high I could barely walk on them. I'd never have picked out those shoes.

I wouldn't struggle. Don't fight it, Ned had said sleazily. But it *did* hurt more if you struggled.

Prey animals had the sense to play dead.

So I leaned down and picked Lena up, though her weight made me stagger on the too-thin heels. But she was real and solid. I knew from her red eyes that she'd been crying and I squeezed her hard, maybe too urgently. Had all of us been frozen there? Had we all been suspended on Ned's whim, or only me? I tried to see if Lena looked older . . . I was flailing. It was possible, faintly possible that her face was more angular suddenly, but whatever slight change I might imagine wasn't obvious like my long talons. I tried to keep them from scraping her back as I held her; I'd rip them off. They were like parasites on me.

"Mommy, I'm hot," complained Lena.

I put her down and as I turned away bit at the longest nail, ripped the white edge of a thumbnail off with my teeth. But then—they weren't long anymore.

And the hairs on my legs? I leaned down to look beneath my tights. They were black tights, semi-sheer, and I could see no hairs through them. The skin on my calves was smooth. I straightened up again and was holding out my hands, looking at them dazedly, when Ned appeared behind Lena in the hall. He wore a black suit, true to his word, and a silver-gray tie, and looked like he'd stepped off the pages of a magazine.

"My *father*," I said, and it hit me whose death this was—I wasn't the ghost after all.

It had happened without me. He was all gone, and I'd missed him. I'd been absent. There was a picture in one of my mother's photo albums: my father as a tiny boy in a white suit, sitting on the back of a horse. Or maybe it was a donkey. It was a blurry, black-and-white picture.

That little boy, I thought.

How would my mother ever forgive me for missing it? How would my brother?

Had my father lain in bed, had he grown thinner, the way the dying do? He might not have missed me. I hoped he hadn't but I would never know.

"You were always a daddy's girl," said Ned.

"You were a rotten son-in-law," I said, as though it was news.

He kept smiling, as always. His smile never wavered now. It was a rictus.

"You took his money and you even took his dying," I said.

"Mommy?" said Lena. It was as though she hadn't heard me; I was glad and ashamed, ashamed for speaking that way in front of her. "Can we go now? Nana says they're going to play a pretty song for Grumbo at the funeral. She said they're going to play 'The Skye Boat Song.'"

"Take my arm, kiddo," said Ned, bowing his head in Lena's direction.

She clung to Will for a second, she would much rather have walked with Will, it was awkwardly obvious, but finally she lifted her hand up to Ned's.

I walked right behind them, fearfully close; as I stepped into place at their heels, I clutched Will's arm for a moment where she'd let go of it.

"Let go of that thing right this fucking second," said Ned through gritted teeth. But he was facing away from us. As though he had eyes in the back of his head. "You're *my* wife. You remember it."

"How did you know how sick my father was?" I asked weakly. "How did you know before we did?"

"Whatever you *need* to know, I'll fucking tell you," ground out Ned. Then he turned and whispered over his shoulder, almost tenderly, "Bitch."

My stomach flipped but Lena was looking elsewhere and waving at someone: she hadn't heard the tone or the words. Again she seemed to be immune. She was usually so observant—it was as though Ned had a wand.

We stepped out onto the front porch, where I saw my parents' grass was yellow and dry. There were flags flapping from porches down the street: it was Independence Day. Out past the awning, where the shade stopped, reigned a bright blank July heat, cicadas whining in the trees. A small group of photographers stood on the lawn. Had Ned hired them? Would a real news outlet spend money on pictures of a candidate's in-law's funeral?

Ned wore a solemn expression, making the occasion momentous—such was the power of his bearing—and curved a graceful arm around me in a supportive gesture. He was between Lena and me, seeming to shelter us both, there on the porch: the father of the family, presiding over a sad wife and innocent little girl.

Will had fallen behind somewhere—that he had even been allowed to come was surprising. Ned couldn't have liked it; maybe my mother had pushed. There were limousines at the curb, and my mother was getting into the first. We joined her there, Ned and Lena and I (I looked back and saw Will headed across the dry grass for limo number two). My mother slid in beside Solly and Luisa, already seated.

In the cool car with the air-conditioning blowing into our faces Lena sat between Ned and me and sang in a high little voice.

Speed, bonnie boat, like a bird on the wing,
Onward! the sailors cry;
Carry the lad that's born to be King
Over the sea to Skye.

Across from us my mother wore an expression both peaceful and relieved, maybe. Alone now, without my father, but probably also relieved. She avoided looking at Ned as though there was a blank space where he sat.

Lena, who only knew the chorus, sang it again.

I tried to discern from my mother's face, then from Solly's whether they were angry at me for being trapped by Ned this whole time as my father was dying.

But Solly wasn't looking at me at all: he was looking at Ned with open contempt, with raw hostility. Luisa nestled into his side, her eyes cast down. Miserable, I thought, and polite. My mother patted Luisa's knee and they smiled at each other sympathetically.

I turned my head toward Ned, slowly and slightly so that he wouldn't notice. He'd dropped his falsely protective arm off me when we got into the limo and also dropped Lena's hand; now he was looking down at his phone, as usual.

There was his neck, its even tan, the sweep of one lock of hair over his forehead, his perfectly clean ear. There was the faint scent of his cologne. I kept looking, I kept gazing at the graceful tendon of his neck, the clean shave along his jawline. And just when I was about to turn away—feeling my eyeballs throb dully from being rolled to one side too long—I saw a movement on the skin. Just for a second, just for an instant, I saw an L-shape made up of pink-and-white squares flash onto the skin before they disappeared.

I swear I saw him pixelate.

I didn't say anything, my tongue was stuck in my throat, but as we got out of the car I found myself scrabbling at his sleeve. Lena was walking ahead holding my mother's hand; I had Solly's and Luisa's backs in front of me. We were on display again as we stepped onto the cemetery's gravel footpath—I didn't see the photographers yet but there were mourners around us, others were parking and walking over to the gravesite—and so, again in the open air, Ned turned to me smiling. The smile was perfect, too: restrained, as though in grief, and yet compassionate.

"How are you *doing* it?" I asked, a bit pathetic. "What are you doing?"

"I'm playing with you, honey, that's all," he said softly, and tapped one temple. "You let me in when you started 'clearing your mind.' That New Age horseshit is good for one thing: access. Safer when you had the therapist in the room, but then you started to do it all by your lonesome, didn't you. With the little earbuds in, all walled off from other people and with your mind wide open."

"The *hypnosis* tapes?" I squeaked.

"You threw open the doors and I walked in. So now I'm tinkering. I'm just tinkering around a bit with the little wife's thalamic nerve projections. I can do that now. I can make you see what I want you to see."

He'd effected some kind of amnesia. If not a dream he'd given me, it wasn't far from it, I guess, a thought, an idea, a mental frame. Drugs, maybe? Could this be pharmacological, and his mind-control brags just a component of his intricate manipulation?

"But I don't know what you mean," I said. "How can you—anyone—?"

"I have the skills," he said. "Ever since I took the kid. Added bonus. You just take what you want. You know that, sweet thing? The more you take, the more you get. It just starts to *pour* in. Talk about miracles."

"I don't get it," I said. "I don't . . ."

"The same way money gives you everything, so does power. It's like one of them math curves, rising steeper and steeper. That's how power grows once you grab it. How'd you get through thirty-some years without even knowing *that* much? *Stupid.* I can make things happen without even being there. I kept you on your toes. The subway, right? The freeway. And the house. It's nice for me, watching."

"But not—that isn't possible."

"Not only possible. *Easy.* With neurons so *much* is easy. Didn't your little Hearing Voices club tell you that? Haven't you learned anything?"

"So you're saying you can get into my—"

"I have the keys to the kingdom."

"What kingdom?"

"I can slide my fingers," and he leaned over and whispered close, "right into the holes in your head."

His breath was moist and stale on my ear and a sight flashed before me, a black pit. Out of it climbed naked people in stuttering, stiff movements, herky-jerky. I'd seen that movie, I thought, a Japanese horror movie, I'd seen it and it scared me. They were like puppets pulled and released on unseen strings, and their thin limbs were hairy and banded as the tails of rats.

"Like I did with the little doctor girl," he said. "You can't let people like that just keep going. She saw *way* too much. And then she opened her little bitch mouth. So she had to go. Didn't she."

I turned and stared at his smile. Then I bolted ahead, my stiletto heels biting into the turf, until I was near enough to grab Lena's hand and use the contact to steady myself. I walked forward holding that little hand tightly, my mother on her other side, and looked down at her face that I love so much, trusting and bright.

I gazed at her face that banished fear and thought of not looking back—no matter what, I said to myself, no one can make me look back now.

AT THE RECEPTION (carefully steering clear of Ned, who was at the far side of my parents' house glad-handing the mourners) I took Will's arm and pulled him into the kitchen with me, where we could talk. I watched Lena through the open door, carrying a tray of food with my mother at her side. I felt cracked and hollow.

Drinking wine didn't make me less parched but at least it loosened my muscles. I was living in a half-life, I thought, a life of distorted lenses where I couldn't trust anymore that a man's skin wouldn't pixelate beside me. Even my thoughts weren't my own, and without them I wasn't myself. Alone had been free, I saw that now—alone had frightened me but the air was clear there. Now I was in prison, without the privacy of my mind. With those claws in my thoughts I wasn't myself—I wasn't anyone.

Will and I stood and gulped from our goblets beside the trays of brought food, the donated lasagnas and plates of brownies crowded onto the island. I made myself focus on the practical and asked him what had happened over the past weeks.

I didn't say months. I was trying to test the waters.

"You mean—in the news?" he asked.

"I mean with us," I said. "What have *we* been doing?"

"Besides your father—helping take care of him? Besides the illness?"

"We've been here at the house for a long time," I repeated, tentative. "Just here with my parents."

I saw in his face: Of course. Yes.

So it *had* been a nightmare, I'd been here, where I needed to be, with them. That motel room and fluttering fast-forward of days and weeks and months had been a memory Ned implanted when he took away the rest.

"Is he threatening you again?" asked Will urgently. "Did he say something threatening?"

"It's not what he *threatens*," I said. "He said—he said *he* did it to Kay. He said she saw t-too clearly. Somehow he *did* it, Will. She d-didn't do it to herself."

I was starting to stammer, a habit I thought I'd gotten rid of as a child. Will reached out and held my shoulders.

"And now I don't have the right memories. This—it's like I wasn't here till today. I don't remember anything since March. Right after the fire, after Kay. And he says it was him. In my head. He did it to her and he can do it to me."

"You don't have the right memories," repeated Will.

I mumbled what Ned had said—his fingers, the holes in my head. My hands had started shaking. "You were reading *Goodnight Moon*. I had this—I thought my hair was growing just, just fast—"

"Anna," said Will, and moved his hands onto my own to hold them still.

"That's all I have since then, all I have since *March*, since we moved back to the motel—it was the week after your house burned, remember? Listen. He *robbed* me of this time. These *months*. His face talked to me from the computer . . . ."

I looked down at my nails, my nails on the fingers held by his fingers, wanting some evidence to show for all of it, but the evidence was gone. It was my interior life Ned commandeered, that was all. Not time. He couldn't do that. I was half-comforted.

"My fingernails were never long," I said dimly.

Will was looking into my eyes intently, but I couldn't describe it any better. As he stared at me, waiting worriedly for me to explain myself, I thought of checking this journal—I'd open this document, see what I'd recorded. Maybe, in the real months that had been taken from me, I'd written real entries. I'd check tonight, I decided.

"I have to tell Don," said Will. He was patting his jacket pockets, searching. "This has to be it. This is what we expected. He wants you to look fucked up. Depressed and grief-stricken. After your father's death, you're going to . . . he's going to do it. Maybe just pills, like Kay, but he's going to make you—he's down in the polls. He could actually lose this. He and his people are desperate. He needs the sympathy vote."

He found his phone and dialed it.

"Sympathy?" I asked. I noticed I was holding the stem of my wineglass too hard. I set the goblet down on the countertop, then picked it up and drained it. "I don't understand it, Will. Do you?"

But then he was saying he couldn't get cell service in here and headed out the kitchen door, slipping his phone against his cheek. "Stay here, stay right here," he called back. "OK? Don't get near him."

Lena, I thought: Where was she? Still offering her tray of food to guests? I'd forgotten to watch her for maybe five minutes by then and my mother might not be vigilant enough. She knew Ned had taken my daughter before, but she didn't know this new Ned, this Ned phase-shifted into pixels and a grin that was a rictus. This one who said *bitch* instead of *honey*, whose skin had pulled back from his face to reveal bone and metal . . . I looked down the hallway at the milling people, pushing away the fact that Will had asked me to stay here: it didn't include panic over having to look for my girl. Then I was out of the kitchen, rushing to get to the living room.

There was my mother, talking to an old woman with a walker, and there was Solly, there was Luisa.

I couldn't see Lena. I didn't see her.

I pushed my way through the people, made it to the front door, and hesitated. There was a ringing in my ears and my hands felt too numb to turn the knob.

But then I was outside, and I must have left my heels behind because I was standing on the front porch in nylons, feeling the rubber nubbins of their welcome mat against my soles. Closest to me were Main and Big Linda, right there on the path from the street, and Lena was holding Main Linda's hand and picking with a stick at the sole of her shoe—it seemed to have a piece of gum stuck to it. She waved the stick when she saw me, grinning.

They were watching our suburban Fourth of July parade, whose route comes down our street every third year. There were floats and bunting that glittered red, white, and blue; there were some kids in an off-key marching band, a girl turning cartwheels. Up came a horse-drawn buggy decorated with stars-'n'-stripes and the name of a car dealership, and then, in the bed of a pickup truck, a human-sized blow-up statue of liberty with a big head. Its torch flames were made of yellow plastic streamers, blown upward from a small fan below in the truck bed. They snapped and fluttered in the breeze.

The Lindas were looking out at the street and didn't turn. Nearby Don and his aged father stood near a waxy rhododendron bush, the father leaning on his cane; up toward the sidewalk, on the burnt July grass, were the other motel guests, Navid and the Dutch couple. There were Burke and Gabe, just getting out of a car parked at the curb. I thought maybe I should talk to them, thank them for coming, but they were watching the parade, all of their faces turned toward it. I would wait, I decided.

I walked down the sagging wood steps and went over to Lena, feeling the grass poke between my toes; I took the gum-stick from her gently and tossed it into a bush. With her hand in mine I turned to look at the parade.

But as I gazed at it—the high school marching band passing—the marchers changed. Their uniforms faded to drab brown and gray; some of them were wearing hoodies or hats, some dragged bags after them, scraping the street—their instruments were gone, and instead of the instruments they carried sacks full of trash, sacks leaking fluids I couldn't make out, leaving brown-red streaks on the road. Their heads hung down. Their passage had a dreadful weight.

As I stared at them, all at once, they raised their faces to me. Hideous. Some seemed to be wearing gluey, primitive masks; some looked like burn victims and others were pimply teenagers, some were middle-aged with bad teeth and glasses. Some were diseased, their eyes red-rimmed, lesions that looked like eczema or leprosy splitting the skin of their faces. The worst were crones with thinning hair, clumps of ragged gray sticking to yellow scalps.

But they were all Lena.

"No," I said out loud.

They were Lena old, young, wretched, in a hundred distortions. That's why we have to die first, I thought, panicked: before they get so old. I shook off the urge to throw up.

Around me the motel guests were watching the parade and smiling. They didn't see what I saw.

I had to be defiant. It wasn't the time to play dead.

"Is this show all for me, Ned?"

The parade shifted so that, for a moment, I saw normality—a second of cheerleaders with pompoms. Then the ruined Lenas were back, deformed and crooked, shambling. They made noises low in their throats. I saw a toddler so thin she was almost a skeleton.

"This is ridiculous," I said, summoning a desperate bluster. "Give it up, Ned." I moved my eyes off the parade and fixed them on the solid, actual Lena beside me. No one seemed to be hearing what I said.

I looked over my shoulder and saw the front windows of the house and sure enough there was Ned, his grin a death's-head rictus through the glass.

"They got here fast, didn't they," came a voice. Will's.

He was on the porch. I pulled Lena with me, stepping back onto the lawn to meet him as he walked down the steps and grazed my cheek gently with the backs of his curled fingers. Once he was near us the yard felt more physical, the house—and when I turned back to the street the parade was normal, just a small-town parade befitting my parent's sleepy suburb.

My body slumped in relief.

"I thought we were supposed to be the ones that *didn't* go crazy," I said, and leaned against Will, my whole body sagging against his side.

"You're not crazy," he said. "He just wants you to feel that way. And look like it. So your suicide's credible. Do you believe me?"

I cocked my head at him and nodded slowly.

"The others are here," I said.

"They came when they heard about your father."

"But Will. Ned's calling the shots. He's still—he's in my head, messing around with me. The parade? To me it looked different."

"So," said Main Linda, approaching. "Hey. I'm sorry for your loss."

"We're all so sorry," added Big Linda.

Navid hugged me lightly. He wore a dark suit almost as expensive as one of Ned's, I noticed. And he was clean-shaven again.

In the street several jeeps passed by with banners supporting the armed forces.

"Soldiers," said Lena helpfully.

"Brave young Americans," came Ned's voice from behind us. "How do you like the parade, Anna?"

I opted not to turn around. The others barely acknowledged his presence either, but I felt them tense and stiffen, I felt their mood turn gray.

"Can we see fireworks?" asked Lena.

"It has to be dark for fireworks," said Will.

"That's later on tonight," said Big Linda.

"But can I stay up late?"

"Of course you can," I said.

"I'll see you then," said Ned, and he strode down to the sidewalk, two suited bodyguards converging on him as he went, the engine of a parked car revving.

Watching him get into the backseat of the car, hearing the curt slams of three car doors in a row as the bodyguards got into the front, was when it hit me: one job remains to me. However bad it is now, I saw—his cartoon-thug tactics, the way he used my love for my daughter against me—it will be far worse if he wins. And not just for Lena and me, not only for us, not at all.

I've been blindered for months—maybe the whole length of my life. These visions and pixels make it obvious. Around me is the desperation of others, the arms of supplicants growing out of the dirt, and I've walked through those fields as though there's nothing there but tall grass. I should have played dirty long ago.

The living spring from the dead, was the first thing I had heard.

I smile thinking of it. Maybe the dead had been me.

I won't have Lena if I don't even have myself. And Ned has a sociopath's overconfidence, that's his weakness. Maybe he's made mistakes that can be used against him, one or more of his obvious, arrogant, flagrantly taken risks.

"Why are they *really* here?" I asked Will as we headed back into the house with Lena. The motel guests were drawing closer together on my parents' lawn.

"To be of service," he said.

And there was war in heaven: Michael and his angels fought against the dragon. —*King James Bible, Revelation 12:7*

62 percent of Americans . . . think recent natural disasters are evidence of global climate change while 49 percent say such disasters are evidence of biblical end times. —*Washington Post, 11.21.2014*

I WRITE THIS in my old room with the bulletin board, where among the dust bunnies on a closet shelf I found a fortune-teller made of pink construction paper. It's numbered with blunted pencil on the finger flaps, and inside each flap is an outcome scrawled in miniature writing. My friends and I made them up, giggling hysterically, during a sleepover when I was in sixth grade. *You will be Famous (for Burping the national Anthem) / You will be Rich but Really Dumb / Our Love will never Die.*

In the corner is a crate of my old records, on top of which an LP lies flat. It bears a once-famous logo, a black-and-white dog staring into the cone of a gramophone beneath the words *His Master's Voice.*

When I looked into this Word file to see what I might have written during my lost spring, all I found after the cut and pasted-in email from Kay's parents were two fragments.

I assume I wrote them, but have no memory of it.

Say God is a complex grammar that doesn't coexist with our own language, its ego-driven structures. Say Kay is right and dolphins or whales can be its hosts for their whole lives, instead of funneling it briefly as Lena did, because the form of language that emerges in those animals doesn't displace the deep grammar the way ours does. Say that deep language, whose name may also be God, stays with them because their communication systems, though capable of individuation, are not *devoted to the self.* Say we're left on our own, as Kay had it, when we pronounce our first words and God deserts us, and it's in that respect that we're different from the other beasts and different from the aspen trees. Then it has to be said also that instead of being raised above the other kinds of life—instead of being special as we have always claimed—we're only more alone.

That one was peppered with errors of rapid typing that I've fixed. The other was this:

Some people hear more, some less, some nothing at all. What we hear is what we *can* hear, its content minutely tailored to our character and biases. That means, if I believe her, that even we, who should be outside the range of any dogmatic faith, even we *only ever know the God our personality describes.*

Lena, living out a fixation on the cute, has made the screen on our tablet into a picture of a fawn in a snowy forest glade, looking over its shoulder with big dark eyes as flakes fall and soften the world around it. The only moving elements are its eyes, which every so often blink, and the snow. I look at it now, while she runs through the sprinkler in the backyard with Will.

I can see them out my window if I scooch my desk chair sideways—there. Better.

The fawn with its dark, slowly blinking eyes takes me back to Ned's beautiful girlfriend, the young model or model lookalike. Where is she now? I could do so much good mischief if I had just a little time-stamped footage of her and Ned together.

Of course any action I take is a risk to Lena and there's no way to attack him from anonymity. Everything's obvious now that I know he actively wishes me harm. It's transparent that nothing binds him to the norms of decency—no guarantee exists, none ever did. There was never a contract to rely on, some solid agreement that could be wielded in a court, only my naive belief that such abstractions have any weight at all.

All my credulity is out the window now, that frail screen of written-on paper I let myself believe would keep the world predictable. Ned's handshakes add up to less than nothing—or nothing but the flag my gullibility flew on. Don and Will and their fears, well, those fears were only a slice of the malice that Ned is.

Maybe the knowledge is chilling—it is, when I don't block it out stubbornly—but it also means I have no reason to jump at his command anymore, there's nothing left to make me do what he wants me to. So he's now lost his postcard family. He shouldn't have shown himself, and I wonder why he did, because he could have strung me along forever, practically, while I still believed he could be bargained with.

Now I know he doesn't bargain. He only pretends to.

And he has nothing left to get from me. Nothing but the last thing.

It must be his narcissism that's to blame, maybe he couldn't help showing me how powerful he is. Maybe he had to flaunt it.

And all I have left is this: my girl and her uncertain future.

She used to look forward to every new day.

THE OTHER MOTEL GUESTS insisted on staying close, crowding around Lena and me as we walked across the parking lot. We'd left Solly and Luisa and my mother at home, my mother so she could help the caterers clean up, Solly and Luisa so they could pack to leave for Manhattan the next day. But they urged Will and me to take Lena out. Let the child see the bombs bursting in air, at least, on this death-textured day.

The show was being put on at a Minor League baseball stadium about twenty minutes from my parents' that's always been the perfect place for pyrotechnics; we used to go there for the Fourth when I was a kid. Until I went to college I came here every Independence Day, first with my parents and Solly, then with a swarm of classmates, and by my last years in high school with guys in their hand-me-down family cars—not watching the show, just using the dark and crowds and noise as camouflage. That was when the stadium was small and dilapidated, with wooden seats, before it was renovated into the slick behemoth it is now.

I led the others into the elevator and we went all the way to the last row, where the view was worst for sports but best for fireworks. It had been a hot day but now a breeze swept up and chilled me; I'd remembered to bring a jacket for Lena, but not one for myself. As we filed along into our seats my arms came up in goosebumps.

Ned would have to work hard to find us, I figured, and of course there was no good reason he should try: no photo op, no obvious prospect of gain. Then again, hounding me seemed to be its own reward. He was always able to trace my movements. And he'd said he was coming.

Tumbling acrobats erupted onto the field, frolicked and ran off again; lumpy costumed creatures ran out next, waggling their top-heavy bodies, possibly cartoon animals connected to a TV show. Tinny pop music blared loudly from a bad sound system to accompany their antics, then mercifully cut off. Vendors of popcorn and glow-in-the-dark novelties moved among the seats; I bought Lena a whistle in the colors of the rainbow. Finally the main show started, a local orchestra that tuned up and launched into a jumbled rendition of the 1812 Overture.

Maybe it wasn't jumbled, I thought, maybe the flaw was in my ear, maybe Ned's long fingers had twisted even the music that I heard.

Lena bounced off my lap in delight when the first firecrackers shot into the sky. She'd moved along to sit with Main Linda by the time, a few minutes later, her father appeared at the end of our row.

He wasn't wearing a suit and tie for once; in a jacket and a polo shirt he was strictly business casual. Where was his bodyguard, I thought, his driver, the fake Secret Service guy? There was always one of them at least, but I saw no one near. Maybe they were seated somewhere, hidden in the crowd.

I moved out toward him instantly, exactly as though I *wanted* to be in his company and sought it out—and I *did* want to, I wanted nothing more than to reach him at that moment. Instead of a rush of adrenaline or heavy dread it was a stolid calm that guided my progress; I barely noticed the guests as I inched myself along between their jutting-out knees and the seatbacks in front of us. It was almost romantic, as though, beneath the falling pink stars and showers of green, there was no one anymore but Ned and me.

Stepping onto the catwalk I remembered parking with a boyfriend senior year, just a few steps from the stadium wall. I knew the moldy smell of the seats in his car, the lacy brown rust along the bottom of the doors, and how we'd thought of the fireworks as our soundtrack—the world was about us. We were sure of that as we made out, moving in the darkness of the car with our long, lean arms and legs bound up in each other, that soft skin tingling over the curves, thrilled by the conviction that this here, this was the only and the all. There was no question, then, that the world had been created as our scenery.

That was the bliss of being young, the pure egoist joy. But if you get old and don't grow out of it, I thought, looking up at my husband, you are ruined.

Maybe he'd never had a chance for that. Maybe he never had that kind of youth. Maybe he could only feel it now.

I leaned in as though I wanted to kiss him, and though I don't think he believed or wished for that anymore he must have been surprised for a moment. He's always assumed I'm harmless, pathetically harmless, and that gave me a couple of seconds' grace to slam my hands against his chest. I was feeling nothing for him then but a pity that stretched all the way back to his childhood, all the way back to before he was him.

At the second of contact I saw how the guests had been drawn together, dots gathering around a node or birds flocking to a flyway. I saw Ned and his ominous host converging on us like a machine army—even the child in the subway train, even the air in the tires of my car, even the fire that had burned the house, all these were his armaments. I saw in every granule and wave how my husband's power had seemed impossible, how it had borne the sheen of dark magic for me but was constituted of energy, energy subverted.

And when the heels of my hands came off him again, the images faded.

But it wasn't easy to send him over the rail. I didn't have enough weight behind me or enough leverage; maybe the angle of my approach was weak. I felt the bulk of his chest against my hands, the shock of his unyielding body as he leaned back. The chest was the wrong place to hit, a mistake that almost cost me my life: he was well-balanced with the rail against the backs of his thighs. Instead of toppling backwards he grabbed me and steadied himself—a strong man as well as a beautiful one. With his disciplined allegiance to fitness he'd always had strength. Discipline equals strength, though the coldness of the equation is depressing—unfair, it seemed to me as I felt instantly shocked and made foolish by the feebleness of my attack.

I'd felt its prospect tingle on my skin and seconds later that prospect had ebbed. My chance had passed. Why does strength hold itself so stubbornly away, why can't it be that we can summon it out of feeling or impulse, out of just wanting to? Fear made my legs weak. I couldn't move.

One hand grabbed my right shoulder and the other dug into my left wrist like a claw, and then it was twisting me there, by the wrist, and I don't know if I gasped or shrieked.

But all the time he was smiling.

Then he raised his hand from my shoulder and, still smiling, punched my face with it, sideways and hard. I felt my nose crunch and the pain was blinding; my eyes squeezed shut and now he was punching me again. And again. My tongue felt a loose molar and my mouth was full of blood.

I was willing to fall with him if I had to. I feared being crippled, but dying I could stand, as long as I could hold a picture of Lena in safety as I fell, Lena in Solly's care, Solly and Luisa keeping her safe from harm. Before I could push myself forward and topple us both there was a rush of others around me, a cluster of people, and it's hard to say what the geometry was. Ned must have known I wasn't alone, but only then did his smile flicker. Or so I believe. I couldn't see much by then, was blinded by the blood in my eyes.

I know there were others all around me but I couldn't say if we made noise, I couldn't say how our hands moved or our feet, couldn't say much about who did what, whose bodies pushed or pulled, all I can say is that at a certain point I swiped at my eyes and saw we were by ourselves.

Ned was gone.

And when we looked around us—after we leaned over the rail and stared down into a pool of black that didn't tell us anything—we found the crowd seemed to have ignored our scuffle. But I wasn't paying attention, I was preoccupied by the pain in my face, the blood dripping down my chin. My nose made a high wheezing noise when I breathed. Will took my hand, Navid was squeezing my shoulder, and then we turned and in a rush we pounded down the stairs—other than me it was all men, Will and Gabe and Burke and Navid and Don; Lena was away from all of it, back in the seats, deep into the row surrounded by the Lindas.

We pounded down and out and around, running hard until we got to the right stretch of pavement. In the dark I breathed my fast, wheezing breaths, tried not to faint from the acuteness of the pain. There wasn't a floodlight anywhere near us and I couldn't see his face. I wasn't sure I even wanted to.

Finally someone found a penlight—I think it was hanging off a keychain—and its weak light was dancing over Ned's head and shoulders, a small spot unequal to the task, lighting the planes of his face in a piecemeal way. I clenched my hands into fists so the pressure would anchor me against unreality.

But he looked as real as anything lying there, real and even alive, his magnetism intact despite the white polo shirt that should have left him looking like an out-of-place golfer. His jacket was spread open at his sides like wings, his arms were flung out, eyes nearly closed, well-shaped mouth just a bit open. The skin of his face was stainless, almost without a pore, its same delicate hue of salon gold.

Only the pebbly asphalt around his head was stained.

NEWS OF HIS death ran in Alaskan media outlets: heroically trying to save a fellow climber, he'd lost his footing in the mountains and plummeted. On the main street in Anchorage there were altars of flowers and photographs. People held candlelight vigils, although (said Charley) they were notably more modest than for fallen celebrities.

There are cameras at the stadium but maybe it was too dark for them to capture what had happened: in any case none of us were ever contacted, none of us were questioned. I have to conclude this was intentional—that it wouldn't have jibed with the narrative.

We stayed in my parents' house for two weeks after the Fourth. I had to have my nose reset and the bruises around my eyes are still fading; the tooth I lost was at the back so the gap doesn't show.

Lena asked about the nose and the bruises, of course. I thought about not telling her, but then I thought again and I did. "I pushed your daddy," I said. "Listen. I'm not proud of it. It's not the way to solve problems. But then he hit me back. Harder. Men shouldn't ever hit women."

"He should have only *pushed* you back," said Lena, pragmatic. "It's not fair. I'm glad I don't like him."

"Lena," I said, holding her hands, "your daddy's not coming back. We won't see him again."

"That's good," she said.

I'VE BEEN HELPING my mother with the funeral aftermath. Solly had to go back to work, so we said goodbye to him and Luisa and waved to them from the front porch as they drove off.

After they left we moved at our leisure through tidy rooms, curating the many vases of cut flowers as their rotting stems sloughed off into the clouding water. We sorted clothes and shoes into boxes for donation, read and acknowledged condolence cards; we cleaned out my father's desk, his chest of drawers, the file cabinets and high-up shelves at the back of his closet. I drove my mother to the bank to fill out forms, went online to switch her utilities and other services out of his name, made sure she filed a claim with the life-insurance carrier.

While we were going about these dull tasks, Will walked with Lena to a nearby park, a nearby pool. He took her to the movies, to a beach in Connecticut, and once to a state fair, where they went on a Tilt-A-Whirl, ate funnel cakes with powdered sugar and, by shooting a water gun, won her an orange stuffed giraffe.

Those public places, open to the world, the two of them were able to wander through in liberty.

For me it was a melancholy, dreary time with a curious softness. I kept waiting—I wait even now—but so far I've found no moral torment in being a murderer.

None at all.

· · · · ·

IF WHAT SLIPS through to us from the deeper language is filtered and textured by our own interests and affections—our ties to babies or animals or trees—maybe I heard only what I could.

Maybe our gods are as small as we are or as large, varying with the size of our empathy. Maybe when a man's mind is small his God shrinks to fit.

Because if you're the kind of person who wants to know what's at the end of the universe, what's at the edge of being, and you grow older and older and comprehension settles on you that you'll never know, despair can well up. The question of what we don't see, what's beyond our capacity—in the space where the answer should be, in the knowledge that nothing will ever give us that answer—we have to pass through all the dark nights we live until we die. Never to see what's at the end of infinity, never to see the future of what we love, even the hidden lives of our children— the knowledge breaks our hearts. It nearly cracks us open as we walk.

It's enough of a burden, that futile desire to know more than we ever can. But worse than the mind's natural limits, far worse is the invasion of its privacy. Ned's desecration of my thoughts, *that* was a distortion I could never have kept living with, that conversion of the world's airy expansiveness and wild unknowns into gray squares. Compared to that violence the presence of divinity was gentle.

With language, with the splendid idea of an intelligence that lasted forever, at least I still had my own perceptions, my own moods. I had room for doubt, plenty of space for movement. That room and space could be inhabited. But Ned's monotony of empty assertions in the service of self-promotion, self-replication and mastery for its own sake, his reach that extended past the boundaries of even the body—that was a weapon without end.

· · · · ·

DON CALLED ME tonight, just called me on the cell phone. Slowly I'm learning to live with his pronouncements. It wasn't over, he said, as I had to know: in fact we were still at the start. My husband happened to be the first we met, he said, the first we encountered *personally*, but another had already risen to take his place. There are many like him.

They are legion, said Don. They speak in false tongues and want to own the world.

No, scratch that, he said. We both know they own the world already, but now they want even more.

Now they want to make it over in their own image.

"Are you ready?" he asked me.

I THINK OF what Kay wrote in her mania.

> Deep language is in all living things but all the others, it stays with. Only not humans . . . God leaves us, Anna, God leaves us.

Yet we're the children of that language—not the *only* children, that boast was always a rookie mistake, but among their multitudes. We still swim in the shallows of that vast and ancient sea, the water that runs through us, a coding of genes and flesh that lives on in beings and cultures. We are those bonds that make our nervous systems, our circulation, our lungs exert their miraculous intelligence without our direction—the beneath and always, the insane, preposterous motion of life.

Let God leave us, Kay, if what you mean is constant company. Let God leave us! Let us grow up. Let us walk forward on our own. Because we *need* the silence of the holy: we need the sacred and equally we need its maddening silence. And in the curious privacy and relief of that silence we can go out into the chaos and commit a thousand acts of minor and gleeful splendor all our own. If it's our tragedy to be left by God, then let it also be our luck.

Our loneliness *is* our strength. It's not the same as being alone—almost the opposite. Loneliness is the sense of others, present but beyond our reach.

We feel a terrible tenderness, a terrible gratitude, and at the end we see that face and know the moment is here. The beast has come for us at last.